About the Author

Chris Bailey-Green was born in Suffolk in 1973. He spent almost twenty years in the police both as a civilian member of staff and as a police officer, before leaving to become a full-time writer. He has a degree in philosophy and lives in Norwich. *Crossing the Thin Blue Line* is his third novel. He can be found on Twitter @CBGreen9

Crossing the Thin Blue Line

Chris Bailey-Green

Crossing the Thin Blue Line
A Fable

Olympia Publishers
London

www.olympiapublishers.com
OLYMPIA PAPERBACK EDITION

A CIP catalogue record for this title is
available from the British Library.

ISBN: 978-1-78830-735-2

First Published in 2020

Olympia Publishers
Tallis House
2 Tallis Street
London
EC4Y 0AB

Printed in Great Britain

Dedication

As always, dedicated to my wife Debbi. I wouldn't be here today if it were not for her.

One

Necessity breeds strange bed fellows. That's what they say, at any rate. Well, somebody probably says it somewhere. At some time.

There are times when the situation forces the individual to do something that they perhaps would never have considered doing under normal circumstances. There is a line that the good can cross; sometimes without even knowing it; sometimes it can be with a very deliberate stride. What few people realise is that the line between good and bad; between right and wrong — is actually much thinner than you might have given it credit to be. So, when it comes down to it; it is really easy to step across, as easily as you might cross a road. Very often, though it is a one directional journey. It is easier to cross from the path of the good to the path of the bad than it is to go in the other direction. You can do it, of course; but the fact remains that when you have been on the side of badness, temptation, and immorality; it is so easy to stray back over to it. It is like being a smoker. Once you have become used to cigarettes you can give them up; but it is so easy to slip back into lighting one up again; and you never really stop being a smoker, even if you haven't had one for years. Old habits will die hard.

Every action or inaction has a consequence. We may not always be aware of what those consequences will be. How can we be? We just don't have the capacity to imagine and predict the course of events that might happen when we make a decision. We can't predict the potential outcomes of everybody else and how they will react. It can make for a very interesting life. Sometimes you make a decision that will seem to be not very important at all; almost entirely inconsequential — and then a few years down the line you look around you and you think: 'How the hell did I end up here?'

Complicated isn't it? So many variables from every decision that you might make. If you really sat down and thought about it then the headache that it would cause would drive you insane. You would never be able to work out whether or not to get out of bed in the morning; and what would happen as a possibility of either decision that you might make. Of course, for the majority of us the small decisions such as whether you want coffee with your breakfast or Earl Grey tea, will not have the consequences of the collapse of an ex-Soviet bloc country or the demise of the polar bear. Although you could never be entirely sure of that.

But then it isn't just about the decisions that we make. It is the decisions that other people make that could have consequences for us as individuals as well. In some cases, these decisions made by others — perhaps people that we would never actually meet — would have far more devastating effects on our lives than any decisions that we might make ourselves. You can spend ages debating what your morning drink will be and the ramifications that it might hold; but it probably won't make the slightest bit of difference if someone else has made the decision that you are going to be handed a rifle that morning and told to walk in a very steady and courageous, but ultimately futile manner at someone else who is armed with a machine gun.

See how it works?

We are all interlinked like a tapestry or spider's web. Remove one thread and the entire tapestry can fall apart. The entire world can unravel before your very eyes. This is a story about what can happen when you start pulling at one of those threads.

****

Simon Orford was an average person who was going about his average life when he reached an age when he felt unsatisfied in what he was doing and the direction that he was going in. In truth he felt that he wasn't going in any direction at all. He had done all the things that you are meant to do in life; or so he had believed. He had been to university where he had gained his degree in English Literature and then he had got married. It might have been because he had fallen in love; or it might have been because he had believed that he had fallen in love; or it might have been because of the fact that he felt that if he didn't marry someone then he could easily spend his life alone and it was perhaps better to be with someone than to be alone. This was the first of many mistaken beliefs.

Simon had worked in a variety of different, but ultimately meaningless jobs before having to make a decision on what to do with his life. To his credit there are a number of people who don't realise this and go through life with no real idea that they haven't made much use of it. They get to the end of life rather too quickly and think: 'Hang on; is that it?' The answer is of course; yes. There are many people who change their direction in life because they are fortunate enough to realise that they are going the wrong way. It might be a change of a job; it might be a divorce or even a marriage; it might be a change in sexuality even. It could be anything. These people get to around forty years old and suddenly realise that after forty years they have been doing it all wrong. Now you have a choice. Do you just carry on and to hell with it; or do you make a stand and go off in a different direction?

Why forty? Well, that is easy to answer. You can rush up to forty doing what you think is right, or what you think you should be doing with your life; or ultimately just doing whatever the hell you want to do; but then you hit the big 4-0; and that is when you realise that up until that point you have been racing uphill. After forty the polarity shifts and you realise that you are probably now coming down the other side of the hill and that it just might be possible that there are less years ahead of you than there are years behind you. With that fact in your mind then you might as well start doing the right thing and making the most of however many years there are left to you before it is too late.

Simon was a man of some intelligence and substance so eventually realised after only reaching the age of thirty that he needed a change of direction. He needed to feel useful. He needed to feel part of something. He needed to feel that he was giving something back. He ultimately needed to feel that he was making a difference.

With all of this in mind Simon decided that he was going to apply to join the police.

****

'Why the police?' asked Amanda.

'Why not?'

'I can't say that I approve of it at all. I never imagined that I would ever be married to a policeman.'

'Police officer,' replied Simon automatically.

'Whatever. I just can't say that I approve of it at all.'

'Yes, you said.'

'But why do you want to do such a thing?'

'I want to be able to help people. I want to make a difference.'

'I'm sure that there are many occupations that you could take up where you would be helping people and making a difference. I don't understand why you want to be a policeman.'

'Officer.'

'I don't understand you at all, Simon.'

Now, much has been written about the police over the years and the vast majority of it is a complete load of bollocks. This is for several reasons.

The first reason is because there are a lot of people who are very anti-police. There can be a number of reasons for this. It might be because they are a liberal who think that the police are in some way more oppressive than the people that they are trying to protect the public from. In other words, they would gladly get rid of a police force in order for them to be mugged and raped for their sandals. This is one of the more stupid positions that there could be and it is a constant source of amazement that people who are in other ways considered to be intelligent can be so bloody stupid when it comes to this kind of thing. Perhaps what it boils down to is the fact that some people like to be able to protest. They like to dress up in tin foil and flowers and stand outside of whatever the protest of the week is and then throw insults at the police, who are for the most part disgruntled and only trying to do what they *have* to do so that they can go home and do what they really *want* to do.

Students protest like this a lot because it is seen as the fashionable thing to do. It is cool to go on protest marches and to complain about things that you really don't have that much right to complain about because you haven't actually lived any of it yet. Try doing it yourself, whatever it is you are complaining about and then go out on a protest about it afterwards. Of course, the vast majority of the students that are there are not there because of any deep held political beliefs. They are there because they think it is cool to be there; or they are there because of the fact that they are trying to get into the pants of the other students that are there with their deep held beliefs.

Once, not so very long ago there had been a riot following an illegal rave that had already caused a great deal of damage and seriously endangered a rare and delicate species of toad that could easily be killed by a fart from the wrong direction. Complaints had been made and the police had tried to break it up. The ravers had turned against the police. Clearly the police were in the wrong in this situation because they had been trying to stop the students from having their fun. The police became the common enemy, as is so often the case. Afterwards a sociology student had been interviewed by the press about her experience. The press is always keen to progress a campaign against the police.

'It was terrible,' she had moaned into the camera. 'The police were using batons, CS spray, and dogs.' The interviewer had nodded sympathetically at her sensing a great story in the making. 'All we had,' she had continued, 'were bottles, rocks, and planks of wood.'

It had never occurred to her that the police might have been annoyed that she had been throwing missiles at them in the first place. So clever and yet so damn stupid. You could just see Charles Darwin sitting in the corner slapping his forehead and wondering where he had gone wrong.

The other reason for dislike of the police was the fact that you were a criminal and you didn't like the fact that these interfering men and women in blue kept stopping you from having your fun and then banging you up in prison all of the time. Damn them for their impertinence to think that they should stop crime from happening.

In a nutshell if you hate the police that much then you probably have got something that you are trying to hide. You may not like them, but what kind of a world do you think it would be without them? Would you *really* want to live there?

Of course, the real villains are well aware that what they are doing and what the police are doing is all part of a big game. It isn't something to be taken personally. The majority of the police realise this as well.

Both sets are playing by different rules, but there are set moves that have to be marked out and played to their natural conclusion. Each has a role to play. It might surprise some of the more liberal elements to realise that the real criminals view their activities as a career. They realise that they can make more money from a life of crime than they can from a more legitimate job. They also would probably not have to put as much effort in as a normal job would require. You certainly have the right to set your own hours.

And if they got caught? Well, that was just an occupational hazard to them. They understood that better than most; but they also understood that for every crime that they were caught for there were several others that they had managed to get away with. It was all just part of a big game. Both sides were playing the parts that were allocated to them, and the one who is caught in the middle, could be you, the victim. But if you still hate the police that much then next time that you are burgled or mugged or a victim of any crime, rather than call the police, why don't you call the local smack dealer and see if he can be of better help to you.

There were other things that had been written about the police before as well which were also a lot of rubbish — this was called crime fiction. It was staggering the amount of crime fiction which was factually inaccurate and unrealistic. Of course, a really realistic police drama, or novel would probably be very boring to the general public that knew no better. If it were to be true then the majority of the time would be spent waiting whilst nothing happened. A surprisingly large amount of police time was hurrying up to wait. Waiting around for things to happen. Waiting for people to do things; both public and other officers. Percentage wise perhaps 40% was spent waiting and about 55% of the time was filling in paperwork explaining and, in some cases, justifying what had happened in the remaining 5% of action.

There were several amusing things that were noticed largely in police television dramas for instance. The first was the director's desire that if he had a marked police car then it had to be made full use of the blue lights. Even if in reality there would have been no logical reason for the lights to have been used. Perhaps the director felt that he may as well get his money's worth out of it.

It was also amusing the amount of time that you would see an officer standing in the corner of an interview room watching a suspect and saying nothing. This caused endless amusement that there were officers to spare for this when in reality your suspect would just be banged up in a cell until you were ready to talk to them. It was also amusing to see how these interview rooms were so large when in reality they were often the size of a cupboard.

Police officers often found it amusing as well how the promotion systems were obviously not fully understood. You had to take exams to make sergeant and inspector; they didn't just promote you because you had done something worthy. Any idiot who could sit an exam could climb the ranks of the police even if they normally wouldn't be able to find their arse with both hands.

After the rank of inspector, you didn't have to sit exams any longer. You were then promoted on merit; or to be more precise on your ability of how much arse licking you could do. It was a completely fair and impartial system.

Simon didn't know any of this though so it was with a sense of pride and determination that in the summer of 2003 he posted his application form off to try and become a police officer.

At that time, he had no idea the future that fate had lying in store for him. If he had then it was debatable whether he would have chosen to go down this path.

Two

The first thing that took Simon by surprise was the fact that the application process for joining the police took a long time. It would not be the first time that things in the police took a long time to happen. There were a lot of hoops that needed to be jumped through. First of all, there was the application process itself. During the course of this application you had to demonstrate that you hit certain frameworks. He had to demonstrate that he had the necessary communication skills — both written and verbal; evidence of team working; evidence of respect for race and diversity; evidence to support community and customer focus and finally evidence of personal responsibility.

He examined these one at a time. Written communication skills could easily be incorporated by the fact that you were filling out the application form in the first place. If you couldn't fill that out then you weren't really demonstrating that you had the required skills. Verbal skills could be demonstrated later on; however, it was possible to waffle on and say enough on your application form to show that you could read, write and talk without making too many screw ups.

Team working was again something that could easily be shown by the fact that almost anyone who had at some point had any kind of job had needed to co-operate with a colleague. He wasn't really worried about that one.

Respect for race and diversity was something that he could show by merely pointing out that he was not a racist. He didn't think it necessarily meant that he had to go as far as to provide evidence that he had once met a suicide bomber and whereas he hadn't agreed with his views he had consented to carry his bomb for him. He didn't think that was what they were really looking for. Very possibly they were looking for something quite opposite to that. It was possible to take respect for diversity a little too far.

He based his evidence on community and customer focus by stating that he had been involved in charity work for the local community and had been able to deal with a number of customers when he had worked in a supermarket. It wasn't ideal, but he wasn't entirely sure of what community and customer focus meant anyway. He hadn't really done any charity work either, but it was a difficult thing to prove otherwise and it sounded good.

Personal responsibility he imagined was really just showing that he had the ability to do things for himself. It contradicted the team working side of things; but he was sure there was a fine balance to be had with it all. All applications and interviews were like exams at any rate. You had to spin doctor it. Take the question you were asked and spin it into an answer that you actually knew and hope that nobody noticed. You saw it in interviews with politicians all of the time.

Once the application was completed there was the long wait whilst the submission was read and the decision was made whether you passed the paper sift. This was the long moment of agony while you waited as some unknown person sitting in an office read through your application and then made a decision on your life. It was surprising how long this took to happen. It was probably because the person sitting in the office was someone that had actually never done the job that you were applying for so really didn't know what they were doing.

If you made the grade in the paper sift then you were invited to the local police headquarters and took part in a fitness test. After this if you were successful then you had the chance to attend a half day assessment centre. This was a matter for contention. Previously the assessment centre had been two days in length which meant that as well as covering lots of different tests the examiners had a chance to find out what candidates were like when they thought they were not being examined. This usually took place in the bar during the evening where candidates relieved their tension with alcohol and then tongues were loose and you could observe whether some of the things that they had said on their application form were in fact true; particularly with reference to what had been said about race and diversity.

Having been reduced to half a day you were then rushed through a maths test; a written test; a logic test and then to conclude a carousel of five role play scenarios where you were given the chance at only five minutes a role play to demonstrate how good an actor you were if nothing else. Get through that and then there was a final interview in which you had to give a five-minute presentation on a given topic and then answer questions. If you were accepted at that stage then you had the joy of taking part in a medical examination.

If you had been successful in all of this then you were in and you were going to be a police officer. The fitness test would be repeated on the first day of your new job that you would have to pass in order to proceed with your training. Training would be split into several parts over a series of months and then you would eventually be released solo onto the public, but the entire process of training from day one until the day you were confirmed in the rank of constable would take two years.

It wasn't like applying for a lot of other jobs. Simon was sure that the entire process was designed to see how determined you were to do the job. The risk was that you would get fed up with the long process due to the need for things like money to buy food and you would go and get another job. The application process from submitting the form through to turning up on day one of the new job could take anything from eighteen months to two years; in some cases, even longer. The important thing was to not look at the process as a whole, but to take it one step at a time; otherwise it was too big a feast. One thing was certainly clear; you had to really want to do the job in the first place.

****

'So why the hell do you want to do this?'

It was a reasonably fair question and one that Simon could have probably predicted from his rather difficult and complicated wife, Amanda. Amanda would probably consider Simon to be a rather difficult and complicated husband. It was one of the few things that they really agreed on. You may ask why they were together if this is how they felt about each other. It was also a reasonably fair question and one that requires an explanation.

Simon and Amanda had married after a reasonably short courtship and to begin with things had seemed to progress as normal. He would have been foolish to marry her in the first place if he had not thought that the lead up to the marriage was as he expected at least. Once they had married within four months things seemed to change. Simon would say it was Amanda's fault and Amanda would say it was Simon's fault. Who knows where the blame truly lies in situations like this? Four months after the wedding day the arguments had started and they had continued ever since although at the time of him applying for the police they had only been married for a couple of years.

'I think it is because I want to make a difference.' He had been expecting the question to come from her for some time so had been ready with his answer. He knew that she disapproved of the application; on principal more than anything else probably.

'Huh! Fat chance of you being able to do that,' she had scoffed and wandered off leaving him with his thoughts.

'It's nice to know that I have your support,' he muttered under his breath as she walked away. He could have said it aloud for all that she would have cared; or for all the difference that it would have made.

Since this brief and somewhat limited conversation, they had not spoken about the application process or his intention to change career again. There wouldn't have been much point really.

****

It was at some point in 2004 that he had been going about his normal business when the post had arrived. He had always found the post most annoying. It was not the fault of the individual delivery person, but it seemed to Simon that the mail deliveries had gone rapidly downhill over recent years. He was sure that when he had been growing up the post had arrived twice a day and that it was so prompt that you could set your watch by the sound of the letterbox flapping. Now this had been reduced to one delivery a day that could arrive anywhere in an eight-hour period. To top it all the cost of a stamp had done nothing but rise whilst it seemed that the service had done nothing but decline.

It was something to do with the fact that people were more inclined to send electronic mail these days rather than put a stamp on a piece of paper and trust it to a stranger to delivery when they felt like it. You could probably see the point really. It was sad though. History was full of interesting letters that had been preserved between scientists, artists, writers, musicians, politicians and God knows who else. We knew a lot about the period because of people like this. What would the future hold with electronic disposable mail? Simon bemoaned the fact that nobody kept diaries any longer either. We gradually seemed to be losing our ability to be a literate nation that liked writing to people and recording our thoughts on paper. He was pretty sure that the future would pay for this loss.

All of this was rather a distraction from the fact that the post had arrived that morning. Simon had shrugged his way up the hall with the depression of knowing that as no one wrote to each other any longer all that awaited him on the mat would be bills and junk mail. He gathered up the pile of envelopes from the mat and trudged back to the kitchen.

Back in the kitchen he sorted through the mail. There were numerous requests for him to take out credit cards and the odd magazine from a book club. He then reached a small brown envelope at the bottom of the pile and noticed that it had been franked by the police.

With a certain amount of trepidation and slightly shaking fingers he slowly opened the envelope and folded out the crisp, white paper. He slowly read the letter and found to his utter amazement and pleasure that he had passed the paper sift and he was being summoned to conduct a fitness test at the nearby police headquarters in a few weeks' time.

He was rather amazed by this. He had got through. He had passed the first test. He sat in bewilderment for a time whilst his coffee grew cold. The first hurdle was over, granted there were a lot more to be accomplished before his target was achieved, but he was on the move. He then began to think about what the fitness test would mean.

The police fitness test had changed over recent years. It had, in fact become easier. It was now divided into a couple of parts. The first part was what was called the beep test. This consisted of running from one end of a gymnasium to the other with the aim of reaching the other end before a recording gave a beep. Each time it beeped it moved up a level with the gaps between the beeps becoming smaller.

As a test of fitness, it was entirely inadequate. Perhaps if it had been a test to run in a straight line for a certain distance it might have been more relevant to discern if you were fit to perform the office of a constable. It was difficult to work out under what circumstances you would be required to run from one place to another and then turn hard to run back again repeating the process becoming faster and faster as you did it. On the other hand, life in the police was made up of strange occurrences, so you never knew. It was a pointless test for testing fitness really.

Once this had been completed you were then required to undertake a test of strength. This really wasn't all that hard and all it needed you to do was to sit at a machine and gripping the handles push it away from you as hard as you could. This would test what your strength was like at pushing. You then repeated by pulling it towards you. Guess what this was a test of?

To anyone who was reasonably fit it was not the most difficult of fitness tests in the world. The worry that Simon had was that he was not a particularly good runner. He had never been much of a runner if the truth be told. He could never really see the point of it. The chief problem that he had was the fact that for some reason that he was entirely unaware of he had developed a habit of holding his breath whilst running. This was sub-conscious really and had probably got something to do with the fact that he was concentrating so much on making his legs move that he had forgotten to breathe. The obvious problem with this would be the fact that he would eventually not be able to run at all — possibly on account of having died.

There was no doubt in his mind that he would have to get his arse in gear. He had been training, there was truth in that. Unfortunately, it had not all entirely worked the way that he would have liked and last time he had gone out for a run in the forest he had run over a dew covered little wooden bridge which had caused him to slip and go flying off the end of the bridge only to land and invert his ankle.

His first thought was that he was glad he had been running in the woods so that he did not have an audience to see him fall like a colossal dick. His second thought was that his ankle now appeared to be the size of a tennis ball which with his limited knowledge of medical science he was sure was not how it was meant to be. His third thought was now that he was in the middle of a forest with a buggered-up ankle how was he going to get back to where he had parked the car? His fourth thought was how he would work the pedals in the car now that his ankle was trying to escape from the inside out. His final thought had been — 'fuck.'

Three

The fitness test had actually turned out to be not that much of an effort when it had come down to it. It is true that he had turned out to be one of the first people taking part to drop out, but taking all things into consideration he was thirty-one years old and not overly someone who had been that fit for most of his life whereas the majority of people that he had been running against were between nineteen and twenty-three and looked like they had been born in gyms. There was an element of unfairness in this as it didn't matter whether you were nineteen years old or fifty years old. You had to do the same test. Obviously, some people were going to find it easier to deal with than others.

The push-me pull-me test had been a piece of piss. He left the police building feeling satisfied that he had at least achieved something on that day. This was an unusual feeling as there would be many times in the future when he left a police building feeling that he had achieved nothing at all.

Going home to face his wife was not something that he was overly happy with as he doubted that she would share anything of his happiness at demonstrating his ability. Indeed, they had spent a quiet meal together eating microwavable dinners sitting at the kitchen table. Simon found it hard to believe that they had so quickly reached a point in their marriage where they had run out of things to say to each other. Not entirely true, however as they had plenty to say to each other in argument.

That evening they spent a cool night in the living room not talking to each other and separated by their individual activities and a wealth of bitterness. Simon did ponder upon the fact that matters had so quickly come to a head like this. Nobody enters into a marriage with the belief that it will fall to pieces. You marry because you hope it is your life partner that you have found. For the life of him he could not understand why it was that Amanda had wanted to marry him now that he looked back at it.

'There is something that I have been meaning to say to you for some time now,' her breaking the silence shocked Simon and for a moment he was in a slightly confused state unsure of what it was that was going on. He then began to wonder what it was that she had been storing up to say to him. She had not mentioned his career plans for a while now so he imagined that it probably was another attack on that.

'Oh?' There didn't seem to be anything else to say and experience had taught him to play things as neutral as possible, to begin with at least.

'Yes, when you get out of the bath can you not stand on the bath mat.' He had to hand it to her he had not been expecting that.

'What?'

'Pardon, Simon; not "what?" How many times do I have to say it "What?" is so common.'

'Pardon?'

'The bath mat, Simon it's a simple enough request.'

'Why?'

'Why? Because every time I go into the bathroom the mat is soaking wet after you have had a bath.'

'Yes, but isn't that what it is there for? The mat is there to stop the floor from getting wet.'

'That's as maybe, but I would appreciate it if you would dry yourself before stepping on the mat.'

'What am I supposed to do, levitate?'

'Don't be facetious.'

'I suppose you don't want me to dry myself on the towels either because it will make them wet?'

'I really don't think there is any call for this. I am merely pointing out an observation. It is very irritating, that is all and I would appreciate it if you would do what I asked.'

Simon lapsed into silence. He hadn't been expecting that but he was just as shocked by it and he sat in the resumed silence wondering just how big the gulf was between them now and how big it was going to get before it was impossible to bridge it any longer.

***

The next test was the assessment centre and it was a couple of months before he was to attend that. Like all things he had faced so far there was a concern about this. Despite the fact that he had a degree he was not particularly good at mathematics. He had barely scrapped through with the requirement that had been needed to carry on his academic career. It had been a struggle so he was not confident that he would be able to pass the maths side of the assessment centre.

Simon had not entered blindly into his application. He had sought out and spoken to a number of police officers from the rank of constable through to inspector to see what their thoughts were and what advice they had been able to offer him. He had been able to meet with a rather laconic inspector at his local police station.

The interview had not been easy to arrange. It would seem that Inspector Jones was not an easy man to get hold of. From the little that Simon had been able to find out about the man he had realised that Inspector Jones was a man who was months from retirement. He had probably spent the majority of his career in retirement mode.

As a matter of fact, Inspector Jones could have retired several years ago, but he had realised that there was no rush in giving up what was for him the easy life in order to go into retirement where he might be expected to do things. At the office he could get away with lounging around doing nothing whereas in retirement there would be trips to Tesco and to the garden centre, DIY and decorating and all the other things that he avoided doing at the moment by going to work and leaving it all to his wife to do.

The rules regarding retirement, at this time, were that police officers had to retire at thirty years of service or at the age of fifty-five years old; whichever was sooner. However, if you were at the rank of inspector or above then you could extend this period if you wanted passed the age of fifty-five.

Inspector Jones had joined the police at the age of twenty-two and had been serving for thirty-four years. Now at the age of fifty-six he was finally prepared to ease into retirement. This was chiefly because of the fact that his superintendent had realised that Jones had blazed through the ranks and had been made inspector in 1987. He had then stopped; grinding spectacularly to a halt and had remained at that rank for the last seventeen years doing as little as possible. The superintendent had reviewed his file and politely offered him the chance to retire. Such things would obviously make the superintendent look good as he was no doubt eyeing up the chief superintendent role.

Inspector Jones had spent a great amount of time over his career avoiding his colleagues as much as the public, but had received orders that he was to grant Simon an interview before he was politely shown where the door was and then less politely shoved firmly out of it.

Inspector Jones had moodily sat across his desk and tried his best to listen to what Simon was saying and at least try and look like he might be interested even if he really couldn't have cared less. After some time, he was aware that a question had been asked which he had missed.

'I'm sorry?'

'I said how do you get along with mathematical knowledge?'

'I have never really considered it,' Jones was very puzzled and wondered just how much he had missed of the conversation.

'Only I bought this book called "*How to Pass the Police Initial Recruitment Tests*".'

'A gripping read, no doubt.'

'And in it there is talk about the maths test, which I have never been all that great at. One of the questions for instance — as an example — is how many pallets which are five feet by six feet in length and one foot in height, could you get in a warehouse that is thirty feet by seventy feet in length and forty feet high?'

'I see. It's rather difficult to know under what circumstances I would need to know that as a police inspector.'

'But if you did?'

'Then I would probably say something like "How many pallets can you get in there, sergeant?"' It wasn't the most useful of answers that he could have expected, but it was pretty obvious that he wasn't going to get all that much out of Inspector Jones. Well what could he expect when the police service had not got all that much out of him either?

The problem as far as Simon saw it was that he didn't *see* numbers.

He couldn't visualise them and retain them in his head in the same way that he could with words, for instance. Even the simplest of sums would be something that he would have to write down otherwise he would never retain them.

He was very pleased when he was able to find out a thing or two about the assessment centrè from a more obliging police officer. Firstly, he had found out that you were allowed rough paper when working out the maths questions which was a God send to him as he was not sure about this and rough paper was the very least that he felt that he would need. A calculator would have been even better, but you can't have everything that you want in life.

Secondly, he found out that the grading is an average taken of all your scores, rather than you having to specifically pass a certain grade in each individual test. This was good news, because if he did fall down slightly on the maths test that still gave him an opportunity to retain an overall decent score.

Before he knew where he was the day of the assessment centre had arrived. He had travelled down to the assessment centre and had gradually grown in nervousness with each mile that he progressed along the road. The good thing was that everybody else who was there appeared to be as nervous as he was. He found himself thanking his lucky stars that they had reduced it to half a day and he had been lucky enough that his turn had been in the morning rather than in the afternoon session which would have driven him nuts having to wait throughout the whole morning. At least this way he could get it over and done with.

His first test had been to write a letter on a given subject regarding someone who had written in to make a complaint. It was stipulated that none of the tests had anything to do with the police so that no prior knowledge of police practices or procedures would be required. It was an easy enough test as far as Simon had been concerned. As with any examination though there was not really the amount of time that you would have in real life to work on things at your leisure. If you had to write a letter in reality you would almost certainly take longer than twenty minutes to do it. Twenty minutes; this incidentally included the reading of the letter that you are replying to.

After this it was time to move on to the interactive exercises which were frankly very nerve racking. Five interactive exercises which take the form of five minutes of preparation about something that you have no previously knowledge about. This is followed by five minutes of interaction role play with someone else where you attempt to resolve a problem that is being presented. The problem is that it is just impossible to truly resolve these problems in the five minutes given. You can only make a certain amount of progress before your time is up and you have to move onto the next five minutes of preparation.

Simon had no idea if they were particularly looking for you to resolve any of the problems. If he had only known what being in the police was like then he would have known that members of the public frequently expected police officers to resolve problems in five minutes which had probably taken years to deteriorate to the point that they were now at. All he tried to do was to show as much diversity as possible. He felt that he was bound to have forgotten a great deal, however. You can't help but come out and wonder if it has all gone wrong.

After this it was the turn of the competency-based interview which was basically a repeat of the core issues that had been spoken about on his application form. He had to admit that he felt he had done better on the application form when he had been able to sit down with a coffee and a cigarette when writing it out. Once again you have twenty minutes for this interview, during which you have to answer four questions on various areas of competency.

From there it was on to the dreaded maths test and then logic tests. By this time Simon felt that he was very much on a conveyor belt and that the 'startled rabbit in headlights' look on his fellow competitors made him think they were probably feeling the same as he was.

Simon had to admit that the maths test had not been as hard as he thought it was going to be. He had perhaps expected to be questioned on calculus and trigonometry, but that had apparently not been deemed necessary. It was something that he was eternally grateful for. These were words that he could spell with ease, but had no idea what they actually meant. It was like algebra. The hours he had spent labouring over algebra at school only to discover that it was something that he would never have any use for again for the rest of his life. He had ultimately become convinced that the only use for half of these things was to employ maths teachers to regurgitate it out for another generation of maths teachers. At any rate he had been able to answer all twenty-five questions in the twelve minutes that were allotted. Whether they were right or not was another matter.

He had walked out of the assessment centre into the bright sunshine that had glared viciously at him after the reasonable darkness of the centre. As he had walked out, he had joined up with a girl called Julie that he had met during the course of the day. They had decided to go down the pub together. This was very quickly revealed to be a mistake as Julie had wanted to dissect the entire assessment centre process — Simon instinctively thought this was a bad idea as this is only bound to cause a high level of depression in one or both of them. She obviously had some kind of sadistic streak as she also wanted to exchange numbers so that she could keep in touch and share results when they came in.

Simon thought this a very bad idea, but being quintessentially English he found himself caught in a situation where etiquette would not really have allowed him to refuse to go along with it. From his way of thinking if he were to fail this then the last thing he would want to do would be to be sharing the failure with the entire group.

Whatever the result was going to be the chances were that he would never be seeing any of these people again at any rate.

Four

Simon found that time was moving as swiftly as something that was moving really rather very slowly indeed. There were some agonising weeks whilst he waited for the assessment centre results to arrive in the post. It seemed to be taking forever as every morning he checked the post. Most of the time it was the usual rubbish that he had come to expect from his postman each day, but he nevertheless approached the pile of mail with the same expectancy as a child on their birthday; and each day achieved the result of the said child realising that he didn't have any friends after all.

Despite the fact that all of this was taking a great deal of time, matters were in hand and moving very quickly. There was no time to rethink his decision. He was on a rollercoaster ride now and things were moving quickly. Yes, he could have halted it and pulled out if he had wanted to, but that would have been disastrous at this stage. He was pretty certain that if you changed your mind at this stage, they were not going to let you back again if you changed your mind back in the future. He felt that these people had very long memories indeed.

One morning he had picked up the pile of mail from the mat when he had come down to breakfast and seen that there was nothing in the pile that required his attention in the least. He had been sitting at the breakfast table when his mobile phone had bleeped in his pocket. He had fumbled to get to it and then looked at the screen as his half-awake mind came to the realisation that he had received a text message. A quick investigation revealed that it was from Julie. He had not heard from her since the day of the assessment centre so with a degree of apprehension opened up the message.

The text was short and to the point stating that she had received her assessment centre results and that she had failed by three per cent. What a bugger! Three per cent! Jesus! Simon's heart immediately went out to her in sorrow. This is exactly the situation that he had wanted to avoid. After the initial concern for her had worn off, which didn't take all that long, he had immediately riffled through the letters once again trying to find out where his results were. They weren't in the pile. He raced down the hall and started to search the mat. If Julie had got her results, but he had not then what would that mean? Probably nothing, but he was feeling paranoid enough to worry about it nevertheless. It had to be here surely.

Yes. There it was. It had fallen behind the curtain. He picked it up as if it was radioactive and carefully, almost at arm's length carried it back down the hall to the kitchen. He delicately placed it on the kitchen table propped up by the salt and pepper pots and then sat and stared at it for some time.

He was convinced that he must have failed. If Julie had failed by three per cent then his failure could only be more so. When they had been in the pub and Julie had insisted on dissecting the tests and had brought out the same book on passing the application process for the police that Simon had bought. She had compared the answers that he had given to the answers that she had given and then whenever they differed, she had looked them up in the book and found that her answers were always right. With results like that given her mild failure then he was doomed.

The pass mark was 50%. It didn't sound all that much, but now she had failed at 47%. It was hopeless, but as long as he didn't open the envelope then he wouldn't have to face the truth of the matter. It was a situation that really could not last forever. He would have to open it eventually; it was just a matter of time. After twenty minutes he sighed and reached for the letter. There was no sense in delaying any longer. He carefully slit the envelope open and unfolded the letter. He looked at it, and read it, and then he read it again. He had to make sure that he got this right with no mistakes.

He had passed. Overall score 68%. He couldn't believe it. He had passed. He read the letter again. He had not been mistaken; it was true he had passed. This meant that even if he did not now get into the force of his choice, he could still take the result to any other police force and try again without having to go through another assessment centre.

He calmed himself and started to breathe as he had suddenly realised that at some stage he had stopped breathing. The letter went on to break down all of the individual results. In respect for race and diversity the pass mark was again 50% and he had scored 67%, that wasn't too bad he reflected considering how it had never really been an issue that he had been required to evidence before.

In written communication the pass mark had been 44% and he had scored 78%. Not too bad although he was a trifle disappointed that his degree in literature had not stood him in better stead there.

The final breakdown was for oral communication. Again, the pass mark for this was 50% and he had scored 93%. That was pretty respectable really considering how he had felt that he had fluffed that area completely. Guess that meant he could certainly talk. Ultimately it did not matter although he had scored more than enough to pass and to get him onto the next stage.

The letter did not finish there and he was beginning to grasp the idea that if nothing else the police really liked statistics. There was a comparison of how you scored compared to other candidates. He found this to be rather shocking and he couldn't help but wonder what the other candidates had been like.

In the area of evidencing team work Simon had scored 80.4% higher than the other candidates. In the area of community and customer focus he had scored higher than 91.9% of the other candidates; that was rather remarkable as he was still not sure what that was really all about.

When it came to personal responsibility, he had scored 88.6% higher than the other candidates. The big surprise was that he had received a grade B in the maths test. He really found this hard to believe and was pleased that he had spent a lot of time studying up on his maths before the test. He would surely have failed if he had not have done so. He had been convinced that this would have been the area where he would fall down. It just went to show you that sometimes you just had to have a little faith.

The letter, which seemed to go on forever, concluded by summoning Simon to his final interview which was due to take place two weeks from now. In that time, he had to prepare his presentation which was to be on the topic of speed cameras.

Well that was interesting. Simon was like the majority of motorists in the fact that he hated speed cameras and wanted the things to be taken down. He hated them with a passion. He was not entirely sure why really as speeding was breaking the law as much as theft was after all. Although the clarification of which laws were more morally acceptable to break than others would be an interesting debate; but perhaps one for another day. Still, he supposed that he ought to find something positive to say about them.

He secretly thanked the fact that Julie had sent him the text or he might not have looked for the letter and it would have been ages before he had found it and then it might have been too late. He wasn't sure of what he should send back to her as he didn't want to appear gloating or in any way rubbing in the fact that he had passed where she had failed with such a small margin. Perhaps it might be better if he just didn't respond to her at all, but then he considered that might be a bit rude and he certainly had not been brought up to be rude.

He put the matter to one side for a minute and went to get his laptop so that he could start to get some research done on speed cameras.

He really wanted to share his good news with someone. It felt like it would be rubbing salt into the wound to share it with Julie. The only other person he could share with was Amanda, and she had already made it clear that she was not remotely interested in his flirtation with the police and wouldn't be remotely interested to hear that he had passed the assessment centre. He would just have to celebrate on his own.

***

The first thing that he had discovered about speed cameras was that the common belief that the fines that were collected by them went to the police was not entirely accurate. He had done some further research and had been able to meet with a Chief Inspector who headed up the local Traffic Department. He had explained to Simon what it was all about.

'People think that the money goes to us and we are making loads of money on the amount of people that are caught going through the cameras,' the Chief Inspector had said.

'And does it?'

'Not entirely. We have to pay for the upkeep of the cameras and also the running of the camera vans. There is maintenance and supplies as well as the cost of the staff and the processing of the data that is received from the cameras. We are allowed, by the government to re-coop the costs of the running of these cameras.'

'Okay.'

'Anything that is left over after that is sent to the government.'

'So, they get the money out of it all.'

'Yes. Well, they would if we allowed a profit.'

'I'm not sure I follow you.'

'We always try and make sure that if the costs of the cameras were, shall we say approximately £80,000 a year then we would make sure that there were just under that amount in fines; or if we were feeling generous then maybe just a little over that.'

'You don't sound as if you have a great deal of respect for the government.'

At this the Chief Inspector just tilted his head and shrugged slightly as if he was not prepared to confirm or deny any suspicion on this front.

'So,' Simon continued deciding not to press this point. 'These speed cameras—'

'We prefer to call them safety cameras.'

'You do?'

'Yes.'

'Why?'

'Speed is an emotive word. We prefer to look on them as safety cameras as primarily they are there to promote safety to all road users.'

'Would the public agree?'

'Probably not; but then they rarely do. Of course, the public belief that we have set these cameras up all over the place so we can make money is just another excuse for them to hate us even more than they would normally. People get so very emotive about traffic issues. The simple fact remains that speed is a contributing factor to road accidents and fatalities. If we are able to reduce speed in certain accident hotspots then we stand a pretty good chance of reducing fatalities.'

'Hotspots?'

'Yes, well they used to be called "accident black spots", but we aren't allowed to call them that any longer.' Simon decided that he would not press this issue either.

'Do you think they work?'

'Most of the time. I think that anything that stops people from dying is a good preventative measure.'

'But the speed limit is well known.'

'Yes, it is, but numerous members of the public don't seem to think that it applies to them; or that they don't need to adhere to it because they are somehow better drivers than the rest of us.'

'Do they use a lot of excuses?' Simon was becoming rather fascinated in this, despite himself.

'All of the time. I have had people tell me they were speeding because of the fact that they did not know that speed limits counted at night. I have had people tell me they have just washed their car and were driving fast to dry it off.'

'Really?'

'You would be amazed at the bollocks that most people are prepared to come up with. I suppose you have to give them some degree of credit for their originality and inventiveness. The truth of the matter though is that they are probably just very stupid and actually believe all this shit that they come out with.'

'You don't sound like you have a lot of time for the public.'

The Chief Inspector made the same gesture that he had made when the comment had been made about the government.

Simon was beginning to think that perhaps an extended period of time in the police and all that it exposed you to was likely to turn you into a cynic about a number of different issues. He made a promise to himself as he left the meeting that if he was accepted into the police then he would make every determined effort not to become as cynical. He wasn't to know then that it was not only a promise that he would be unable to keep, but that he would go a lot further than he could have imagined.

Five

Amanda wasn't really sharing in the enthusiasm that Simon was feeling for his attempt at changing his career as well as his life. She failed to see why he should want to better himself and change things in his life when surely just being married to her must be all that he could possibly ever have wanted. She came from a background where you were expected to know your place and get on with things without this strange need to want to change careers and other aspects of your lifestyle.

They had talked about the application process and what it was that he was hoping to do; and the talk had developed into a discussion about what was going on in their lives; the discussion had moved onto the level of a debate which had in turn made its way into the inevitable argument that was always going to happen. It was predictable because arguments were what they were all about these days. Their relationship had seemed to reach the point where it was defined by their level of argument.

If either of them actually stopped to think about it then they would have realised that there was little point to their marriage any longer and that they would be better off giving it up and parting for their separate ways. It was the logical thing to do. The problem with this was that Simon was not someone who was a quitter. He had not been brought up that way and he didn't believe in walking away from things. It was an attitude that would probably change as he got older.

He had not bothered to discuss anything further with her about the police after she had laughed herself silly when she had caught him practising his five-minute presentation out loud in front of the bathroom mirror. For reasons that had not been entirely clear to him she had found this extremely amusing. He had probably realised at that point that he was not really in love with her anymore. It is one step from thinking this to wondering if you ever were.

The realisation of these dramatic life changing things often happen at the smallest of moments in your life. When you are having a shave or making a cup of tea, or something so seemingly trivial you can suddenly be hit by the thunderbolt of realisation that you are entirely wasting your time.

He continued all of the rest of his preparation when she was out visiting her mother. Simon had stopped accompanying her to see her mother as it had been clear to him from a very early stage that Amanda's mother did not approve of him. It was pretty fair to say that she would probably not have approved of anyone. As far as she had been concerned nobody was good enough for her daughter whom she had raised to be treated like a little princess.

The problem with being raised to feel like a little princess was that you would only really have been happy if you could go on to grow up and marry Prince William. The other problem was that everyone else read 'little princess' to mean 'spoilt little bitch.' It was a pretty accurate description if the truth were told.

If Amanda's mother did not like Simon then it was equally as fair to say that Simon did not like her. Mother-in-law jokes are two a penny, but he had considered laying a minefield for the rare occasion that she visited them — which was not all that often as she had not considered that the house that they had set up together was good enough for her daughter. It is possible that only Windsor Castle would have been good enough and only then if you could ban all the tourists and she could have changed the décor. Simon had also briefly considered the possibility of setting up surface to air missiles in his back garden, as their house was on a flight path which her mother regularly used when flying to warmer climes. The unfortunate thing about her flying out of the country was that she always insisted on flying back into the country again.

Amanda's father had died a number of years ago and Simon was secretly of the opinion that he had died as a pleasant alternative to having to live with his wife any longer. To an extent Simon could understand and sympathise with this view entirely.

It was amidst all of this domestic bliss that Simon prepared for his final interview and presentation. The two weeks had passed quickly and it was soon time to dig his suit out again and prepare for another nerve-racking experience.

***

Simon had to admit that he was more than a little nervous about this interview board. He had been through a great deal already that was very true, but this was the final moment when everything could turn out to have been for nothing. He was aware of the fact that his entire future rested on the outcome of the hour or so that he was in this meeting. It was whilst he was sitting outside in the foyer of the police headquarters that he had been unfortunate enough to bump into Inspector Jones.

'You here for the interview then?' the Inspector had stated as he had stood in front of him slightly hunched and looking like the most unlikely of police officers that there could have been. Simon had confirmed that he was indeed there for the interview.

'We do them all the time.'

This did not seem to warrant much of an answer and Simon couldn't really think of one so he had just sat there trying to look polite and attentive.

'Don't worry about the first question,' the Inspector said looking as if he had just imparted a secret piece of information so great that at any minute people would jump on him from several different directions at once for breaching both the Official Secrets Act as well as the Data Protection Act.

'I'm sorry?'

'The first question,' the Inspector went on. 'Ignore it. They only ask it to set you at your ease and let you get into the flow of talking. They don't grade you on the answer.'

Simon was surprised by this level of helpfulness that he had not expected from the Inspector. It was a feeling that was about to be entirely changed with the Inspector's next comment.

'Of course, they routinely reject 50% of the candidates on these final interviews. It's our way of sorting the wheat from the chaff. Got to have some standards after all, haven't you?'

Simon just stared at Jones not quite believing that the man had told him this just before he was about to go and face the firing squad.

'Not entirely sure why you would want to join this circus though if I am honest. Still I suppose someone has got to do it. Would you believe that I am here on a retirement course? Amazing really. This organisation has courses on absolutely everything, including how to retire. I would never have imagined it. Still good luck, hey.' With this the Inspector moved off to see what other useless things he could get up to that day.

As he walked off, he passed a short frumpy woman that was hurrying along like a ship in full sail. This turned out to be a woman from Human Resources who introduced herself to Simon and with whom Simon immediately forgot her name the moment she said it. He guessed that this was probably something that was usual for her. She struck him as someone who was very easy to forget. She had come to conduct him to the interview room where his future would be decided.

Mrs Frumpy, as he had already begun to think of her conducted him into a small airless and windowless room. In front of him was a table where sat a Superintendent who introduced himself as Superintendent Norman Bean and an Inspector who didn't bother to introduce himself at all. Mrs Frumpy joined them at the table. Six feet in front of the table was a single, uncomfortable looking chair. To one side of this chair was a board on which Simon could place the flipchart that would form part of his presentation. Mrs Frumpy had grabbed this as she had conducted him in and fixed it to the board before she sat down.

With a polite nod of his head Superintendent Bean indicated that Simon was to begin. The Superintendent then folded his fingers and looked attentively at Simon as if the very future of the human race hung on every word that he was about to say. The Inspector looked slightly bored and gazed around the plain room as if he was planning a re-decoration; whilst Mrs Frumpy eagerly and almost sadistically clicked a giant stop watch which she would stare at intently during the course of the next five minutes. It had already been explained to Simon that if he went over his five minutes then the presentation would be terminated no matter where he was in it.

Simon began to speak and as he warmed to his topic he began to relax and flipped through the charts that he had prepared before with magic marker. He spoke about the merits of speed cameras drawing the ultimate conclusion that they were a good thing in the grand scheme of things. He had rehearsed this speech a great deal in front of the bathroom mirror so if nothing else he knew about timing. He concluded his presentation, took a deep breath and said 'And that concludes my presentation, thank you.'

Mrs Frumpy clicked the stop watch and looked up at him with a form of amazement as if he was bringing the word of God to the savages.

'That was exactly five minutes,' she said with a degree of awe in her voice. It immediately gave Simon the impression that this was perhaps the first time that this had happened so exactly in all the interviews that they had done so far.

'I know,' he replied and then immediately regretted saying it; thinking that perhaps this was going to come across as too arrogant. Truth be told the timing was more due to luck than judgement. He was just trying to appear cool and as if he had perfectly timed the presentation to the second. Well, you got nothing for want of trying.

The Superintendent smiled and thanked him for his presentation. It was then that the Inspector who had looked like he had been asleep spoke up.

'Your conclusions are all wrong, of course.'

This threw Simon slightly off his guard. 'I'm sorry?'

The Inspector took a deep breath as if summoning patience to talk to a particularly difficult child who did not understand a basic maths equation.

'Your conclusions,' he repeated waving vaguely in the direction of the flipchart. 'They're all wrong.'

'I don't agree.'

There then followed a three-minute debate as to why the Inspector felt that Simon had got everything wrong with Simon finding himself on the back-foot having to justify everything he had said. The Superintendent just sat there benignly smiling as if indulging a favourite child. Everything that Simon said to justify his research and conclusions was immediately shot down in flames. After a while he became aware that they were going around in circles and did not seem to be gaining anything. It was then that he had an inspiration.

'I'm sorry you feel like that, sir, but those are my conclusions and I stick by them.'

'Thank you,' the Inspector said and lapsed into silence with his hands in his lap and his head down. The Superintendent nodded his head slowly.

So that was the test, Simon thought to himself. The Inspector is briefed to argue with anything I say, to see if I will collapse and admit that everything I have said is bollocks, or whether I will have the courage to stand by my convictions. He was pleased that he felt he had passed this particular test.

It was then that the general questions that formed the main part of the interview began. It started with Superintendent Bean.

'What are the aims of the Constabulary?'

Simon started to panic. It was on the tip of his tongue to say 'Fucked if I know,' but he resisted and for a couple of minutes waffled on about preventing and detecting crime as well as protecting the public. It sounded like complete rubbish to Simon, but the Superintendent was nodding as if he was receiving the word of God directly from the source. He seemed to have got away with that one and hoped that Inspector Jones was correct that they didn't grade the first question.

After that the questions came one after the other for almost an hour. The three people on the board all looked at each other and nodded their heads to agree that they had concluded. Mrs Frumpy then stood up.

'If you would like to take a seat outside, Mr Orford we will consult privately for a few minutes and then let you know our decision.'

This took Simon by surprise; he had not realised that he would find out then and there what his result was going to be. He had assumed that they would send him a letter in the post. It was far easier to let someone down by letter, but it seemed that these people had the balls to tell you to your face whether or not you were any good.

Simon stood up and walked out of the room and sat on a plastic chair that was positioned opposite the door of the interview room. Simon considered that this was probably the worst and longest five minutes of his life. He then began to wonder how it was that they could make such a big decision in five minutes anyway. Surely, they needed to debate his future over the course of several hours? He then turned the other way and felt that they were taking too long to decide. It was then that he became convinced that he was going to be rejected.

The door then opened once again and Mrs Frumpy appeared and invited him back into the room. He entered and was invited to take his seat once again whilst Mrs Frumpy resumed hers. He felt that he was being kept in suspense for ages but in reality, it could only have been a few seconds. It seemed like an eternity as far as Simon was concerned.

Superintendent Bean looked Simon directly in the eye.

'Mr Orford. We are going to put you through and you will be required to go to the next stage which will be a medical test. Pass that and you will be very welcome to join the family.' He smiled.

Simon was in shock. He was being asked to be a police officer. All he had to do now was get through the medical and that is it. After the medical there was passing the fitness test once again; followed by two years of tests and exams as a probationer, but it was just about confirmed for now that the worst was behind him.

He shook hands with all those present and then left the room and the building feeling as if he was walking on air. He had expected to be rejected, but they had accepted him and he was to all intents and purposes a police officer in all but name.

He didn't know it then, of course, but if they had of rejected him at this stage then his future would have taken a very different course to the path that he was now set on. It was very possible that he just might come to regret that he had been accepted.

Six

With every step of the application process Simon would find that there was something that he had to worry about. This was just something that he did naturally anyway. He was one of those people who would probably worry about the fact that he had nothing to worry about, if that had been the case. He just seemed to like to worry about things. In truth there were a number of things that he did have to worry about and a number of hoops that had to be jumped through in order to get to the successful level. Even though he had to all intents and purposes been selected and successful in his application it could still fall down when it came to the medical. This was a fact that Amanda took great pleasure in reminding him at every step of the process. She was the kind of person who only seemed to be really happy when she was making other people unhappy. It was more than a hobby for her; it was a passion and a vocation. It was probably something that she had inherited from her mother. Obviously being an evil bitch was something that ran in the female line of her family.

Simon did not have to wait all that long for the medical to come around. When the day arrived, he was up early and arrived at the headquarters at nine o'clock where he found himself waiting for a short while until he was approached by a member of staff whom he was tempted to call a nurse, although he very much doubted that she actually was one. She conducted him along a passageway to a toilet where she asked him to provide a urine sample in the small bottle that was provided inside. He didn't really know it at the time, but this would only be the first time that they took the piss; it was not going to be the last time by any stretch of the imagination.

This test was partly to see if Simon was shot up to the eyeballs on cocaine, but was also to test to see if he suffered from diabetes. Either result would mean that all of the hard work that he had done so far would be a total waste of time. Simon wasn't too worried about this though as he knew that he wasn't a drug taker and he was pretty sure that he didn't have diabetes.

After this he was conducted back to the corridor where he was asked to stand and then read from an eye chart that was at the other end of the corridor to prove that he could see. He was slightly concerned about this test as he was aware of the fact that he did not have the best eyesight in the world. It would be a complete bugger if he had failed on this front as they most certainly would not have accepted him if he had turned out to be as blind as a badger. He was pleased, therefore, that he had managed to sail through this; but then it was not over.

Having done this he was then conducted into a small medical office where he was asked to sit in front of a machine that resembled a microscope. He was then shown a variety of images which he had to look at whilst they judged if he could see them or not. This test provided them with the ability to see if he could see objects at night as well. He was asked to have a look at a variety of circles and identify, if he could, the one that was not complete. This was a test that became progressively more difficult as time went on. He was, nevertheless, pleased that he managed to pass this test as well. Being a police officer was obviously about being able to pass a series of tests. He had no idea just how accurate this statement really was.

Having checked to ensure that he could see, they progressed next to see if he could hear. For this he was placed in a small cubicle facing a wall with a pair of headphones and a plunger button in his hand. He was required to sit in this little box whilst the assistant outside played a series of high-pitched beeps in either ear. Every time that he heard the pitch, he was required to press the plunger and keep a hold on it until he could hear it no longer when he was to let it go. Simon found this to be a bizarre test as after a while you began to imagine that you were hearing the beep even when it was not there. It became difficult to tell the difference between reality and the imagination, therefore. Perhaps this was part of the test as well. The ability to differentiate between fact and fiction.

When he was released from his little booth he was then sat in front of another machine where he was asked to blow into a tube so they could see what his lung capacity was. He was an infrequent smoker so had wondered if this would be as easy to pass as it might have been if he had never smoked, but it turned out that it was not all that difficult and he had never suffered from asthma either so it had been a breeze.

He had to hand it to them that they had the ability to be very thorough. It was almost as if they were determined to catch him out and find that he had something wrong with him. The next test was to see how much he weighed. It turned out that he weighed fifteen stone and two pounds. The medical assistant then took a little time debating on whether this was acceptable as he looked at various charts and examined it against the Body Mass Index. This was a ridiculous and pointless test as it was based entirely on the fact that it gave you a weight that you should be for a certain height. This assumed that you did not have an ounce of muscle or fat on you. Taking this into consideration a rugby player who was covered in muscle and not an ounce of fat would be rejected for being fat. Bloody silly idea really.

Having been conducted through all of this and having found nothing wrong with him whatsoever; a fact that the medical assistant appeared to be disappointed with; he was left to wait for a little while until such time as he was ready to be examined by the doctor proper. When he was conducted into the room with the doctor, he was asked to lie down on the examination table whilst the doctor felt Simon up in a manner which can only really be described as an indecent assault thinly disguised as a medical examination.

Simon was then very surprised to find out then and there that he had passed the medical. In the true spirit of the way things had gone so far, he had expected to wait until a couple of weeks had passed before they had told him whether he had passed or not.

***

'I really don't understand why it is that you are continuing to bother with this charade,' this was a comment that came from Amanda as they sat at breakfast the next morning.

They only really seemed to meet at breakfast most of the time, if they ever met at all. They went through most of the day without seeing each other and very rarely ever sat down to eat an evening meal together. Most of their married life seemed to be spent in avoiding each other. It wasn't much of a marriage. It wasn't much of a life.

'What charade would that be?' Simon asked, knowing clearly what it was that she was referring to, but choosing to be deliberately obstinate.

His wife smeared marmalade over her slightly burnt toast and tried to give a dignified air of one who had been sinned against.

'This whole charade of wanting to be a policeman.'

Simon decided to not say anything at this point which seemed to be the best thing to do under the circumstances. He certainly wasn't about to remind her that the correct term was police *officer*, as they tended to try and be less sexist in the terminology.

'I mean what are you thinking? I don't understand what you are thinking at all. Are you thinking anything?' This much was really clear without the need of having to express it in speech. Simon watched her attacking her toast and tried to remember what it was that he had liked and loved about her in the first place; but found that it was becoming increasingly difficult to drag this particular memory from deep within his brain. Clearly there must have been something that had attracted him to her in the dim and distant past; but he was damned if he could remember what it had been.

'Well, are you going to answer me; or are you just going to sit there sulking?'

'I don't really think there is anything that's worth saying.' He also didn't think that he had been sulking, but there was little point in expressing that view to her.

'Well, that's just typical of you really. You have no understanding or appreciation of anyone else; or what their feelings might be.'

Simon thought that this was a bit rich, but had learnt that nothing would be gained by him saying so. Amanda was someone who only ever saw things from her point of view as she seemed to hold onto the belief that anyone else who had an opinion that differed from hers was not worth entertaining. Clearly anyone who had an opposing view was wrong so not worth spending time on. This was probably some ancestral, genetic inheritance that dated back to when her family had helped the monarch of the day to rule the country. She and her mother were inordinately proud of their family and the long history that they shared. In fact, her mother had once told Simon with a degree of pride that her family could be traced back to having arrived in England with William the Conqueror.

Simon with his sense of history had replied: 'Actually at the time he was not known as William the Conqueror, but William the Bastard. An interesting model to align yourself with. Of course, I never realised that your family were, to all intents, descended from illegal immigrants.' You can probably imagine how this comment had gone down. When you are on the slippery slope downwards the best thing to do is to just strap some water wings to yourself and get on with it.

Simon dragged himself back to the current moment and the situation that he was in. He sighed deeply and took a sip of his coffee.

'I have nothing to say because no matter what I say you will not understand why it is that I am trying to do this.'

'You're not even trying to make me understand.'

'I've tried, but you're not exactly open to understanding what others want.'

'And just what is that supposed to mean?'

'I'd have thought that it was a reasonably clear and unambiguous statement, which an intelligent woman, like you, should have no difficulty in understanding.'

This was something that was called fanning the flames. Amanda seemed to be turning a peculiar colour. Ultimately, she resorted to doing what she and her class always did in these circumstances. When someone made a comment that you really didn't like to hear then you just ignored it like it was something that simply had not happened. She sniffed the air as if an obnoxious smell had just entered the room; which as far as she was concerned was probably the case.

'Why you should wish to become an agent of the state is anybody's guess.'

As was often the case Simon was dumbfounded by the illogical position of her argument. Her family were proud of the fact that they had served under numerous kings and queens so you couldn't really be much more of an agent of the state than that, surely?

He sighed quietly to himself and pushed his breakfast away having lost his appetite completely — not for the first time either.

Seven

Although he had passed every section of the recruitment process, Simon found that he still had to wait for a few months before he was given a start date. It would take some time before a date was available as he had to wait to be fitted into the next intake that had any spaces on it. Eventually, he was given a date to start in January 2005. As the date approached, he began to wind down his affairs in his previous job, tender his resignation and then allow himself to have a few weeks of leave before he would be due to start his new career and new life as a police officer.

During the course of this time off he made the most of the winter and developed a raging cold which ensured that he looked and felt his best for his first day as an officer. The very first requirement was the need to pass the fitness test once again which was no means a certainty when he felt like shit.

Despite feeling so crap, he did appreciate that there had been a lot of hard work and a very long road to even have the privilege to be standing where he was that morning; of course it is rather difficult to think like that when it is seven thirty in the morning and you are facing a fitness test of running up and down a sports hall about forty or fifty times. Simon could understand that this might be some people's idea of having fun; but it was not something that featured anywhere in his top one thousand fun things to do. It seemed to be an interesting start to his new job though.

Before long the fitness test time had come and Simon had lined up with the other eleven people on his intake whilst trying to remind himself that he needed to breathe. The test was repeated as it had been before and despite the dregs of his cold, he was amazed to find that he had managed to get through it once again. Due to his general feeling of ill health and the fact that he was not much of a runner in the first place, he only ran for the minimum of time that he was required to do whilst some of the others seemed to want to carry on running until the tape ran out; or until time itself ended. He was not entirely sure what it was that he thought that they were trying to prove by this.

After that they were all given the opportunity to have a shower and freshen up before being marched off to the Uniform Stores Department where they were all given the amount of uniform that they would be required to use. Bags became full of shirts, ties, epaulettes, trousers, riot boots, helmet, soft cap (for when they weren't walking), two types of high visibility jackets (one heavy, one light weight), a standard issue set of handcuffs and a baton followed by a stab proof vest. They were all required to get into uniform without the need for the vest and other bits and have their picture taken for their future warrant cards.

From there they went off and had a group photograph taken with them all wearing their dress tunics. Looking smart and fresh for the first and possibly last time in their careers. This all took a large amount of time and they were then given an opportunity to have a brief rest before lunch.

They would only be here for two weeks, but they were all required to stay on site and sleep in the accommodation block. This was so that they would have the opportunity to bond and get to know each other as a team. This was compulsory even if you lived five miles away. Simon was distinctly happy about this as it would give him an excuse to get away from Amanda and their three-ring marriage which had followed the procession from engagement ring to wedding ring before ending with the bickering.

After lunch they were ushered into one of the classrooms where they would spend the majority of the rest of the day being introduced to the Police Force and told how wonderful it was. They all sat in a semi-circle whilst their trainer stood in front of them.

'Welcome. My name is PC Thomas Cartwright and I'm going to be your trainer for the next two weeks before you all go off to training school. These next two weeks will be an introduction to the police and where I will endeavour to introduce you to the basics of what it means to be a police officer. Many of you will find that your lives will change now, forever.' He paused to allow this to sink in.

'You will find that many members of your family and friends will tell you that you have changed. This will be true. You will change. This job changes you; there is no way around this fact. You will see things that nobody else will see. You will do things that nobody else will do. Most of the time nobody else will want to see or do these things; but you will be expected to do it anyway — because that is now your job.'

This wasn't perhaps the introduction that a lot of people had been expecting and was probably something of a shock for the majority of the people in the room. PC Cartwright appeared to be satisfied with the reaction which was clearly something that he was used to experiencing at this stage. He continued.

'Some of you may even find that you lose friends because of what you have done by putting on the uniform you are wearing. Not everyone understands or respects the police or the job that we do. As a result, you may find that some people that you called friends no longer want to be your friends. This is because of the fact that they were never really your friends to start with. Try not to worry about this too much if it happens. You have joined a big family now and you will get a whole lot of new friends; should you need them.'

The group was starting to feel distinctly uneasy by all of this as it was most certainly not the introduction to the police that any of them had been expecting. They were all starting to realise that things were beginning to change. This was not a game and what they had been the day before they were no longer.

'You all have a lot of responsibility now and you also have a great deal of power. More than you perhaps realise; but within a few months you will have the power to stop people going about their business. Under certain circumstances you will have the power to search them, their cars and their homes. Most importantly of all you will have the power to take away their liberty. This is a power that you must use responsibly, without fear and without favour or prejudice.'

He took the time to look each of them in the face as he said these words. The importance of the decision that many of them had taken was being brought home for perhaps the first time; which was a bit of a shame as this was a lecture that could really have been given before half of them had actually put the application in. Some of them may not have then completed the application in the first place.

'As I mentioned fear, it is perhaps a good time to make some comments on that. From time to time you will be asked to do things that are frightening. You will find yourself in situations that are scary. You may even come across people that want to hurt you or perhaps even kill you. You will meet the lowest level of scum that society has to offer. Murderers, rapists, paedophiles maybe even politicians,' he smiled slightly to indicate that this may or may not be a joke.

'So, what do you feel when you're in these situations? Do you feel like a hero or a coward? Perhaps you will not feel any fear at all; in which case you should probably find yourself another job. It's only natural that you will feel afraid in some situations; that is what will keep you alive. Being a hero is having the ability to feel the fear and get on and deal with it anyway.'

There were some heads starting to nod at this.

'Police officers routinely run towards what most people will run away from. That is why you are here. You wouldn't be here if you were not like that. The public will look to you and in many cases, they will look up to you; not all cases and not all people, of course. When an emergency situation takes place, whether it is someone who is in a domestic and needs your help or whether they have been the victim of an assault or perhaps involved in a car accident; they will look to you to take charge and tell them what they have to do. This doesn't matter whether you have one day of experience or twenty-five years. All they will see is the uniform and they will have no idea how long you have been wearing it and they will care even less.'

'What if we are the first to a scene of something like a car crash and we don't know what to do because everything is chaos?' PC Cartwright looked slightly miffed that this question had been injected in what was obviously a well-rehearsed opening speech that he had probably used a number of times before.

'I find that the best thing to do is to issue orders. Even if the orders are not important, trivial orders that don't matter in the least. Doing this will achieve two things,' he marked them off with his fingers. 'Firstly, it will reassure the public that someone in uniform has turned up and is issuing orders and appears to be taking control. Secondly, and most importantly, it will give you time to assess the situation and think about what you really should be doing.'

There appeared to be a certain degree of sense about this.

'I don't want to put any of you off. This is a good job and it's unlike any other job. You should know the realities of what you're up against. Just in the same way that from time to time you will hear swearing during this training. Someone from a previous intake made a complaint that one of the trainers had sworn during the classroom exercises.' He looked everyone solemnly in the face.

'I only have one thing to say about this,' he paused again for dramatic effect. 'During the course of your day to day jobs now you will hear people swearing and most of it will be directed at you. If you are going to get prissy about this kind of thing then it is probably a good idea if you fucked off right now.' He pointed at the door for emphasis.

Nobody seemed to be even remotely inclined to take him up on this offer, but he nevertheless kept the suspense up for as long as he could to see if anyone would take him up on the opportunity to walk out. When it became clear that he was not going to be taken up on his offer he smiled and sat down in the chair in front of them all.

'Good. Now let's begin.'

Eight

That evening the twelve people in the group got together and decided to walk into the nearby town to find themselves a pub to sit down in, have a few drinks and get to know each other. As was the case they all sat about and discussed who they had once been. Simon was surprised about the variety of people that the police attracted. In this group of twelve there was an ex-postman; an ex-supermarket worker; an ex-army corporal; an ex-RAF sergeant; an ex-social worker; an ex-primary school teacher; an ex-student straight from university who hadn't done anything else; an ex-dustman; an ex-used car sales man; an ex-bank clerk; an ex-fitness trainer; an ex-unemployed person who didn't seem to have previously done anything and then there was Simon. All in all, a lot of exes, who now seemed to want to be something other than an ex-something.

Simon was rather surprised at how they all seemed to become firmly friends despite not knowing each other twelve hours before. He wondered how long this bond of friendship would last. He wondered whether or not they would all make it. Just because of the fact that they were now police officers did not mean that they were going to remain so for the rest of their careers. The Force reserved to right to get rid of any of them during their two years of probation with little or no warning; or even with all that much explanation as to why. It also worked the other way around, of course, and if you wanted to you could walk away a lot easier than it would be after your two years.

After having had rather a few too many they all staggered back to the accommodation block giggling at nothing in particular. The walk back in the winter air sobered them up a great deal which was just as well given that they would have things to do when they got back. The next morning PC Cartwright had announced that they would all be inspected before the lessons started. This meant that he expected boots to be highly polished; trousers to be neatly pressed and shirts to be smartly ironed.

This, unknown to them, was an exercise in teamwork. There was one iron and one ironing board to be shared between the twelve of them. Some among them knew exactly how to go about such things; whereas there were others who would have to think twice before they were able to work out how to plug the damn thing in. The idea of ironing a formal shirt was a complete mystery to them. Some had led rather sheltered lives in this regard and it had been their mothers who had sorted this kind of thing out for them. The organisation was well aware of this and was also aware that there would be some among the group that had been involved in such parades in the past.

The ex-forces members were a God-send when it came to ironing, putting creases in things and polishing boots to such a high level that you could see your face in them. It was something of a pain in the arse to them that they had to spend most of the rest of the evening showing everyone else how to go about doing these things correctly. In the end, more by luck than planning all twelve of them felt that they had reached a point where they would be able to pass the inspection.

The next morning, they all ate a cooked breakfast trying desperately to make sure that they didn't drip egg or baked beans down their crisp new white shirts. Simon could not help but notice that the rest of the police officers who were in the room also eating breakfast and who weren't on an intake of new officers all looked rather different from the twelve of them. The other officers were not as clean shaven as the twelve of them. They did not have uniforms that were as fresh and clean, in fact they looked rather slovenly compared to the other twelve. The most disturbing thing as far as Simon was concerned though was the fact that they all looked so damned tired. Not a one of them looked like they were getting enough sleep and most of them looked like they were on the point of physical collapse.

Simon had a rather disturbing feeling that he was looking at his own future staring back at him. He wasn't sure that it was something that he was too happy with. They all filed out of the canteen passing two officers that were sitting near the door. One turned to the other as he tried to destroy his bacon butty.

'You can always tell the new recruits.'

'Yep,' said the other as he pushed food around on his plate, 'they don't look as fucked as the rest of us.'

***

As PC Cartwright entered the training room, they all stood up as they had been taught to do whenever a trainer or a senior officer walked into the room; at this particular stage in their career, senior officer meant just about anyone. He glanced briefly at each of them as they proudly stood with everything shiny, sparkling and creased.

'Yeah fine,' he said as he moved to his chair. This was something of a let-down. Simon wasn't sure what he had been expecting, but he was learning pretty soon that praise and compliments were not something that were freely forthcoming in the police.

'You are all ambassadors,' PC Cartwright said as he settled into the lesson for the day. 'You will all be judged on what you do and say, both in and out of uniform. That does mean whilst you are off duty in case you are in any doubt.'

Simon was sure that there were a lot of revelations that would be coming over the weeks that were to follow. They never told you half of it before you joined up.

'If you are not aware already,' he continued, 'you are not employed.'

This raised a few eyebrows and a slight number of knitted brows. They were pretty certain that they were getting paid so that made them feel like they were employed.

'No. In almost any other job you would be employees; but not in this one. In this one you are servants of the Crown.' He looked around the group letting this sink in. 'If any of you are republicans and have any Cromwellian thoughts in your head then you may as well remember that Her Gracious Majesty Queen Elizabeth, second of that name, is *your* boss.'

He pointed around the room taking in each of them.

'Now, we may all hate our bosses, but that is the way that it is. I expect you to show respect for the Crown regardless of what your personal thoughts might be. The crown is on your badges — when you get them — it is on your epaulettes, on your helmets and cap badges and everywhere else that the Force crest appears. It is on the buttons of your tunic — which whilst we are at it I expect you to always have the correct way up — after all you don't expect the Queen to stand on her fucking head do you?'

This did raise a few smiles.

'You will also be sworn in as police officers shortly, and when you are you will swear your oath of allegiance to the Queen. The *Queen*,' he said again for emphasis. 'Not the Chief Constable, not the Home Secretary and certainly not the fucking Prime Minister.'

'Surely the Queen doesn't take that much of an active interest in us?' piped up one of the group, who was feeling braver than the rest.

'I very much doubt she even knows who you are or fully understands what it is you do; but then again I very much doubt that the Prime Minister has much of an idea of what it is that the police are about either. That is the problem with politicians. They control our lives and our destinies without having a bloody clue what we do on a day to day basis. No one can, that is the problem. You only understand this job if you have done it. No amount of reading books or anything else will tell you what it is like to do this job. If you want to find out then you have to do it. Simple as that. That does mean that everything that you saw on *The Bill* is nothing like reality. Sorry folks, welcome to the real world.' This appeared to make a certain degree of common sense as far as the group could see.

'Nevertheless, despite that given fact; you will find that you come across people all of the time who tell you exactly how to do your job. Politicians, victims, suspects, offenders, witnesses and oily little tykes who have never done so much as a day of work in their life. Despite the fact that many of these people have never worked or paid so much as a pound in taxes for as long as they have lived, they will nevertheless tell *you* that *they* pay *your* wages.'

He paused once again and looked around the room.

'This is, of course, complete bollocks. I pay your wages, and you pay mine. Look at it from that point of view.'

'Are we not servants of the people?' another asked.

'No. We are servants of the Crown, I just told you. The thing to remember about the public is that they are divided into a couple of groups. Those that are criminals, or lily-livered liberals who hate the police; and then there are those that will do everything that you ask them to do because they have grown up to believe in the police. If you told them to stand on one leg, they would probably do it because they think you have the power to do this kind of thing. This is why I told you yesterday to be aware of the power you will yield. You will find that it is too easy to abuse.'

They all looked at each other as if very unsure of what to say.

'With this power and authority come restrictions. You cannot, from this day forth strike — you have no industrial powers the same as other peoples. You also cannot become actively involved in politics. Some of you may not want to. You cannot stand in elections or be an active canvasser for any political party. You are also unable to express a preference for any particular political party in public. Like the Queen, herself, you are now neutral. No one doubts that the Queen has an opinion on political matters, however she tends to keep those views private and they are not known. This will be you from now on. You are also not allowed to be a member of the British National Party or any other fascist or pseudo-fascist group. If you are members already then frankly you shouldn't have got through the selection process. If any of you are thinking of joining in the future then you may as well know that the choice will either be that or to be sacked.'

***

'What do you think?' This was Suzanne asking, one of Simon's fellow recruits.

'I don't really know what to think,' Simon admitted.

They were sitting in the canteen once more thinking over the morning and the revelations.

'He seems very negative.' Suzanne continued.

'Perhaps he is just trying to show us the way that it is rather than paint a little rosy picture that will be blown out of the water.'

'Perhaps,' she didn't sound too certain. 'He doesn't seem to have much respect or faith in the public or the politicians either.'

'I suppose that will be up to us to work out if that is a valid position or not when we are eventually let loose on the streets.'

Suzanne seemed to grow in statute at this suggestion. 'I can hardly wait,' she said.

Simon nodded his head, but didn't say anything.

'You know I will never truly be happy until I have a crown on my shoulders,' she stated.

Simon looked at her incredulously and then tried to hide the expression on his face. Jesus, he thought to himself. This woman wants to be a superintendent already and she hasn't as much as stepped foot in the public arena in uniform yet. What the hell does that say about her motives for joining? Perhaps PC Cartwright had developed his deep-felt level of cynicism over years of practice and experience.

Nine

The next two weeks of training went very quickly. The way that it was formatted is that they would train for two weeks in their home Force and then they would transfer to Kent for twelve weeks where they would train at a big training school that included officers from all over the country. This would be their chance to meet a number of people from different Forces and see how things were done differently around the country.

There were still a number of things that caused issues and worries amongst the group; of course, there would be, it was only to be expected. These were very early days. One fear that Simon felt was the fact that he was not sure of his ability to make decisions correctly and solve problems. He knew that as a police officer he would be required to make decisions very often on the spur of the moment. In other jobs and other areas of life you might actually have a chance to sit down and discuss what it was that you were going to do, but the point had been made clear that in this job you had to think and more importantly act quickly. In many cases lives might depend on the decisions that you made and how quickly you were able to make them.

Very quickly they had the moment of their official swearing in as police officers. As a special moment they had been allowed to invite friends and family to see them being sworn in. This was the first time that they had been given the chance to stand outside in the compound in their high visibility jackets and helmets or hats. It was something that brought them a level of satisfaction of achievement.

For this brief moment, if at no other time Simon actually did feel like he was 'authority,' probably for the first time in his life. He also began to notice that people's attitudes changed towards you when they saw you in uniform. Rather amazing what wearing different clothing and acting differently could do to people.

Simon already knew this. He had conducted experiments in the past. If he walked into a newsagent where he was not known and bought a copy of *The Sun* newspaper whilst wearing jeans and a T-shirt; the shop assistant would invariably refer to him as 'mate.' However, if a few days later; or even a few hours later he walked into the same newsagents to buy a copy of *The Times* whilst wearing a suit then he would be called 'sir' by the same assistant.

People made judgements about you all of the time based on stereotypes and first glances. Yet, PC Cartwright had already stated that as police officers they were not expected to have prejudices and play up to stereotypes. He wondered how practical this would be given that whatever else they were, or were going to be, they were still human.

Simon could see how people's attitudes could change towards you. People have faith in you even though you are on day three of training and know nothing. He could see how this power, this authority can all too easily corrupt and go to your head. He felt that it was something that could happen to any of them and it was a bubbling volcano that they needed to keep a cap on.

He felt a mixed bag of emotions about how people reacted towards him in uniform. He felt pride, almost embarrassment and a degree of fear. Pride because he was proud that he had made it through a difficult process. He had arrived. He felt almost embarrassment because everyone looked like they were relying on him and he didn't know any more than anyone else. Finally, he felt fear because he was aware that this was something that could certainly go to your head.

When the time came to be sworn in, they were marched into a room and in front of their friends and family they stood up one at a time and in front of a superintendent, PC Cartwright and a Justice of the Peace and were then sworn in as police officers. They pledged their allegiance to the Queen and received their warrant cards. They were now officially warranted police officers. From tonight they had to take the words that they had spoken in front of the JP very seriously because they now mattered. They had each sworn an oath to uphold the law and that is something that had to be taken seriously.

After the swearing in they all mixed with their family and friends. It was a relaxed atmosphere and there were some soft drinks and slightly odd-looking sandwiches for the going. PC Cartwright worked the room and eventually found himself standing in front of Simon with a drink in his hands.

'Your wife here, Simon?' he asked as he looked suspiciously at what he had been reliably informed was a ham sandwich.

'No,' Simon said as he scanned the room. 'No, she doesn't appear to have turned up.'

***

The following day they were all hit hard with work. It was all pretty intense and they guessed that now that they were fully fledged police officers 'the powers that be' had decided to bring the heavy guns up and by the end of the day all or most of them were feeling very brain numb and could do with something of an intellectual rest. It had been a very busy week and there had been a lot to know and learn.

Simon was something of a reflector and he found very quickly that with all the hard work that was going on, there really was not all that much time to be able to sit back and reflect upon it all. It was ironic really as they had all been actively encouraged to do the work that they had been set and then have moments of reflection upon it. Nobody had said where and when this was meant to take place.

As their two weeks had progressed the group had gelled more and were getting on far better than it had to begin with. It was hard to believe how far they had come in such a short space of time. Simon had been on a long journey; as had they all and it already seemed like the group had known each other considerably longer than they actually had known each other.

By the time of the second week they had the dubious honour — if it could be called that of meeting the Chief Constable. They were all aware of the fact that meeting the Chief was a rare occasion, and it was not something that they expected would happen on a regular basis. It would seem, however, that this particular Chief liked to meet new recruits.

Simon could not help but feel that the entire thing had been a little too staged for his liking. The Chief tried to come across as too friendly and as a mate when that isn't necessarily the image that most of them wanted from a Chief Constable. In this regard at least he seemed to have his priorities mixed up and was somewhat confused about what it was that he wanted. There simply was no way that you could be everyone's mate whilst at that high a rank. It would not work. He seemed to be the kind of person that would be all matey with you and act like your best friend, but would then discipline the hell out of you if you did not stand up when he walked into the room. Perhaps that was what a number of senior officers were like. Simon had not really known enough of them at this point to be able to comment on it.

A few days later they had the opportunity to go to a real police station where some of them would be working in the future. There had been a level of excitement about this, but the truth had been somewhat boring. Welcome to the real world of policing, Simon thought as he listened to one of the shift sergeants droning on and on about something that they had all stopped listening to pretty much from the moment that he had started talking.

As the final week progressed, they all started to become a little concerned about their transferring the base of operations to Kent. This concern was largely based on the unknown. Simon felt that the twelve of them were a good group. He was aware that they would all be spread about when they got to Kent and be swallowed up into the mass of one hundred and fifty or so police officers that there would be down there. They would then have to start all over again.

Simon also felt that it was a long way to travel and with the rising cost of fuel it would not be the cheapest of things to have to cope with. Still things were always in a position where they could be worse than they were.

***

At the end of the two weeks Simon returned home where things were worse than he thought they were.

Whilst the rest of the group went back and spent a weekend with their wives, husbands, boyfriends and girlfriends and a mixture of more than one of the above and spent their time in having a relaxing weekend, in some cases with those that they loved; Simon spent the weekend as if he had decided to visit the North Pole. It was that frosty an atmosphere between Amanda and him that it probably would have been hotter at the Pole.

Most of the weekend was spent in not talking to each other and avoiding each other whenever the opportunity arose. Simon was upset and annoyed that Amanda had not come to his swearing in and had not provided him with a reason as to why. Amanda was upset and annoyed because Simon was a police officer despite all of the objections that she had voiced about it. She felt very strongly that he should have listened to her opinion, taken it on board and then acted on what it was that she had wanted him to do. This rebellious streak that he had developed of wanting to do his own thing was something that she found very hard to be able to stomach and smacked of insolence.

Both of them were as entrenched in their positions as much as the soldiers from opposing sides had been during the First World War. From time to time Simon had considered the possibility of trying to make a peace offering so that he could go off to Kent feeling a little better and with a clearer air. He quickly came to the conclusion, however, that he would be unable to make it across no man's land without a substantial amount of shrapnel in his arse.

Some fights were just not worth the fighting. And so it was that Simon packed his suitcases that he would be required to take with him to Kent on his own and in silence. A lot of the luggage that he was taking down there for the first trip would be left in Kent and from then onwards for the next twelve weeks he would just be ferrying his washing backwards and forwards with each trip.

In order to be ready for Monday morning it was necessary to leave Sunday night and so it was that fully packed up he walked out of the door without so much as a goodbye from Amanda and loaded all his bags into his small ten-year-old Golf.

Ten

And so it was that they all journeyed from various different directions to the location that was Kent. Simon arrived at the Police Training School to discover that there was a very long queue of cars that were winding for about a mile down the hill from the entrance gates. A lot of people were trying to get in. Presumably all of those trying to get in were police officers although Simon did not have much faith in their ability when he saw that some of them were not acting any better than what he would later learn to describe as 'boy racers.'

Simon sat in the queue for an hour moving forward a few feet at a time and winding his way closer to the sentry box that marked the entrance to the compound which he was soon to discover was massive. As he slowly crawled forward, he saw the sentry in the box with his hat on his head and a little moustache that made him look somewhere between a bus conductor and Hitler. Before long he drew level with the window.

'Name?' The little officious man demanded with no preamble or attempt at civility.

'Simon Orford,' said Simon Orford.

The nameless official looked down the list and found the name that he was looking for.

'Drive up the hill and park in the large car park on your right. You will be required to park in this car park and then take all of your bags up to your rooms. You are not allowed to drive into the residential area so you will have to walk it from the car park.'

'How far is that?'

The official sniffed as if to say this was an irrelevant question that was taking up time and slowing down the progress of the cars that were behind Orford.

'It is about half a mile up the hill. Display this in your car at all times,' he handed over a permit. 'If you don't display it in your car then it is liable that you will get towed.'

Simon nodded and carefully placed it on his dashboard as if he had just been handed the Holy Grail.

'You are in residential block B. When you get to the top of the hill you will see the old mansion house.'

Simon smiled at this and thought that this was sounding good.

'Block B is opposite the mansion house in what was part of the old tuberculosis hospital during the War.'

This wasn't sounding quite as good; at least he hadn't said which war it had been. Some accommodation information was passed over to Simon and then the conversation appeared to be at an end as he was waved up the hill. He parked in the car park as he had been directed to do so and began to carry the first amount of his luggage up the hill.

It was a good brisk five-minute walk up the slight hill to where the accommodation block was. This would not normally have been much of a problem under normal circumstances, but it was a complete pain in the arse when he was lugging so many bags and equipment with him.

He eventually found his accommodation block. He had not been remotely surprised to learn that they were all segregated in what would probably turn out to be a futile attempt to keep the sexes from mixing. He walked his way down the corridor to his own room and finding the right door he pushed it open to find his heart sinking when he saw that there were three beds in the room. He had not considered the possibility that he might be sharing a room. Twelve weeks would go by in this room so he hoped that his roommates were going to be of good character and with a decent sense of humour.

Well, you can hope, can't you?

***

Instructions had been given that they were all to be on the parade square at nine o'clock the next morning in full uniform where they would be split into their classes. This was something that took about an hour to complete and as it was February it was not the warmest of weather to be standing about doing nothing; other than catching a mild amount of hyperthermia.

It did not take Simon too long a time to decide that there were a lot of arseholes amongst his fellow recruits. His thoughts the night before when seeing them in their cars was already beginning to show a degree of truth about it. He tried his best to ignore them otherwise they would grind you down until you could not take it any longer.

When they had been divided up into their new classes they were taken to their main classroom for the coming weeks and introduced to their main tutor. She introduced herself as Sharon Morgan, which was presumably her name.

'Good morning and welcome to the Police Training School which will be your home for the next twelve weeks. I will be your base tutor and from time to time you will have other tutors who will teach you specialist subjects. There are some ground rules that you should be aware of first.'

'I thought there might be,' muttered the person to Simon's left.

'Many of these rules we will establish as you go along. However, you should know immediately that all members of the training branch whether civilian or police officers will be addressed as "staff" unless they are sergeants or above in which case they will be addressed as appropriate to their rank. Be advised that it would be foolish of you to pass a staff member or officer senior to you without acknowledging their presence. They won't take too kindly to that.'

The person on Simon's left sniffed as if disgusted by this.

'Next you should also be aware that at no time whatsoever will any of you be seen outside of the buildings within the compound without your hats or helmets on if you are in uniform. You will be appropriately addressed during working hours unless directed otherwise. You will also not put your hands in your pockets or run unless taking part in a role-playing exercise. For those of you that smoke, you will only be permitted to smoke in the designated smoking areas. These locations are clearly marked on the maps that you have been given. I have no doubt that most, if not all of you have already located the canteen and the bar. Now, any questions?'

***

Days passed into weeks and it is not really necessary to go into too much detail about what was taking place. After a couple of weeks Simon went out for dinner with his roommates as a method of getting to know them a little better. They walked down to the bottom of the hill where there was a Harvester restaurant considerately located.

Tim was twenty-two years old and spent the majority of his time not saying anything. Gavin was twenty-four and made up for Tim's silence by saying more than enough for the three of them. Simon certainly felt like he was the old man of the group. By the time that they had got onto the desert course and consumed a little more alcohol, Gavin was beginning to be a little too loud for Simon's tastes.

'I have wanted to be a police officer since I was about five. It is so amazingly cool that I'm now able to wear the uniform.'

Simon was aware of the fact that a number of other people were looking at them throughout the restaurant. He was also aware of the comments that PC Cartwright had said about discretion and being judged on and off duty. It was probably the case that the majority of the people that used this restaurant were from the college, but there would also be civilians mixed in amongst them; or 'normal people' as some of them had already begun to refer to them. It probably was not wise bragging about being a police officer in front of these people who could have any background at all. Furthermore, the other students that were amongst the diners could easily be listening and waiting to report back any indiscretions to the college.

'Perhaps you should keep your voice down a little,' he said as diplomatically as he could.

'Why? Are you ashamed of being a police officer?'

'No, I'm very proud of it actually. I just believe that there is a time and a place for everything and I don't think an appropriate place to be talking about this is in a restaurant and public bar after several drinks.'

'Sounds to me like you are ashamed of it,' Gavin concluded as he returned to his drink and ice cream.

Simon thought that Gavin was lacking in common sense and he tried to put it down to his age and perhaps lack of maturity. He also imagined that Gavin was the kind of police officer that would eventually say the wrong thing to the wrong person and would end up getting his head kicked in; assuming he managed to last that long in the police in the first place.

Simon was pretty amazed at the number of officers that he had come in contact with over the last couple of weeks and was frankly gobsmacked that they had been allowed to join the job in the first place. There were some real idiots in this job; that much was becoming clear. They weren't just idiots; they were stupid with it. It beggared belief, really.

It staggered him that there were so many people that had no idea of whom, or what, they now were. It came across in the behaviour that he saw almost every day that he was training in Kent. He saw numerous people, particularly in the bar who did not seem to realise that they couldn't continue to act in the way that they used to act before they became police officers. They still thought that they could act in a drunken and loud way when they went out for a few drinks. It was beyond belief really when they did not seem to realise that in a few weeks they would be required to go out on the streets and prevent the public from being drunken wankers and yet still acted like it themselves.

Some of the trainers were not particularly that much better either if the truth were told. Simon would remember the good trainers as well as he remembered the poor ones. The mediocre ones would slip by the wayside and be forgotten.

Two of the bad ones that would be unforgettable would be the ancient looking Mr Carvel who was a retired police officer and, as Simon suspected, a retired human being as well. His lectures were heavily centred on PowerPoint presentation; which considering his advancing age more credit should be given to him for being able to work the technology, or even to know of its existence in the first place. He would display the PowerPoint on the screen; but he would also give an exact hard copy of the PowerPoint to all the students in the class; he would then insist on reading aloud everything that was on the PowerPoint. He did not divert from what was on the PowerPoint and say anything else; or elaborate, for that matter. It seemed that he had nothing else to say.

This triple form of PowerPoint presentation was, everyone agreed, death by PowerPoint.

The other really bad one was one of the fitness instructors whose name was one that Simon never remembered because he was never entirely sure that he had even ever known what it was. This particular instructor had introduced himself by sticking a twenty pence piece to the top of the whiteboard. He had then stated: 'For those of you who have questions, that twenty pence piece is so you can go and ring someone who gives a fuck.' It made you wonder why some of these people had been drawn to the training environment in the first place.

There were others who were really good. There were those who still clearly loved the job and relished the idea of shaping the minds of the police officers that were to form the next generation. It wasn't always that bleak a picture, although it was clearly possible to view it that way. As was so often the case you tendered to focus more on the negative than the positive — in anything.

At the end of each week there was a knowledge check which you were expected to score well in and you also had to write eight statements over the course of the twelve weeks. All of these were scrutinised minutely for the smallest of mistakes. If you made huge errors continuously and scored badly in the knowledge checks then there was always the threat of 'being returned to Force.' This meant that you would be sent back to your individual Force in disgrace and then they would decide whether you would suffer the indignation of being re-coursed or just simply dismissed.

Staff would check to see if you were breaking any of the rules as well so that they could jump on you. One of the biggest flagrant disregards for the rules was attempting to leave the compound in uniform, or partly in uniform. This was a big no-no. Leaving wearing half your uniform, such as trousers or shirt, or maybe even just slipping a jacket over the top was referred to as 'half blues.' This was something that was unacceptable. No matter how late you were or how desperately you needed to leave the compound, you were expected to change out of every bit of uniform before you did.

Before too much longer it was time for the final knowledge check. Simon sat it with a degree of trepidation that he had not felt since he had been at university. He had done okay in all of the knowledge checks so far, but there was still plenty of time to screw things up. This was the mother of all knowledge checks.

He was delighted to find out that he had ended with a result of 82%. This brought his overall final course result to an average of 84%. He was happy with this and hoped that his force would be happy with it as well. There were physical tests as well, including tests in handcuffing and unarmed defence tactics. He worked hard and managed to get through them all and survived to tell the tale.

It had not seemed all that long ago that he had arrived at the Training College and now he was packing his bags once again and making his way back down the hill to his car.

Eleven

As Simon started the long journey back home, he reflected on the events that had taken place over the previous twelve weeks. There had been high moments and there had been low moments. For many of the people present it had been something of a wrench being away from home for so long; granted you were allowed out at the weekends and could return home if you so wanted to do so. Most people elected to go home at the weekends and would spend a lot of the time during the week cooing into mobile phones and pay phones assuring their loved ones that they really did love them still. Simon had decided not to bother with this. He didn't really think that Amanda would have been all that interested to have him call her and tell her how he felt. There was always the danger, as well, that he would call her and tell her what he actually felt. He rather suspected that she had enjoyed not having him around during the week as well.

He did return home on some of the weekends; chiefly because it was easier to do his washing at home then it was to do it whilst he was at the training college. Every now and then though he had told Amanda that he would not be home at the weekend as he needed to study for an important test that was coming up the following week. Amanda had taken these announcements with her usual blend of indifference and indignation. Having been able to secure his release for the weekend he would then shun study completely and would more than likely sod off to Canterbury where he would spend a very enjoyable day or two looking around the cathedral and other associated and non-associated historic attractions.

From time to time his thoughts would be dragged back to Amanda and he might feel a moment of guilt that he had lied to her about the reason for his weekend stay in Kent. He would then feel less guilty as looking at the area where Thomas Becket was murdered, he reminded himself that Amanda would consider herself even more of a martyr than Becket was. He wouldn't have been surprised though if you had told him that one of her ancestors was involved in sticking the sword into the former Archbishop. It would have made him feel quite certain that one of his ancestors would have been the one tasked to clean up the blood.

He had met some very nice people at the training school and he had also met some complete and utter wankers. Were he to know it, but this was a pattern that would be reflected throughout his entire police career.

He had met the wankers like the guy who had resigned after two weeks. Standing in front of the superintendent of the college he had been asked why it was that he had jumped through so many hoops and so many difficult tasks to become a police officer only to throw it away so quickly. The superintendent had been baffled to say the least and had politely asked for an explanation.

'Well, I didn't realise that we had to work nights.'

Silence had greeted this for some moments whilst the superintendent had digested this information and then felt his grip on his patience begin to wane. He had asked the soon to be ex-police officer to repeat what he had just said. The soon to be ex-police officer had duly followed this last lawful order.

'What on earth did you think happened at night then? Do you think we just shut up shop and leave a fucking answering machine on, or something?'

The soon to be ex-police officer had admitted that he had not really given the matter the full thought that it perhaps deserved.

'You aren't kidding me,' the superintendent had said and had waved the soon to be ex-police officer away and had then gone on to compose a letter of explanation to the soon to be ex-police officer's home Force where he had seriously questioned their vetting and recruitment standards before concluding: 'Really?'

Simon had also met the lout who clearly had joined the police because he had thought it was the SS and had smilingly admitted during the lessons that he had received every fixed penalty notice that was going. Simon didn't rate his chances of staying in the job all that long. In fact, his mid-course review had diplomatically suggested that 'Maybe you should consider an alternative career away from the police.' This had not gone down all that well and he had accused the college of discriminating against him. Simon had thought this one over and came to the conclusion that if he believed that the training college was discriminating against him on the grounds that he was a thick, useless twat then he probably had grounds for a grievance.

Everything so far may have appeared negative, but it is fair to point out that Simon had also met some very nice people who had been serious and dedicated to the job that they had undertaken and would undoubtedly eventually turn out to be a credit to the uniform. As well as a lot of negativity he had started to realise that there were a lot of people who had joined up because they wanted to make a difference; because they wanted to stop bad things happening to good people and to ensure that justice was metered out to the villains. Of course, there were those that had joined because they wanted to drive fast and break traffic laws, legally.

Simon had also met a very nice officer from another Force called Laura and he would certainly not be mentioning her to Amanda; assuming that Amanda would have been interested to know anything about what he did at training college in the first place; which she thankfully wasn't. Laura was evidence enough that you couldn't keep the genders apart just by having segregated residential areas. There were some forces of nature which were impossible to control.

Thinking about Amanda had darkened his mood — as it often did - and not for the first time he wondered why it was that he got married in the first place. Like a lot of things, it had seemed like a good idea at the time. Looking back, he realised that he had been a complete idiot about the whole thing. He wondered what the future would hold for them both. They had drifted apart in so many ways over recent years and if everything that he had been told so far were even slightly true then the chances were that they were going to drift a lot further apart over the coming years.

A number of people had told him that the divorce rate amongst police officers was uncommonly high. He supposed that the reason for this was that having a spouse who was not in the job meant that they couldn't really relate to the things that you did or saw on a daily basis and had no common frame of reference.

'People think that they live in the real world; but they don't,' one of his trainers had said. 'You now live in the real world as you will see things that nobody else sees. You will see what is really going on. People will walk through life and not see the things that you will see or understand the things that you understand.'

If there was some truth in this, then most people probably would not want to live in the real world, given the chance. The real world was dark, nasty and violent.

He also supposed that working so closely with a colleague you were forced to rely on each other for your very lives. This formed a bond and you were very often together more than you were with your families. This led the way to affairs happening for those that were inclined to go that way. Simon didn't think that the police were to blame for affairs though. If you were going to have an affair then you would have one no matter what it was that you did for a living. In order to 'go over the side' as one person put it then there had to be something that was fundamentally wrong in your relationship to begin with.

He was not looking forward to the week of leave that he was now to 'enjoy' after the intensity of training. Training college had, on the whole, been a warm, friendly, happy time where he had been able to spend company with like-minded people that were, on the whole, all there for the same reason. To return home to the coldness that awaited him was not an attractive proposal.

One week off and then it would be blissfully back to work where after a couple more weeks of localised training where they reinforced the way that they preferred to do things — each Force has its own nuances — and then after that he would be out on the streets with his tutor doing the job for real and meeting the public in all their fragile and angry states.

Perhaps things would change with regards to his social life, but if they were to do so then they would have to be done one slow step at a time. He was on a journey now and it was just a matter of working out whether it was going to be a journey that he would be making on his own or whether Amanda would be coming along as well. He was pretty sure that he knew the answer to that one already.

Twelve

There isn't really much point in dwelling on the week of annual leave that Simon had as it was a time that passed in frosty silence for the most part with not all that much passing between Simon and Amanda other than the barest of essentials. This was so common place now that it was something that he was used to. He had spent the majority of the time split between reading his law books and reading novels for pleasure. In particular the ones that he had read during his degree were ones that he liked to return to whenever he could. It reminded him of simpler days. Days when things seemed to be easier than they were now. It was also much more fun reading the novels for pleasure rather than reading them for study.

The return to work had been a lot more boring than he had anticipated with a great deal of the time dedicated to studying the way in which local forms were completed and in studying things that they had not taught him at training college; such as the delights of the Countryside and Wildlife Act, which was something that try as he might he really could not get his head around. A secret part of him that would not voice itself aloud couldn't help but wonder that with all the murder, rape, burglary and theft that was going on in the world that really people wouldn't be all that concerned about the odd badger here and there. He was, of course, entirely wrong about that. The English people were a nation of animal lovers and would often care more about animals then they would about their next-door neighbours. It was just one of those things really.

After the course, which had been delivered in a monotone for the most part, he was assigned a tutor that he would be working with over the coming weeks. This was PC Jayne Arnold who was about five years older than Simon and had been a police officer for eight years. Simon was noting already that whenever a police officer introduced themselves, they largely would follow with how long they had been in the job. If they didn't then it was a question that someone was likely to ask very soon within the conversation. The reason for this was that people felt that they could judge your level of experience and competence by the amount of years that you had completed. It was all about being placed within the hierarchy as well and knowing your place.

There was a degree of logic to this, but there was also a major flaw. Length of service was not an indicator of how competent you were. You could have worked for only one year, but in that time done more than anyone else. You could have worked for twenty years, but just have repeated year one over and over again without making any progression or development.

They worked in a rural county so spent a lot of their time driving around in a three-year-old Ford Mondeo with one hundred and twenty thousand miles on the clock exploring the depths of rural England. PC Arnold encouraged questions and would answer truthfully whatever she was asked. Most of their conversations took place in the car as they drove about, particularly at night.

The structure of the police was such that there were numerous departments. The front-line uniform patrol officers were known as response officers. These were the people that would turn up if you ever dialled 999. Then there were the officers who made up the Safer Neighbourhood Teams, or SNT for short. This was a relatively recent thing that had been formed because the Government thought it would be helpful to have a team of people that would concentrate on things like anti-social behaviour and neighbour disputes. They were also people that would attend parish council meetings and allow the members to moan at them about how little the police were doing about anything. Usually this involved speeding through villages and dog mess on the pavements.

From there you could go in a number of different directions as the specialist departments were virtually endless. There was the Traffic Department, no prizes for what it was that they concentrated on. From there you had your Criminal Investigation Department, Rape Investigation Department, Domestic Violence Unit and the list went on and on becoming more and more obscure as you got deeper into it.

Simon was a response officer, but he was keen to know as much as he could about the other departments so had asked Jayne to give him an overview of how things worked. She had thought about it for some time before providing him with an answer as she negotiated the country roads in the darkness.

'Key departments consider what they are doing to be essential work,' she had eventually replied. 'Whereas there may be elements of truth in their importance — essential, they are not.'

'Why not?'

'Well without a Domestic Violence Unit then Response would do it. Without a Rape Unit then Response would do it. Without an SNT — well nobody would notice or probably care. Without Response though the whole thing would fall to pieces.'

'But would it really?'

'Who else is going to do it? How many CID officers turn up first on scene at a murder or a burglary?'

'I don't know.'

'None. Do the Rape Unit turn up at the scenes of rape? Of course, they don't, it's us. Without us it all falls apart. We are the backbone of the entire structure and the pressure is on us.'

'The pressure?'

'Of course. We are always first on scene to everything. We have the most to do. We are meant to be experts in everything that we go to. You may see people from other departments spending a lot of time sitting around and as far as you can see they may not appear to be doing all that much. You must remember that they are the experts in their fields and as such they need a lot of spare time so they can scrutinise the work you are doing at jobs that they should attend in the first place so they can then tell you in detail what you are doing wrong.'

Simon thought about this as the car continued on its journey of endless patrol from place to place. Something was bothering him slightly and had been for some time so he decided to eventually voice his concern.

'I can't help but notice that the vast majority of police officers that I talk to are somewhat...'

'What?'

'Cynical and rather depressed frankly.'

She thought about this as she continued to drive. She sighed deeply.

'Well you're right, of course.'

'Why?'

She sighed again. 'Well, I suppose we all start off excited and enthusiastic. We are keen on the job and we want to help people and make a difference. The problem is that this is not a job that anyone else understands. Not the public and certainly not the politicians by any stretch of the imagination. The politicians sit in judgement over us deciding our future and our fate, but they have no idea of the reality of the job that we do.'

'Some would argue that politicians have no idea of reality full stop.'

'I wouldn't disagree with that. Well, as time goes on the unique nature of this job begins to wear you down. Slowly, a day at a time. If you are unfortunate then you become "job pissed"'.

'Job pissed?'

'Yeah, pissed on the job. You see them all over the place. People who live and breathe the job 24/7. These are the ones that are most dangerous because they have ambition and don't mind who they crap on in order to work their way up to the top. The saddest thing about these fuckers is that they are too stupid to realise that one day they will retire; and the day after they retire nobody will remember them or give a toss about them ever again. They will go into retirement and then realise that they have nothing at all. Their entire lives have been made up of this job and then there is nothing left for them to do any longer. As such, they will probably be dead five years into retirement.'

'Doesn't sound very appealing.'

'It isn't. Be wary of these people. Our Chief Inspector is one of them. A more heartless, ruthless, ambitious man you will never meet. About as diplomatic and as subtle as Hitler at the Nuremberg rally. '

Simon snorted.

'And the other sort of people?'

'The other sort are the ones that make up the majority of us. These are the ones that are not on the drug of the job and eventually become disillusioned with it. We are worn out, pushed to the limit of our endurance. Each job that we go to wears us down slightly. The senior officers and the politicians grate on us and, it becomes harder with each day that passes. That's probably why so many people go into specialist roles so that they don't have to stay on front line any longer. It's the hardest.'

'Why do you still do it?'

'I don't know. It's just what I do. I can't imagine that I will stay here for the whole of my career. At the end of the day there is only so much of this you can take before the tiredness and the injuries get the better of you. That's why it's not like any other job either. We are pounded and pounded hard.'

'It all sounds like a bit of a joke really.'

'Well, never fall into the trap of treating this joke as a job.'

'It amazes me that so many people are in this job, but hate it.'

'I suppose we are all trapped into it now. We are tied up and there is nothing that we can do. Getting out is not so easy. In the meantime, we have to put up with all sorts of shit.'

'Like the Chief Inspector?'

'Yes, well we are led by idiots masquerading as fools.'

'So many officers I've spoken to seem to act like it's some kind of conspiracy theory that's going on and that the job is personally out to get them.'

She snorted at this.

'The job's not out to get them it's just the way that the job is. Remember this; if it's ever a choice where you think there is a conspiracy in this job against you, just consider that it might just be incompetence. We are not organised and intelligent enough for conspiracy; but incompetence — well we have shed loads of that.'

'Any more wisdom to pass on?'

She thought about this for a moment and then decided to come up with some answers that he had not expected.

'Never stop any vehicle that you can't see over.'

'Why not?'

'Because that's heavily into the world of Traffic and you're talking tachographs and a whole host of weight regulations and other stuff that nobody really understands.'

'I see. Anything else?'

'Yes, run to a fire and walk to a fight.'

'Really?'

'Most people who are in a fight are because they want to be in it. A lot of others are in it because they have done something to deserve being in a fight. From time to time there will be the innocents of course; but it's worth keeping in the back of your mind when you're speaking to a victim remembering that they may well have done something to deserve what has happened to them.'

'Really?'

'Yes. I'm not saying it justifies it, of course. However, if you go about your everyday life without antagonising others than the chances are that you won't become a victim of an assault. It does happen, of course. There are exceptions to every rule. The fact of the matter is though that people lie to us. Offenders lie to us. Suspects lie to us. Witnesses lie to us and yes, victims lie to us.'

'It doesn't sound particularly encouraging does it?'

'No. That's because it isn't.'

They drove on in silence for a few minutes. Each drowned in their own thoughts thinking about the job that it was that they had signed up to do. Eventually she turned to him again.

'It isn't what you expected is it?'

He thought about this for a few minutes as he stared through the windscreen, following the light of the headlights as they picked out a path on the country road.

'No. No, it isn't what I expected at all.'

He had no idea just how different it was going to get before the end came.

Thirteen

Whatever illusions Simon may have had destroyed by joining the police he was nevertheless still pleased to have got into a job that he liked so much. This was something that would probably change as his tutor had predicted. We are all brought up to have dreams and it often happens that the reality is not what we would have expected. This is why they tell us that we should never meet our heroes. This was not really a problem for Simon as all his heroes were dead so the chances of meeting any of them was rather slim to the say the very least. Simon's heroes were Thomas Hardy, Charles Dickens, Albert Camus and of course, William Shakespeare.

One thing that Simon was noticing was that the police was run on cakes. There were numerous occasions when cakes were deemed appropriate to buy. There was a whole list of cakeable offences. If it was your birthday then you had to buy cakes for the rest of the shift. Simon found this a little converse as he was pretty sure that when it was your birthday people were supposed to buy you cake. You had to buy cake for finishing your tutorship, for being confirmed in rank. You had to buy cake for every mistake that you made. If you said something silly over the radio, or if you pranged a police car, forgot your pocket notebook, or left it out so that someone could draw a penis in it (and they would); these were all offences that were deemed suitable for cake buying. In fact, the list was not exhaustive. New offences could be added at the drop of a hat.

Simon's tutor period introduced a world of firsts. As was to be expected he experienced a number of things that he had never experienced before. There was his first blue light run. Although he had only been a passenger, there was something thrilling about being in a car that was driven, safely, at speed. Going through red traffic lights and on the wrong side of the road. He looked forward to the day when he would perform his own blue light run for the first time. He was sure that it was something that he would remember for the rest of his career.

There was the time that he saw his first dead body. He had never seen a dead body before. He was not to know that he would see a lot of dead bodies throughout his police career. Some freshly dead, and some long dead and decomposing. He would remember some detail about all of them, even if he remembered nothing else about the job.

His first sudden death was an eighty-nine-year-old woman who had died at home where she had been living with her son and his family. It was a natural death with nothing suspicious about it at all, but because she had not seen a doctor for the last two weeks and the death had been unexpected, the police had been called. Now, in these circumstances the police are acting as agents of the coroner. And the coroner carried a lot of power. The police gathered evidence about the death for the coroner so if there was a court hearing it could all be presented in detail, although this only tended to happen for car crashes, suicides and murders.

In all deaths the police were required to obtain all personal details about the deceased and to view the body, just to make sure that there was not a knife sticking out of the back, or something like that. That was the kind of thing that could ruin everybody's day.

The son led them to the room where his mother was at rest. As they did so Simon noticed Jayne nodding towards his belt. He looked down and noticed that his baton had come loose and was in danger of falling out on the floor. This would not be a good thing to happen at such a sensitive moment and so he began to fiddle with it to put it back in its holder.

Unfortunately, the son chose that moment to turn around to say something. He immediately noticed Simon fiddling with his baton. He gave him a sympathetic look.

'You won't need that, son. She's dead.'

Time went quickly, as it has a want to do, and before too much longer the tutor period was over and then it was back into training for three weeks where he was attached to the Driving School. Now, some might think that the idea of being taught how to drive was a strange concept. Recently a civilian had taken over the job of trying to save

Simon's Force money. He had looked at the Driving School and then without any trace of stupidity in his voice had announced in a budget meeting: 'Why do we actually need a Driving School?'

Stunned silence had greeted this comment. The man had progressed forwards with the confidence of someone who feels that they are out for a pleasant afternoon stroll in the country rather than walking across a mine field.

'I mean, we all have driving licences, don't we? '

With the patience of a saint the Head of the Driving School had explained that there was more to it than that.

'We are, after all, letting a large number of people out on the unsuspecting public. We are expecting them to drive fast and, in some cases, break traffic laws in order to get to an emergency call with as little delay as possible.' He had rubbed his forehead gently as if his brain was trying to escape from the meeting that he was in. He continued as best he could.

'Now it is up to you; but we traditionally think that it is important that police officers are given the best level of training possible to ensure that they can drive not only at speed, but safely as well.' He was being met with a blank expression.

'Or perhaps you think it would be best to just give them a silly hat to wear and then let them drive like cunts and hope for the best?' It might be imagined that his patience had worn out at this stage.

'The thing is,' interjected his deputy in a desperate attempt to save the meeting. 'There is much in the press about police officers inflicting injury or death on members of the public because of fights, baton strikes, Taser shots and of course by being shot—'

'Although thankfully there has not been a shot fired in anger in this Force,' interrupted someone from the Health and Welfare Department.

'Indeed,' continued the deputy. 'Now, what we tend to forget is that out of all of these items which can be used to cause injury or deadly force, the most common and perhaps the deadliest of them all is the motor vehicle.'

'Really?' said the budget manager who had already clearly lost interest.

'Oh yes,' responded Health and Safety. 'More people are killed in the UK each year in car crashes than are killed by a firearm.'

'Road Traffic Collisions,' said the Traffic Inspector.

'What?'

'They are not car crashes. They are Road Traffic Collisions.'

'I thought they were Road Traffic Accidents?' This was from someone else at the bottom of the table.

'No. Accidents suggest no fault.'

'If we could just get back to the point,' pleaded the Budget Manager who was beginning to wish he had never raised the point in the first place now.

'The point is that we still think it's a good idea to train people to be able to drive to a system that's safe as well as progressive,' replied the deputy.

The Budget Manager gave up and decided that the Driving School was something that would have to wait for another day. He decided to turn his attention to other things.

'Well, do we really need to have a Riot Squad?'

'More than we need you,' muttered someone from the end of the table. The Manager chose to ignore this last comment.

'We don't have a Riot Squad,' spoke another Inspector from further down the table.

'It says here that we do,' said the Manager.

'Well we don't,' explained the Inspector with firmness.

'Perhaps you would care to explain?'

'Not really.'

'I think what the Inspector is trying to say,' started someone from Human Resources.

'Please don't tell me what I'm trying to say,' interjected the Inspector. 'At least let another police officer try and do that.'

'If I may,' said one of the sergeants. The Inspector nodded. 'We do not have a Riot Squad. Riot is such an emotive word. What we have is Public Order Units and Police Support Units.'

'I'm sorry?' The Manager was confused; it was easily done in all fairness.

'Don't be,' said the Inspector.

'Are you telling me that we have units made up of police officers who support police officers?'

'Yes,' said the Sergeant.

'Well why are we supporting police officers with other police officers? Surely they can support themselves?'

The Sergeant sighed deeply. It was always the way. Every now and then the Chief Constable would appoint a high-ranking civilian like this to come in and shake the Force up. There was nothing wrong with this in principal, but the fact of the matter was that they would have next to no knowledge of the police at all or how it was expected to work. Worse, they would try to run it like a business when a business was something that it most certainly was not. They would come up with these schemes to cut costs and save money and then it would have to be carefully explained to them why it was that what they wanted could not be done. They would just about get used to the idea of what could and could not be done when they would move off to pastures new and another high-ranking civilian would come in and the entire process would have to start all over again. Most of those sitting around the table had been through all of this several times before, which perhaps explained their lack of patience with what they were going through now.

'We need a PSU—' began the Sergeant.

'A what?' asked the Manager.

'A PSU, Police Support Unit. What we have been talking about,' he said with perhaps just a slight amount of over emphasis.

'Oh, I see,' that was an annoying thing. The damn police had so many acronyms for things. It was like you could only understand what they were saying if you were in the same private club as them. If he could have done, he would have banned all acronyms, but it would have been slightly out of his budget remit.

'We need PSU,' resumed the Sergeant. 'Because of the fact that not all police officers are trained in the level of public order that is required to deal with highly volatile situations.'

'Why not?' asked the Manager.

'Because it would be too fucking expensive,' said the Inspector. 'I'd have thought that would have been right up your alley.'

'To be PSU trained requires a number of skills that officers have to be trained for on a regular basis. It also costs to fit them out with the relevant clothing and equipment.'

'Why can't they just wear the same uniform as everyone else? Why do they need special clothing?' asked the Manager.

'Oh, Jesus-fucking-Christ-on-a-stick,' mumbled the Inspector, not entirely under his breath.

'Because,' continued the Sergeant with his endless patience. 'PSU officers require full cover helmets, they require shields, they require flame retardant clothing—'

'What on Earth for?' asked the Manager shocked.

'Because, in the situations that PSU are deployed to they are likely to have petrol bombs thrown at them,' smiled the Sergeant indulgently.

'Good God,' replied the Manager shocked. 'Do people really do that kind of thing?'

'Yes,' replied the Sergeant.

'They throw petrol bombs at the police?' he asked again.

'Yes.'

'Good God why on earth would they do that?'

'Because,' said the Inspector. 'Although it may come as a shock to you, not everyone likes us.'

'It's outrageous,' replied the Budget Manager.

'I'm suspecting,' the Sergeant said as he twiddled with his pen. 'That you have had something of a sheltered upbringing?' The Manager chose not to say anything in response to this.

'Can we, therefore, accept the fact that we do need a PSU?' asked the Inspector.

'Yes, yes I see what you mean,' said the Budget Manager coughing slightly and shuffling his paperwork whilst he tried to find a piece of dignity left. He found a sheet of paper that he had been looking for.

'Ah, yes. Well leaving the Driving School to one side, what about the Training School in general?'

'What about us?' said the Inspector who was head of training.

'Well, it seems to me that you have a lot of police officers in the Training Department,' said the Manager.

'Yes, we call them trainers,' said the trainer.

'It isn't cost effective. I don't understand why you don't have civilian trainers in there instead of police officers.'

The Head of Training rolled his eyes.

'Here we go again,' said the Inspector.

'We do have civilian trainers in training,' said the Head.

'But why have police officers doing it as well?'

'We took all the police officers out of training a number of years ago and put them all back on the front line,' continued the trainer.

'Oh, jolly good,' said the Manager.

'And then within a very short space of time we had to re-advertise and put them all back in again.'

'What on earth for?'

'Because it didn't work.'

'Why not?'

'Well, the problem is that civilian trainers; no matter how qualified and good they are, just don't know what it is like to be a police officer. So, when they were training new recruits, for example, they would be asked questions about being a police officer that they were not able to answer.'

'Because they didn't know,' said the Inspector.

'Precisely, so we soon found out that the civilian trainers were asking police officers to come into the lessons and act as guest lecturers and answer questions. We were, therefore, rather redundantly paying for a civilian trainer and for a police officer to be off the streets. It was not cost effective.'

The Budget Manager had to hand it to them they certainly knew how to appeal to his better nature. He decided to try a different tactic.

'Well, are there any suggestions that you may have on how we can cut money?'

'I have,' said the Inspector.

'I thought you might,' muttered the Budget Manager.

'To start with I think we need to start at the top. The Chief Constable has a brand new seven series BMW which he is driven around in for the vast majority of the time.'

'You want your Chief to arrive at places in style, don't you?' the Manager asked weakly.

'I personally couldn't give a crap if he turned up in a dustcart. I think it's an insult that he drives around in that at the taxpayers' expense whilst the majority of response officers have to drive around in clapped out Ford Focus' that should have been decommissioned years ago.'

'We also seem to spend a fortune wasting money on things that we really don't need and I don't see the point of, despite the fact that they seem to make the hierarchy pleased.' This was from one of the Traffic Officers.

'Like?'

'The Strap line,' said the Sergeant.

'I beg your pardon?'

'The Strap line. You know that catchy little phrase that we seem to have that fits on everything "Protecting the Community" or whatever it is that we have now.'

'I am in favour of "Hitting the Target; Missing the Point,"' said the Inspector.

'The point is that we have had four of these things in the last five years. We keep changing them all of the time on whatever whim the Chief Constable decides to be on.'

'So?' asked the Budget Manager.

'Well,' continued the Sergeant. 'Every time that we change it we have to change it on all the cars and then on everything else that the crest is on, the name badges, the note paper, everything.'

'I also think that we waste too much time,' this was from a constable who had so far felt that he had wandered into the meeting by accident and was not sure it was where he belonged.

'What do you mean?' asked the Budget Manager looking down his glasses at him at the bottom of the table. The Constable fidgeted slightly under the gaze that he was now getting from everyone.

'Well, I used to be a response officer, but I have recently been moved to SNT.'

'Safer Neighbourhood Team,' interjected the Sergeant looking at the Budget Manager.

'Thank you,' said the Manager trying to contain his annoyance at being informed about something that he didn't know without having first had to ask what it was that he didn't know.

'Well, in response it is all about getting on with the job. One of my first tasks in SNT was to help set up a Pub Watch Initiative.'

'Ah yes, very good,' said the Manager, making a mental note to find out what a Pub Watch Initiative actually was.

'Well, being ex-response, I would just expect to go and do it. But it was ludicrous. First of all, I was told that I had to have a meeting with a number of other officers who were involved in the project with the Inspector who was over-seeing it.'

'Seems reasonable to me,' said the Manager hoping it was not going to lead him to disaster.

'But that wasn't good enough. First of all, all the officers involved had to have a meeting to discuss what we were going to discuss when we had the meeting with the Inspector. We then had the meeting with the Inspector. After the meeting with the Inspector we then had a further meeting to discuss all of the things that the Inspector had said in the meeting. A complete waste of time.'

'I see,' said the Budget Manager. He was keen to move away from all of this. There was a lot of negativity here and a lot of the comments had mentioned the Chief Constable. It was certainly not in his remit to criticise the Chief Constable to any extent. 'Does anyone else have any suggestions?'

'Plenty, now that you are asking,' said the Inspector.

The Budget Manager was realising that this would turn out to be a very stupid question to have asked.

Fourteen

Time must move along and so it was that Simon went on his driving course which was something that he considered to be the best bloody course that was ever imaginable.

'On this course,' the driving instructor had said on the first day. 'We will teach you everything from the correct way of holding a gear stick, to driving to the method and ultimately how to pursue a member of the public who is fleeing from you on account of the fact that he doesn't want to stop.'

This sounded very exciting to the members of Simon's little group.

'Where do we do all of this?' asked one of the group.

'We do it in the real world, son. All of the training — aside from the written papers, of course, will be done in the public domain. That means you will act professional at all times. The public will have no idea that this is a training exercise. They will think that your blue light run is for real, the same as everything else that you will be doing.'

'So, they will really think we are chasing people?'

'No.' The instructor looked grave at this.

'Why not?'

'We don't chase people,' the instructor said through grated teeth.

'We don't?'

'No. We pursue people; we do not chase them.'

'What's the difference?' asked one of the braver students.

'Chasing people lacks professionalism and also sounds like we're enjoying ourselves rather too much and you're not here to enjoy yourself you're here to fucking well work hard.' The instructor's voice had risen higher during the course of this little speech and he seemed to be getting angrier until such time as his face was relatively purple. This was obviously something that he cared a great deal about.

'So, the members of the public will think that we are pursuing suspects for real then?' another member of the group had volunteered who obviously seemed to have a degree of difficulty in following everything that was going on.

'Yes, they will,' said the instructor. 'We will, for a brief moment bring a degree of excitement into their otherwise dull and meaningless lives. Now, we will begin.'

He had said that they were there to work and he was right. A lot of them had been foolish enough to imagine that three weeks of driving about the countryside would be really very easy, but it was nothing like how they imagined. At the end of each day they left feeling both physically and mentally exhausted. They would never have thought it was possible. They were certainly learning though and the Driving School had certainly earned the need that it had to exist in the face of the comments made by the Budget Manager. It was one of the problems with the police that the majority of those involved in making the decisions for the police had absolutely no idea what it was that the police did. How they expected to be able to make decisions about things that they knew nothing about was of course a mystery. This didn't stop them from thinking that they were qualified to make decisions though. It was something that politicians did all the time. It would be the equivalent of asking a police officer who had always been a police officer and nothing else to make decisions on how to run the Royal Navy even though the closest that he had come to the water was being in his own bath and the only thing he knew about battleships was that it was a game that you could play.

The world would probably be a far better place if people were just allowed to stick to what they were good at or qualified in without feeling the need to bumble into something that you know nothing about and expect to be treated like an expert. The world moved in strange ways and there was none so strange as politicians who were the strangest of them all. People plucked from obscurity to suddenly become experts on everything and spend the rest of their lives telling everyone else the way that they should live theirs.

Before they really knew where they were the driving course was over and then the group returned to their areas and continued with their jobs. They would be reunited a couple of times for further training over the course of what remained of their two years of probation, but the majority of the training that they must go through was now completed.

As predicted Simon would forever remember his first solo blue light run. The amount of responsibility that he felt as he drove along the road was huge. He was impressed at how all the cars parted for him and he was allowed to move through them with such power. He could understand why his initial trainer had told them that you had to be careful about power.

The blue light run was to a traffic collision and lasted twenty minutes. It felt a lot longer. It was not unusual to do blue light runs of such length when you worked in a rural Force and you were expected to cover such distances.

Simon would remember it as well as he would remember the first person that he arrested, Adam King for shoplifting. He would make scores of arrests over the years and he would not remember them all, but he would remember the name and offence of his first arrest for the rest of his life. It was just one of those things that stuck in the mind.

Simon went home and in the absence of Amanda who had wandered off somewhere else doing her own thing, he decided to get himself a beer and sit down in front of the television and watch *Life on Mars*. With a little bit of imagination, he was able to pretend that this was research rather than escapism.

What interested him about the programme was not only that it was a very well made drama with some excellently chosen moments of comedy; but it also raised a number of very intriguing philosophical questions about whether the main character really had travelled in time; or if he was imagining it all as he lies in a coma. Looking at his own life Simon often wondered if he was lying in a coma somewhere and everything was all an illusion. Particularly his marriage.

He sat there in his chair all on his own and it seemed to be a cliché of all good police dramas that you have to have at least one character who is the police officer who just can't seem to be able to take their mind off of their work. Even when off duty they spend all of their time thinking about their cases and trying to solve murder enquiries or whatever it was that they were meant to be doing.

This is almost as established as the same character that has a broken marriage and an alcohol problem thought Simon as he sat alone in his living room and took another sip from his beer. From what little Simon knew of the police in the real world it seemed to him that the moment the body armour came off they spent as much time as they could in trying to forget that they were police officers at all until they were forced back into the locker room to put the body armour back on again.

As Simon sat there drinking his beer and watching Sam Tyler trying to teach Gene Hunt how political correctness worked, he found himself reflecting on his life and he came to a number of disturbing conclusions. He suddenly realised that despite all of the hoops that he had jumped through and everything that he had striven to do in order to get through to where he was now, he wasn't actually enjoying himself in the least. His sweet tasting dream had proven to be sour in reality. Whether the unhappiness of his home life was seeping into his work life he didn't know; but he had to admit that over a year since he had taken the oath to be a police officer he was not entirely happy.

The problem that he had was that he had nobody that he could talk to about all of this. He couldn't share these thoughts with Amanda as she would only give him one of those looks of hers and tell him that she had told him so. There was no peace and support to be gained from that quarter. He couldn't really put his finger on exactly what the problem was. He just had a sense that there was something wrong and something that he was not happy with. He began to wonder whether he was really cut out for this line of work at all. As you might imagine it was a big admission for him to have made and it was not an admission that he was pleased to have admitted; even to himself.

His dream had been to be a police officer, but the reality of it was so far from the dream that it had become something of a nightmare for him. He saw the next twenty years or so of his career stretching out in front of him and wondered how it was that he was going to be able to make it through. If he was disillusioned after only a year what the hell would he be like several years down the line?

There were certain officers who were a natural at the job. They had an instinct for the job and a nose for things. Simon knew that he might be able to learn how to have the copper's nose for things, but he doubted very much that it was something that would come naturally to him. He found many elements of the job to be tedious and he often found himself not looking forward to going into work at all. It was hardly a good start to his career that he was thinking like this already.

The trainer was right when he had said that police officers lived in the real world and the rest of the public did not. The problem was that it was a world that was far apart from the one that he used to live in and in which all of his family and friends still lived in. He had come a long way from his studies for his literature degree. The world of books, of creativity and of imagination had been replaced for him with this world of violence. He didn't really know the best way forward.

He knew that he did not have the luxury of walking away. He had fought so hard for this career and gone through so many arguments with Amanda that walking away would be like admitting total defeat. Amanda certainly would not be willing to support him if he was unemployed. She and her family would find him being unemployed even more distasteful than being a police officer. Many of them were unemployed, of course, but that was because if you were a man or a woman of money who was without a job it was just because you were someone of leisure. They would look down on the poor unemployed as just being lazy no good ruffians. It was funny how money could make you view things in different ways even though you were looking through the same window.

Did he really hate going to work? Or was it that he just valued his time off more than he valued working — like any sane person would? Rest days meant you had the freedom to do whatever you liked which was something that was obviously robbed of you when you had to return to working once again. He didn't think that this was particularly an unreasonable position to be in. Unless you were in a situation where your job was your life and you lived to work, he thought that most sane minded people would agree with him on this. The Chief Inspector was someone that lived the job. He breathed the job. He slept the job and if there was a particularly good result on a job then it was the general consensus of opinion that he probably wanked off over the job. You had to feel sorry for his wife really. Well, maybe not, she had decided to marry him after all.

Simon had no illusions that the only reason that he went to work was to earn money so that he could then go and spend it. That seemed the logical course of action and was probably what the vast majority of the rest of the human race were up to at any rate.

He was having a stressful time at work at the moment as well which added to the stress of his home life was not making things any easier for him. As a probationer he was expected to constantly prove himself which was not unreasonable given the circumstances, but became a drain on you after a while of having to prove it day after day. He also had a sergeant who pushed and pushed and no matter what it was that you did it was never right. He would always be able to find fault with what you had done. Simon could have gone into work the next day and arrested Lord Lucan; but all his sergeant would have said was 'What took you so long then, Orford?' There was no pleasing some people and Simon did wonder if his sergeant was in some way related to Amanda.

His Sergeant had also put the onus on him to take control of almost every situation that he got into, and to put himself forward for every job that was available regardless of whether his workload would allow him to do it or not. When he was not doing this, probably with valid reason, he was being pulled up about it. He began to feel that the weight that was upon him was unfairly positioned and he was struggling. Was this just him that felt like this or was this something that they all must go through?

The pressure and stress levels in this job were high enough anyway without having some prick making it more difficult; but it seemed to be that no matter how difficult matters were then there was always some wanker who was prepared to make it even worse. He felt that he worked hard at what he did, but he was also aware of the fact that he was constantly being watched and it was going to reflect badly on him if he allowed himself even a moment of peace whilst he was at work. This may sound like paranoid delusions, but it was sadly true.

Fifteen

Simon had learnt very quickly that although politicians may have been strange there was none stranger than members of the public. They had a very strange attitude when it came to everyday life. You only really saw such things when you were in the strange world of policing. Which viewed the world from a very different perspective.

'I tend to view individuals as intelligent,' PC George Lawrence had said. 'Crowds are stupid.' Lawrence was an officer with over twenty years' experience and was not all that far off from retirement. He had, by his own admission seen it all and done it all — several times.

'When I retire,' he continued, 'I intend to write a book on all of the stupid things that people have said to me over the years.'

It transpired that the majority of these comments had been made on road blocks. Road blocks were a curious problem for the public. If there was an accident, or a road traffic collision as they would prefer it to be called these days, then it might be necessary to block the road so that you didn't have members of the public endangering the scene as well as themselves and all the people that were at the scene. If the collision was fatal then the road would be closed for a very long time. The reason for this was very simple. In a collision where somebody had died the scene had to be investigated with the same attention to detail as if it were a murder enquiry; after all it might transpire that it was a murder when all was said and done.

This was perfectly rational really, but the public didn't seem to understand this. If you were unfortunate enough to be on a road block then your troubles would really start. You would place your police car across the road, clearly blocking it with your blue lights flashing away merrily. What was left of the road you would block off with traffic cones and signs saying that there was an accident.

Despite all of this the most common questions that you would be asked by the public would be: 'Oh is there an accident?' Or more often, 'Can I not get down there?'

The only answer to this question was to look at the nice display that you had set up and then look back at the member of the public and say: 'What do you think?'

Sometimes people just didn't think about what it was that they were saying. Simon had once informed a member of the public; 'You can't go down there I am afraid there has been a fatal accident.' He said this to two members of the public on the same day. The first had said in response: 'Oh is it serious?' Simon had to admit that this was dependant on whose side you were really on. The second driver on being informed the same thing had replied: 'What, on a Sunday?' Simon was not sure that you were supposed to have special days for fatal accidents and he was sorry that it had interfered with this particular person's intentions on a Sunday drive.

Some members of the public would actually try to drive around the road block, on the pavement in some cases as they were so stupid that they just didn't seem to think that this kind of thing applied to them. These questions and this kind of action from these kinds of people explain largely why the public were developing a reputation for being a bit on the thick side.

The stupid would quickly develop into the belligerent. Comments from this group of people would include things like: 'For fuck sake you people are always doing this.' PC Lawrence had replied to this particular comment with; 'Yes you're actually right. We were all sitting around the Police Station and we had run out of doughnuts and coffee so thought it would be a good idea to go and close a main road. Otherwise we would have had nothing to do.' You learnt very quickly that sarcasm was lost on the public. It was also the very best weapon in the police arsenal.

Comments didn't finish here but went on to include rants about what had happened. PC Lawrence had been on a road block for eight hours once when he had finally got so pissed off with having to tell so many stupid people to find another route that when at the end of the shift he was confronted by an idiot who ranted and raved about the fact that his journey had been interrupted, that he had turned on him.

'I'm sorry,' he had said. 'If you'd care to give me your name and address then when we have finished shovelling what remains of the motorist up there off of the road I'll pass your details on to their next of kin and they can personally write to you and explain how sorry they are that the death of their son has added ten minutes to your journey.'

It had at least shut that particular driver up. There would always be others. It was a clear way of seeing what humanity was really like and it was not all that pleasant a sight. Simon came into close contact with all forms of humanity every day and it was not something that had filled him with any confidence for the future of the human race. It had also made him realise that everyone was essentially out for themselves and would only think about themselves. They would not be concerned with the death of a stranger, only that their journey and their life had been interrupted and inconvenienced. No, humanity was not his favourite species at all.

It was a source of much amazement that otherwise intelligent individuals that may well lead a successful life would have their brains and their ability turn to jelly when confronted with a road block. They simply wouldn't know what to do. They would stop and slowly crawl towards the road block as if suspecting that it was a mirage that would vanish the closer they crept up on it. When they realised it wasn't going anywhere then they would stop and would not know what to do.

'But I have driven down this road for ten years, I don't know of any other way to go,' they would say whilst nervously fingering their gearstick.

'This would appear to be the perfect time for you to find another way to go,' PC Lawrence would say whilst waving them away so that he could deal with the next lost individual. Secretly he would wonder why it was that the English had once been such great explorers when they now couldn't find their way on a ten-mile journey that they took every day. Life would provide the opportunity for new and interesting discoveries. In some cases, these latter-day Moses' who had lost their flock would return some four hours later having gone around in circles and become hopelessly lost. There was no hope really.

The moral of the story? When the call came up to say that there had been a serious or fatal accident, then the race was on to get to the scene so you could pretend to be important and occupied with something instead of being surplus to requirements and then sent to do the road block.

They were sitting in the Report Room of their Police Station having this conversation as Simon had joined the same shift as PC Lawrence. The Report Room was the room where, as the name would suggest, you came to write reports. It was also a room that was used to chit-chat, unwind, drink coffee and tea, eat lunch and do everything else that you needed to do. Most of the time you ate lunch at the computer whilst filling out a domestic report or putting a crime report on the system or any other of the hundred things that you had to do during the course of an average shift. If you were really lucky you would get to eat a hot meal — a kebab — in the rest room; usually whilst watching shit late night television.

The thing was that there were members of the public that begrudged the police this. They found it astounding that police officers should have time to eat despite the fact that every other job had lunch breaks that they thought nothing of. They found it amazing that police officers should be allowed time to watch television when they should be working. It was difficult to explain. It wasn't like any other job that existed and there were moments when you needed to take a few minutes out to relax, usually because of the fact that you had just witnessed something nasty or something nasty had just happened to you. It wasn't as if you had the luxury of spending all of your time sitting on your arse eating and watching television which is obviously what these people thought you were doing. Simon often wondered how long these kinds of people would last if they had to come and do the job for a few weeks and find out what it is really like.

'The strange thing is,' Lawrence continued. 'I view this job as being something like the fighter pilots must have felt during the war.'

'Which war?' asked Simon who had been drifting off slightly in his thoughts.

'Either the First or Second World War, really; it doesn't really matter all that much.'

'How so?'

'Well, they spent a lot of the time sitting around waiting to fight.

Which is roughly what we do isn't it?'

'I suppose.'

'I don't mean to demean what the pilots went through, of course.'

'Of course.'

'But you can't deny that there are similarities. We get kitted up in all this shit,' he waved an arm roughly over his body armour. 'We then go out in the cars or all on the van and we look for trouble.'

'I can see where you're coming from, I'm just not entirely sold on the analogy.'

Lawrence nodded and continued to eat the sausage roll that he had been slowly munching on as he had been expanding his theory. He didn't seem to be all that phased by Simon's lack of complete agreement on his theory.

'I suppose our vehicles are not all that different from planes at any rate,' he reflected thoughtfully

'Planes?'

'Well they certainly make enough bloody engine noise to be mistaken for planes. I mean what bright spark decided to buy a fleet of shit vehicles like what we have?'

This didn't appear to be a question that demanded any form of answer.

'I mean when you think about it, it really is a fucking weird job that we do,' he continued.

'How so?' Simon had a feeling that he was going to tell him anyway, but he thought he may as well ask the question.

'Well, most people will spend the majority of their lives trying to avoid danger and violence. Which, is only natural and fair.'

'Agreed.'

'But we go out of our way looking for it.'

Simon had to admit that upon reflection this was a rather weird thing to do, although he had never really thought about it like that before.

'It's all rather strange if you ask me.' Lawrence concluded. Simon thought that nobody had asked him but he chose to say nothing and carried on with his attempt at putting a crime report on the system. It always amazed him how much duplication there was on the paperwork front. Very often you would take handwritten details at the scene of an incident and then have to return to the station and put them on the computer. Duplicating everything that had already been recorded. It probably made sense to someone, somewhere; or to be more precise it probably made someone else's job easier somewhere.

'It's a very strange job,' continued PC Lawrence staring at his sausage roll as if he had found something particularly strange in it.

'I suppose so,' Simon muttered as he tried to get to grips with what he was doing.

It was a very strange job when all things were considered. He remembered his trainer in the first few weeks of training talking about fear and doing it anyway. Fear came in many different shapes and sizes. He remembered the first day of independent patrol when he didn't have a tutor there to fall back on. He remembered being on his own when that radio had crackled into life and calling his call sign. They were calling *him*. It was up to him now to answer and get on with whatever they were about to offer him. And the jobs that could come over the radio were varied. They could be jobs sending you to a shoplifting, to a fight, to a death, to a murder or even sending you into something where you might be injured or even die. You never knew what the radio was about to tell you.

Simon had found public order patrols very annoying as well and they were one of his least favourite things about the job. He didn't mind the fighting that happened. By and large when it came to fights it was the police that usually won them. One way or the other. They could actually be quite fun. What he objected to was that there was a lot of waiting around, with the adrenalin running high whilst you waited to see if you were going to be fighting or not. He would rather just get on and fight if there was going to be a fight, rather than waiting for one that might or might not appear.

'I love public order,' said PC Stuart Raymond as they both stood on the street corner watching the people go in and out of pubs and clubs. They were often paid to stand on street corners watching the public and being prepared to intervene in fights when they came along. There was a lot of standing about and it was murder on the back.

'Why?' Simon had asked.

'Well, we get to stand here and look at all these women. I mean look at them. There is some fine totty out and about this weekend. I love the summer.'

It is true that there were options for looking at a lot of 'eye-candy' regardless of your gender or sexual preference. People often went out on night's out, even in the winter, without wearing all that much at all. It was very strange.

'I mean,' George Lawrence continued with a mouth full of sausage roll and showing no sign of shutting up despite the lack of interest that seemed to be forthcoming from Simon, but bringing Simon back to the here and now. 'I have often thought that as we drive around in the big van on public order nights; or when we drive around looking for trouble on night shifts, or whatever we do; I often think that all over the country police officers are doing exactly what we are doing right at that very moment. I suppose there is a brotherhood to it all.'

'And sisterhood,' said Simon despite himself.

'What?'

'Brotherhood and sisterhood. Don't forget that there are female police officers as well.'

'I know. I've not forgotten them. We can't even call them WPCs any longer.'

'You sound like you don't approve.'

'I don't have any objections. I'm not a sexist; or a racist; or anything. I don't have prejudices against the public regards of their colour, race, creed or sexual disorientation.'

'Disorientation?'

George nodded. Obviously despite numerous courses of equal opportunities and the like, diversity was something that had passed PC Lawrence by without much of a scratch being made on his character.

'And then a little while later they accuse us of being institutionally racist,' this was a particular gripe from PC Lawrence who felt that the levelling of such a claim to the police in general had been grossly unfair. 'I mean, I don't even know what that means. I tell you what though; if we are institutionally racist — whatever the fuck it means — then the politicians are institutionally corrupt. Bunch of fucking idiots the lot of them. Haven't got a clue.'

Silence resumed whilst Simon tried to get on with that he was doing and PC Lawrence got on with not really doing all that much at all.

'It's a funny old job,' he said again to no one in particular but allowing this comment to summon up everything that he felt about the job.

Simon felt that it *was* a funny old job and, in many regards, there were some funny old people doing the job for a funny old public. It was all very strange he had to admit. An outsider might take the view that the police were made up of a lot of officers that were outdated, grumpy and miserable about the job. There was a lot of truth in this. However, there were also a lot of really good officers that cared about their job. Cared about the public and did their best to ensure that they did whatever they could to help people. Simon had to admit that these people were dedicated and taken as a whole were very good people who were fun to work with and were right there when you needed them. One of the best things that could be said by a police officer about another police officer was the fact that they backed you up. There were those that didn't. There were those that were not there when you needed someone to help you. There were those that didn't listen to their radio. There were those who were lazy and spent as much time as they could doing nothing. There were those that never arrived first on a scene no matter how close they were to it.

Thankfully there were not too many of these officers about; but one of them was more than enough.

Sixteen

Each successive generation of police officers become convinced that the job was not what it once was. Each generation is certain that the job has deteriorated since the time when they first joined. They can't understand why it is that anyone else would want to join. This has become ingrained so much that there is a rumour that on the second day of the formation of the Metropolitan Police Force, Sir Robert Peel walked into his office slammed some paperwork down on his desk and announced 'The job is fucked. It's not what it used to be.' Every generation has believed that matters are going downhill and it is not what it once was. It was just possible that this generation would be the first generation where it would turn out to be true. It was announced around this time with all seriousness on the news that police officers were apparently doing too much paperwork rather than actually fighting crime.

'And this is news?' PC Lawrence had said although it seemed pretty clear to everyone else in the room that PC Lawrence was not one of the officers who was doing any of the paperwork himself. He probably felt that as he was such a long serving officers that he had done his share of the work now and it was time for someone else to carry it on.

The truth is that there *is* too much paperwork and it does stop officers from fighting crime. A shocking revelation. This was true; but it was something that had been known about for a very long time so it wasn't really news. From time to time it would be raised up again and someone would pretend to do something about it. An effort would be made to reduce bureaucracy. There were too many forms to be filled in so they would have to be reduced; but which ones? Simon's particular Force had come up with a brilliant solution to this problem by introducing a form that people could fill in to highlight which forms they felt were unnecessary or redundant. This was done without so much as a trace of irony, but it does go a long way to explaining the mind-set of management.

Things were starting to go downhill. It began with the Government deciding to issue a pay freeze. Apparently, the country had spent a great amount of money over recent years and a lot of mistakes had been made whilst doing this. The Government had decided that the police were obviously to blame for this and so they had decided to introduce a pay freeze on the police and not grant them their annual pay rise. The police decided to march in London in protest. Now, a lot of the public couldn't see what the fuss was about and couldn't understand why it was that the police were making such a fuss over not getting a pay rise.

The issues were really very simple when you stripped them down. The police had been guaranteed a pay rise every year. Now other people might think that this guarantee is unfair; but the reason for this was as acknowledgement that the police did not have the right to strike. Due to the lack of this right they were guaranteed a pay rise each year. Simple; until the Government decided that they would stop this arrangement and save money whilst at the same time they were fiddling their own expenses and awarding themselves as much money as they could and genuinely acting in as corrupt a way as possible — in other words, acting like politicians.

Many politicians who were so high and mighty and so far up their own arses that they could not have told you the basics of what it was like to live in the real world made comment that they really didn't understand why it was that the police were making this protest and didn't understand what it was that the police expected to achieve by what they were doing. The answer to this was very simple as one officer said: 'What do we expect to achieve? Wait for the next election result and you will see exactly what we hope to achieve.'

Politicians couldn't understand this kind of thing. They had some belief that they were infallible and seemed to forget that they had been elected by the people and were supposed to make decisions for the people rather than for their own ends. However, the truth of the matter was born out when Gordon Brown brought the Government crashing down in spectacular fashion whilst he blamed everyone else other than take responsibility for its destruction himself. Now the police had not brought down the Government on their own; the Government had gone a long way to falling on their own swords; but the police vote was a large one when you took into account it wasn't just serving officers, but retired officers and all their families and in some cases friends whom the Government had managed to piss off. It is in the nature of all governments to piss people off, but normally you would try to do it covertly or with as little fuss as possible so that people would not really understand what it was you were doing. This particular administration under Prime Minister Brown might as well have had 'Kamikaze' tattooed all over it.

The Government followed it up the following year by refusing to issue a pay rise once again. For the second year it went to arbitration, which was really a waste of time given that the Government were very good at pretending that they were listening whilst at the same time not paying the slightest bit of attention as they were really concentrating on how they could cope with their second homes and expenditure forms. It was against the law for the police to strike; and yet the question had not been answered about who would enforce the law if the police were to all strike. The Government had come to realise that they had the police over a barrel, nevertheless, and that they could then treat them like shit and that there was nothing that the police could do about it. (This was not strictly speaking true though. The Government would have collapsed if the police had decided to take the illegal action of striking. With the police on strike and nobody to enforce the law chaos would have ensued. The Government could not bring in the armed forces to take over in the meantime as they were spread too thin due to the increasing cut backs the Government had inflicted upon them and having to cover war zones looking for weapons of mass destruction that didn't actually exist because, shock and horror, the Government had lied again. They would have to agree to the police terms and allow them back to do the job that only they could do. You couldn't really then go about arresting and dismissing the officers that went on strike because that would put you back in the same position of not having any police. The reason why this had not happened was really two-fold. Firstly, the officers were actually too moral to strike because they knew that the people that would suffer were the victims that really did need their help; and secondly, because experience had taught you that if you got one over on the government they would bide their time and find a way of shafting you later on; even if it were years down the line).

It had then been suggested that if the police could not strike then perhaps there could be some kind of work-to-rule plan. This chiefly meant that of all the thousands of calls that the police received each day they would only respond to the emergency ones where there was an immediate threat to life or property. This would cause substantial problems for the public across the country.

'You have returned home and found that you have been burgled whilst out? Is the intruder still there? No? Well we aren't interested then. Goodbye.'

Simon personally felt that this was a little extreme although any job that came in that said the words 'Facebook' or 'Twitter' or something along the lines of 'My ex-boyfriend has been saying nasty things about me,' should be immediately binned or referred to Jeremy Kyle. The public not only had a tendency to not be able to sort their own problems out, but also expected the police to rectify a situation in minutes that had taken years to deteriorate. A surprisingly large number of them were incapable of sorting their lives out or more commonly sorting their children out. Incredible how they expected complete strangers to be able to sort it out for them though.

Now this would seem to suggest that the public were useless and called the police only because they were unable to sort their own lives out. There is only a small percentage of the public that are actually like this. Unfortunately, like most minorities they are a very vocal minority. This distracted the police from the real job that they were there to do which was to look after the people that really needed their help. The vulnerable rather than the needy. Vulnerable because you were a victim of crime, rather than a victim of life or your own circumstances and stupidity.

The Home Secretary, who was progressively useless and seemed to be picked for the job by some kind of lottery rather than by any ability to actually do the job, i.e. the way that every politician was chosen for a Cabinet post, had finally made a decision on police pay after pretending to go through arbitration. Normally the pay increase was 3%. The Police Federation, which were to all intents and purposes the police union and represented the rank and file officers asked for 3.9% and eventually were given 2.5% backdated a few months to when the pay rise should have commenced. The Home Secretary agreed to 2.5% but refused to back date it. This effectively made it 1.9%. She then presumably went off rubbing her hands together in glee and went to torture some children or something.

The world was changing and Simon was not entirely convinced that it was changing for the better. After the protest march in London, Sir Ronnie Flanagan, the Home Office Chief Inspector of Constabulary published a report into the police. The two main points that seemed to come from this was that he believed that 90% of the work completed by police officers could be completed by civilians. This was potentially true.

The second was that he did not believe that it was possible to sustain the number of police officers at the current level for the next three years.

'What the fuck does that mean?' the disgruntled PC Lawrence had mumbled into his coffee.

'It could mean more PCSOs,' Simon had ventured.

'What, plastic, pretend police officers. They are worse than Specials,' PC Lawrence didn't seem to like anyone or understand anyone other than himself.

'Could mean redundancies,' piped up PC Katy Waterhouse who spent most of her time not engaging in these kinds of conversation when it was at all possible.

'Fuck that,' PC Lawrence had stated as he munched on his pastry. 'I can't see how the police could be made redundant. The very definition of redundancy is that something is redundant; that you don't need it any longer. How can you say that you don't need the police any longer? Bloody stupid, if you ask me.'

Simon had been listening to all of this over the time that he had spent as a police officer and he had rapidly come to the conclusion that he would probably never progress that far in the police. He found himself detesting the way that the police were going at the moment and how political it was becoming. He felt that more often than not they were run by foolish chief constables who were only really intent on getting on the next step of the ladder and a way to develop their career as soon as they could.

Simon may not have had all that much experience with the police, but he was certain that he could not play the political game and it was necessary to play politics if you wanted to progress up the ranks. Already in his career he had decided that the first mistake that had been made was to refer to the police as a Service rather than a Force. This seemed to be a way of sweetening the pill, but it did not get away from the fact that they enforced the law and force was often needed in order to enforce. It did exactly what it said on the tin.

The second thing that he felt was total bollocks was the current Chief Constable's emphasis on the fact that they dealt with customers. PC Lawrence's opinion had summed it up in his usual style.

'This is total rubbish. We do not deal with customers. We deal with victims and we deal with criminals. We need to help the victims whenever we can and however we can and do the very best that we can for them and we need to come down heavily on the criminals. They need to be slapped back into place so fast and so bloody hard that it leaves them in no doubt as to who is in charge.'

This was actually something of a revelation from the cynical Lawrence who in this one statement had apparently let slip that he really did care despite his cavalier attitude to his job. This was actually a rather common feature in a number of officers who might have otherwise denied it to their grave.

Some consolation might be gained from the fact that changes did appear to be happening. The general feeling was that things did need to change and a better balance needed to be sought. Some police forces seemed to realise this and had made comments that they were going to ditch target driven motivation with a view to giving the public what they actually wanted. None of this was actually going to happen though. Targets and statistics were something that would never go away; they would just be driven underground.

Simon's career was going to take a drastic turn and events would be completely turned around for him. It was to begin with the moves that the Government were making, but nobody could have predicted the way that it was actually going to end.

Seventeen

'We need to talk.'

This was from Amanda. It was early one morning. Simon had just finished working a night shift and Amanda had just got up for the day. She was feeling refreshed and he was feeling like he had just had the crap beaten out of him. These were the kind of terms upon which Amanda liked to conduct business. This way she felt that she might have the upper hand.

'Well, there is a first time for everything, I suppose.'

'I really don't need your sarcasm today, thank you very much.'

Simon had the decency to feel a trifle guilty at this. Things had gone downhill between them a great deal over recent months. They had never been great to start with, but joining the police had been a sour note that had slowly ripened over time. Things had grown steadily worse. The biggest problem was that they really did not see eye to eye about anything any longer. This was probably something that had always been there, but was something that had steadily grown during his new career. Amanda had never had to work shifts. She had never had to stand in the pouring rain watching people be idiots all around you. She had never had to deal with a dead body — had never even seen one — and she certainly did not have to break the news that a loved one had died to a relative who had been having a good day up until the point when you rang their doorbell and ruined their life forever more.

Simon had tried to involve her as much as he could. He had tried to tell her about the day that he had and what he had been up to, but there were three major problems with this. The first was that she had no common frame of reference with him. The second was that she still resented the way that he had decided to become a police officer against the advice; or rather orders that she had given him. The last, and perhaps more important of all, was that she was just not interested in what he had to say.

'Well what is it that we need to talk about?' he asked as he wearily sat down at the breakfast table and tried to revitalise himself with the cup of coffee that he had poured when all he really wanted to do was to go to bed. She never seemed to understand that when you were working shifts things were a little upside down. She still expected him to stick to conventional time. It was also a matter of fact that Amanda chose the moments when she wanted to talk about things and that was final. Simon had been raised to talk things over and to never go to bed on an argument, but he had discovered that with Amanda it was pointless to try and talk to her about anything until such time as she was prepared to talk about it. It didn't seem to matter if you were ready or not at that point.

'Us.' This didn't sound like it was going to bode well.

'What about us?'

'Exactly.'

Simon was a little confused and felt that he had missed something here. He decided that the best course of action was to just not say anything and wait to see which way the situation went. It was a strategy that he had adopted for some considerable time in his marriage.

'We have drifted apart.'

There was no denying this. They still lived together, but they may as well have been living apart. They hardly saw each other any longer and had stopped sleeping in the same bed for several months now. Sex was pretty much non-existent; not that it had been particularly abundant to begin with. Amanda had a very strange attitude towards sex. She appeared to be of the belief that sex was necessary for procreation. It was one's duty to do it, but it was not something that anybody should derive any kind of pleasure from. You had sex to secure the heir to the line and that was it. Once this mission had been achieved then it was a stand down. She had enticed Simon with the concept of sex during their courtship but she was very much aware of the fact that one did not have children out of wedlock — unless you were male and it was with one of the maids, as tradition seemed to dictate in the upper classes. A female needed to secure a husband so that the line could continue. Having married Simon and then realising that he was not in the business of immediately wanting an heir she had limited his access to sex to once a year or so. As she had become doubtful about staying with him, she had cut him off completely, and chose to ignore the fact that he appeared to be gaining solace in masturbation. He would hardly have been the first wanker in her family.

Simon sat there and digested the truth of what she had said and looked around the kitchen. He noticed that by the bread bin there was an empty bottle of wine that had been full when he had gone to work the previous evening. Amanda followed his gaze.

'What?'

'Did you drink all of that on your own last night?'

'What if I did? There is nothing wrong with that. Grandma always used to have a drink in the evening.'

'Yes, but Grandma was an alcoholic, wasn't she? She used to drink morning, afternoon and evening. Every single day that she could until her liver exploded.'

'Don't you dare criticise my family. How dare you?'

'Oh, good God woman, your family are not infallible. You always act like they are untouchable and are up there in the highest echelons. They are as flawed and as messed up as the rest of us.'

'My family are not flawed.' There was clearly a flaw in this argument. Simon had, perhaps sub-consciously hit upon the matter which was the closest to Amanda's heart. All of those that considered themselves to be either the ruling classes or descended from the ruling classes were very protective of the family tree. It wouldn't really matter that the family tree might have a few murderers, rapists, sodomites, child molesters, servant beaters and God knows what else lurking amongst the branches; you just did not knock the institution.

'Sometimes,' Simon muttered. 'I wonder why it was that you married me at all.' This was dangerous territory that he was straying into here; but the effects of the nightshift and the general annoyance of the entire situation were making him less than cautious.

'Well, I wonder it as well. My family warned me against it you know. My mother said that it was a bad idea.'

'Of course she did,' he muttered under his breath and into his coffee mug.

'What did you say?'

'Nothing, dear.'

'I really wish that if you had something to say that you would say it properly so that you could be understood rather than muttering all the time like some delinquent.'

Simon could feel his hands tightening on the coffee mug. He really didn't need this conversation. Not after a nightshift where he was dog tired after being run ragged without so much as a chance for a cup of tea.

'You just don't seem to want to put the effort into this any longer.'

'Into what?' His mind had wandered slightly in the last few seconds as he reflected on some of the jobs that he had been sent to throughout the night.

'Into this marriage, Simon. That is what we are talking about.'

'Is it?'

'I do wish you would pay attention at least once in your life. As I say you really don't put the effort into it anymore.'

'Effort,' said Simon feeling that he was grinding his teeth. 'Is something that is a two-way street.'

'Well, that is exactly the kind of thing that you would say that you think of as clever.' Simon didn't think that this was a particularly clever thing to say, but rather a factual thing.

'You don't make any effort to be part of this marriage any longer. I can't remember the last time that you took me out to dinner and you hardly ever bring me gifts any longer like you used to. As to your appearance, well!'

'What about my appearance?' said Simon as he looked up from his coffee mug.

'Well, really! Half the time you spend wearing that ridiculous costume —.'

'It's a uniform,' he virtually snarled at her.

'Whatever. When you are not wearing that, that outfit, you spend the rest of the time moping around in jeans and a T-shirt like you just don't care anymore. I can't remember the last time you wore a suit. Do you have any idea how embarrassing it can be when my friends come around?'

'I wore a suit at Christine's Christening.' As a literature graduate, he had always been able to appreciate the alliteration of Christine's Christening.

'Exactly, and that was four months ago.'

'Well what would you like me to do? Wear one whilst doing the gardening?'

'Don't be facetious, Simon. It doesn't suit you in the slightest.'

'So; are we going to talk about this marriage or are we going to dig some trenches and spend the rest of the day firing shots at each other?'

'There you go again with your comments that you think so clever.' She looked at him for one moment with her head on one side. 'You know there was a time when I used to think you were so clever; and so funny. These days I just think you are sad.'

'Well, I can't always be happy.'

'No. Sad as in pathetic.'

Simon thought that it probably wasn't a good idea for him to tell her what he was thinking about her at this precise moment. He tried to pull his mouth back into some kind of level with his brain to prevent him from saying something that later on one or both of them might regret. Some arguments were going to be impossible to win no matter how much of the moral high ground you might have or no matter how much of the better argument you had. There was just no winning some causes.

'You have never been happy about me becoming a police officer have you?'

'Oh, it is so much more than that,' she said with a dismissal wave of one of her hands. 'You had potential. You could have been someone or something, but you just decided to throw it all away in pursuit of whatever it is you think you are achieving by wearing this silly costume—'

'Uniform.' He virtually growled the word this time.

'—and acting like I don't know what at all times of the day and night.'

Simon tried to count to ten under his breath but was discovering that this really wasn't a useful thing to do at all.

'Well, perhaps if things just don't work out then the sensible, adult thing would be to just walk away from it all,' he eventually said.

114

This seemed to stop Amanda in her tracks and she looked at him as if seeing him for the first time. She studied him for a moment as if trying to work out who it was that he was and what it was that he had just said. Eventually she summoned up generations of good breeding.

'I beg your pardon?'

'If it isn't going to work between us. If you feel that it is really not worth the effort of trying any longer and that there is nothing that we can do to put it back on track then perhaps the only thing that we have left to do is to pack it in and call it a day.'

Only a few months before he would not have dreamed of saying these words, but as time had grown on and as the only time that he and Amanda spent together was in argument he had slowly started to become worn down and it was becoming more and more of an effort to put the effort in; despite what Amanda might have felt about his lack of effort.

'What on earth do you mean?'

'Well, I would have thought that it was pretty obvious. Which part of what I said do you not understand?'

'Are you suggesting a divorce?' she almost spat the word out as if it was as dirty in her mouth as words like 'unemployed' and 'social housing' would have been if they had ever been words that she had actually used. She wouldn't have understood what the last one meant at any rate.

It is probably worth pausing in mid conversation here and considering things from Amanda's point of view. Simon painted a picture of her as a dragon breathing fire and making his life a misery and whereas there were elements of this about her and the situation, this is only one side of the picture. Was it really Amanda's fault that she took the views of life that she did? Not really, was the answer. Amanda was the person that she was because of the way that she was raised by her parents; or to be more precise the way that she was raised by her mother as her father never really had an active part in anything.

All of us are the products of the received wisdom of our parents, but also of the culture and heritage that we are born into. If we are strong in mind and body then we may rebel against this received wisdom and strike out into the world on our own and carve our own niche. Many would remain influenced by our parents to some extent. It might be something as minor as liking some of the music that our parents played when we were children or it might be that we vote for a political party because that was what was indoctrinated into us at an early age. It might be that it was more sinister and some racist, sexist or homophobic views that we had were ones that we had because that was what our parents had taught us was the right thing to do.

Amanda had been raised as a princess; as simple as that. She had been raised to believe that she could have whatever she wanted and that nobody ever said 'No' to her. As far as she understood it this was the way that the world was. She had experienced and expected nothing different than this. Was it any wonder that she became so frustrated with Simon and his free will? Marrying Simon had been the one act of rebellion that she had taken against her parents. Her mother, in particular, had not wanted the marriage to go ahead; but Amanda had wanted it and that was where her mother experienced the problem with the person that she had created. Having brought her up to get whatever she wanted, how could she expect her to adhere to her demands not to marry Simon now?

None of it was really Amanda's fault. She had just been brought up to believe that this was the way that things were meant to be and was now struggling with the realisation that the world of her family was not necessarily the world that everybody else had to live in. She was rather taken aback by it all and not coping with the shock all that well.

However, Simon had mentioned the possibility of divorce now and that changed things dramatically and it was not something that she believed could happen. So, she repeated the question, only slightly louder this time: 'Are you suggesting a divorce?'

They had never mentioned the D word before and it had not really been something that had ever crossed Simon's mind with any degree of seriousness; but now, with no warning at all, the subject was not only upon them, but it was out in the open. This is very often the way that things happened. You could spend ages creeping up on something only to find that whilst you were looking the other way it had crept up on you. Simon found that he was on a dangerous rollercoaster ride. He was heading down the track and although he knew that he was heading towards unknown territory he also knew that there was nothing that he could do to prevent the direction that he was going in. It was like knowing you were about to have a car crash and not being able to do anything but feel detached from the reality of the situation and watch with horrendous fascination as events unfolded before your eyes.

'It might be worth thinking about,' was what he actually said.

He watched with deepening fascination as Amanda's face took on the appearance as if he had just slapped it.

'Are you serious?'

Simon took some degree of heart from this as Amanda's reaction seemed to portray the fact that she was shocked by what he had said and that she perhaps did love him after all.

'You do realise that nobody in my family has ever been divorced? The shame of it would be impossible.'

Okay, so maybe not.

'No, I suppose your lot just had them beheaded when they became fed up with them.'

'You have no understanding of family.'

'No, I suppose not. In my family we were all bought up to look after each other rather than the family name and ancestors that were rotting in their graves — sorry, in their crypts — and who could no longer give a toss about what the current generation were doing.'

'How dare you?' She was turning a very strange colour now, but Simon was beginning to feel that he was on a roll. These are the moments when you become detached from what is happening around you. It is like an out of body experience. You are actively involved in what is happening and yet at the same time you feel as if you are detached and watching events unfold from a distance with no control over what is being said or what is about to happen.

'I dare because it's true, but you're too blinded about caring what someone who died in 1823 might think than to understand that it's true.'

'This is intolerable.'

'Well, on that at least we are in agreement.'

'I can't put up with this any longer.'

'Then I suggest you give some very serious consideration to the idea of a divorce then, because currently from where I am sitting it's looking like a really great idea.'

Amanda looked as if at any minute there would be steam coming out of her ears which was a notion that Simon found to be really rather amusing despite the circumstances.

'I warn you Simon Orford, if you persist in this line of thinking then I will get the best barrister in the country and I will take you for everything that you have got.'

Simon mulled this over for a few seconds. He pushed his coffee mug to one side and stood up.

'Well, first of all *you* won't get the best barrister at all; if anything, your evil decrepit, arse-pit of a mother will get the best barrister for you because you have never had to do anything in your life on your own before. Even loading the dishwasher is too much of an effort for you. Secondly, you can hire the best barrister and you can take me for everything that I have got, but as you so often point out to me, I have next to fuck all. So, if you want to piss away some more of Mummy's money on getting bugger all then by all means throw your money away. Now, if you will excuse me, I'm going to bed.'

And so, it was that the path was set for some of the pieces to be put into place before the game really started.

Eighteen

The divorce was something that had been mentioned and Simon suddenly felt like an entire weight had been lifted from his shoulders. It was perhaps something of a cliché to say it, but that didn't stop the cliché from being true. Until this moment he had not realised that he had been walking around in a cloud of depression for the majority of the time. He would not have been able to put his finger on it if you had asked him, but he knew that something was wrong. Now that the ultimate confrontation had taken place between the two of them, he felt the enormous release that came with the release from a lengthy prison sentence. And that is exactly what he felt had happened. He hadn't realised it, but he had been serving time in the prison of his marriage. It had been hard labour as well.

Simon didn't want to get a divorce as it would in his own eyes seem like defeat. He did, to an extent, believe in the sanctity of marriage; which in his book meant you didn't give up at the first hurdle, but nor did you spend your life in misery and torment just because you had a ring on your finger. He had always tried to pacify and calm the waters of the situation between Amanda and himself. He was always the first to make up when they had disagreed. He was always the one that was walking on eggshells around her whilst she bulldozed her way passed him. He was the UN Peacekeeping Force trying not to ignite the tinderbox of the situation.

But then there had been an epiphany. He had realised in a blinding light of revelation that was verging on the Biblical, that there are times when it is noble to be the peacekeeper; and there are times when you just have to say 'Oh fuck it,' and then bomb the shit out of them. This was his 'bomb the shit out of them' moment. For too long he had put up with the misery and the constraints that Amanda had placed on him without him really having the ability to realise it at all. It was over.

Amanda, despite her bravado had realised that he was serious about divorce and despite everything else she didn't really want this to happen. She didn't want to get divorced from Simon she just wanted Simon to do everything that she wanted him to do. If he would only agree to that small concession then everything would be fine between them. As far as she was concerned it was really as simple as that. So, she had tried reconciliation shortly after their early morning argument. The problem was that Simon had already tasted the air of freedom and it was blissful. He had declined her offer and announced that a divorce was on the cards and he didn't really care how she went about it, but it was going to happen.

The divorce was something that took a few months to organize which was something of a surprise as it had been so much easier and cheaper to get married and appeared to be so much more difficult to divorce. Simon supposed the logic of this was that the government felt the need to control everything that you did and if they made it too easy for you to divorce then you might just walk out at the first sign of trouble, rather than stay and work through years of misery, as Simon had done, before then ultimately ending it in divorce anyway.

In the end Simon had decided that it was easier for Amanda to divorce him on grounds of unreasonable behaviour — presumably this was not doing what she told him to do. He could have divorced her, but apparently you couldn't divorce someone on the grounds of 'you are a bitch.' As promised, she had gone off and got a solicitor and having moved out of the modest matrimonial home had left Simon the run of the place. He had been surprised by this, but then he had put down the mortgage on it and she had put down the grief on it.

He soon received various important looking letters from her solicitor which looked good on expensive notepaper and included words like 'petitioner,' 'respondent' and a lot of 'and there upon.' He signed everything and sent it back with diligence and found that he had a Decree Nisi. This was very exciting as he was pretty sure that he had never owned a Nisi before of any description. The required six weeks and a day had passed and then he was very pleased to find that he received a Decree Absolute in the post. He was now officially divorced. It was time to have a small party and he began to look on the internet to see if he could buy a divorce cake.

Now, his one concern in this had been money. He was not entirely convinced that he would be able to take on lengthy legal battles. He certainly was sure that he would not be able to afford it. However, Fate had smiled down on him. Amanda and her dragon of a mother had gone to the family solicitor who had, to all intents and purposes, nicely and smartly rogered them both with his sharp legal fountain pen. In short, he had allowed them to pursue the divorce and then passed it onto a judge who knew the family in the hope that the judge would smile favourably on the upper classes and destroy Simon as much as it was legally possible to do in a divorce court — which was actually quite a lot.

The judge had looked over the papers with care and remembered the times that he used to play golf with Amanda's father. In particular he remembered the time that he used to spend drinking whisky with Amanda's father in the club house after they had played golf. He paid particular attention to the conversations that they had spoken of where Amanda's father had outlined exactly what a horrible family he had. The judge remembered all of this and he remembered how much money Amanda's family had and most important of all he remembered that it was Amanda's mother that had all but hounded his golfing friend to death. He looked sympathetically on Simon and made sure that the family paid all the costs and did not screw Simon over. That was not something that was going to happen every day. Law is meant to be blind, but it rarely actually is.

So it was that Simon found he had been granted freedom; Amanda and her mother had a huge legal bill to pay which they had generated by means of their own fault and greed, and the judge raised a glass of whisky in the club house to his departed friend and felt that he had exerted some degree of revenge on his behalf.

Simon was free and he found something very curious would happen. When hearing that he was divorced people would act in strange ways. One way in which they acted was to appear suddenly embarrassed and falter in what they had been saying and then with much 'umming' and 'ahhing' they would shuffle off to talk to someone else that would be less of a social stigma. It was a strange reaction to have in the early twenty-first century, but it was England after all and there were some members of society that still had themselves rooted firmly in the dim and distant past. They actually probably felt uncomfortable not because they viewed Simon and those like him as being social outcasts but rather because they just did not know what to say to him. Social etiquette of polite society had not prepared them for this situation. For these people it was on a level with bumping into someone at a cocktail party only for them to tell you that they had been diagnosed with an incurable illness. There was just no social breeding that they had been given to deal with situations like that.

A second popular reaction was for people to say 'Oh I am sorry,' when they heard the news of the separation and ultimate divorce. This seemed to be as predictable a statement as any in the circumstances. People said it because they thought they were expected to say it. Simon usually replied with: 'Why are you sorry? I am personally very happy that it has happened.' This would ultimately throw these people into the first category of not knowing what to say next. They would probably go off and pester the vicar.

In the meantime, Simon was actually still thinking of having a divorce party. Nobody enters into marriage expecting it to end in divorce, although Liz Taylor and Richard Burton might have had an inkling when they got married for the second time. It has to be recognised though that despite the best of intentions there are times when it just doesn't work. Divorce was considered a bad thing by many, the Catholic Church for one and King Henry VIII had demonstrated exactly what a divorce could cost you by pretty much ripping the country apart over it. It should also be recognised, however, that there were times when divorce was a good thing. Why should you stay in a loveless marriage? Why should you stay in a marriage of domestic violence? If you had a valid reason then there really was no argument against why you couldn't walk away and start life again somewhere else either with or without someone else. It wasn't as if you were taking a pair of socks back to Marks and Spencer because you didn't like the colour.

Simon didn't have plans to run off with someone else. He actually thought that it might be a good idea to have some freedom for a change. It was a word that kept recurring over and over again and it might sound melodramatic, but it you have not been in his position then you really can't begin to imagine what it felt like. Flowers smelt sweet and the sun seemed to shine brighter than it had a few months before. It just goes to show you what the space of a few months can do as well as a few signatures on a few legal documents. For a moment he did consider having his Decree Absolute framed and put on the wall somewhere, but thought that this might perhaps be a step too far.

**

In all of the excitement of getting his divorce and embarking on a new life Simon had not realised that the world around him was going into meltdown.

It was approaching Christmas 2008 and things were slowly falling apart at the edges. Depending on who you spoke to a different term was used for what was happening. Some would say it was a 'credit crunch,' which sounded like a breakfast cereal or chocolate bar. Others would call it a 'financial crisis,' which was accurate if somewhat understated. Still others would refer to it as 'recession.' PC Lawrence referred to it as 'a fucking disaster.'

'One of the things that really annoy me at the moment,' he said as he chewed his way through a pork pie, 'is that the Government have bailed out all the banks that have screwed the entire system up in the first place.'

This was an interesting point that he had raised and it was annoying to a number of people that the banks themselves gave little thought or cared nothing about their customers when their customers were in financial difficulty. PC Lawrence had spoken to his bank some time ago when a few expensive bills had landed on him unexpectedly. He didn't have any savings and had gone to see the bank with the view perhaps of getting a loan or some kind of help. He had explained to the bank that he was having financial difficulty and the person in the bank had said:

'And what do you want me to do about it?' This had not been said in a helpful way but rather in the manner of 'so what?' They claimed that they were there to help you, but they were really only there to help themselves to your money.

'What annoys me the most is the fact that we rescued the Bank of Scotland.' He was obviously not going to stop now that he was in full vent. 'I have nothing against the Scots…'

'Of course you don't,' someone in the room muttered.

'The Scots have been banging on at us for years about devolution and wanting independence and yet they have to be rescued by London when they can't cope any longer. Well, hang on, I've got an idea. If they want independence then they should have it. Totally. No help from London at all; and then we shall see them collapse when they realise that they can't actually cope.'

PC Lawrence seemed to spend most of this time ranting on like this without actually seeming to do any real work. He seemed to be a police officer that only left the office if it was absolutely essential for him to do so. The others returned to their work in the hope that the rant was over. It was not.

'To rub salt into the wound even further their First Minister; or whatever he is called; was on the news last night blaming the collapse of the Bank of Scotland on the fact that it is being run by the United Kingdom. Therefore, making it very clear that it would not have been in the mess that it is in if it was run by the Scots. Give us the money back and fucking run it then.'

'Well this crisis seems to be dominating everything at the moment,' said Simon who never seemed to be able to resist the temptation of rising to Lawrence's rants. He was the only one who didn't seem to be capable of ignoring him; perhaps the others just had better practice at it.

'And what are the Government doing about it I ask you?' The room audibly groaned and looked at Simon with annoyance that he had thrown lighter fuel on the fire. 'You have that Brown chap on the news saying, "Trust me I am the best man for the job," and yet he doesn't look to me as if he is doing anything. If you're the best man for the job then get on and do the job and stop keep telling us that you are the best man for the job.'

'An interesting point, but he will not admit that the crisis has anything to do with anything the Government have done.'

'He can hardly blame the previous administration he was chancellor ten years before he became Prime Minister. If we haven't got any money then you have to ask yourself what he has been doing.'

'I don't think any of the other politicians or parties are all that better either,' Simon stated.

'Well I think Guy Fawkes had the right idea. The gunpowder plotters seem to have been the last honest men to go anywhere near Parliament.'

'Honest?'

'Honest. With clear intentions. Honest about what they wanted to achieve. No hidden agendas,'

'Hiding a lot of gunpowder in the cellar was not a hidden agenda?'

'Well, I think they had the right idea.' PC Lawrence brushed crumbs from his body armour.

'A little extreme perhaps. I suppose we just have to carry on and make the best of the situation.'

'Maybe.' He didn't elaborate any further on what this might mean.

Nineteen

The slippery slope had started. The Government were making changes because they felt that they had to rather than because they were probably needed. A new Government was ushered in and if anything, things began to get worse. For the police, it was a nightmare.

Having messed about with pay, they now turned their attention to the pension. Before passing onto this though they gave a final kick to the pay by freezing it so that inflation would continue and wages wouldn't; unless you were an MP, of course. Now the pension was really rather simple. It was large with a fantastic lump sum and a lot of members of the public thought this was unfair; but it wasn't really when you looked at it in detail. For starters police officers contributed 11% to their pension each month out of their wages which was considerably higher than most other people. In return they got a bigger pension and a bigger lump sum at the end of it. You get what you pay for.

The other thing that a lot of people could not understand was the fact that police officers retired at the age of fifty-five, or at the completion of thirty years' service; whichever was soonest. A lot of people thought this was too early. However, to be fair, policing — if you were frontline — was a high impact job and there was a life expectancy on it which was far lower than a lot of other jobs. This didn't mean that you were likely to die before the national retirement age, but it did mean that joints would start to ache and seize and injuries received in the line of duty would start to play up and there reached a point where the logic of a sixty-year-old police officer chasing a nineteen year old offender was frankly just ludicrous. Everyone with half a brain could see this, which is why the Government couldn't see it.

The high pension was the reward for thirty years of being abused, being spat at, being assaulted, sworn at and basically having to deal with a lot of shit and a lot of things which were frankly not all that nice. This was your little reward for the service that you had given the state. The Government then had other ideas.

Firstly, they decided that instead of working thirty years, new recruits would have to work thirty-five years. And then came the biggest kick in the balls of all. Ultimately, they wanted everyone to continue until they were sixty regardless of whether they were on a thirty year or thirty-five-year plan. They also increased the pension contributions from 11% to 13% but with less back at the end of it. Many saw the chances of a happy fulfilled retirement where they were comfortably off after so many years of public service disappearing into the sunset with its arse on fire.

Discontent was rife. Gradually a lot of police officers started to wonder what the point of being a police officer was any longer when you gave so much for so little in return. The Government decided that by stripping the monetary considerations down to negligible amounts they would get a better standard of recruit. This was, of course, complete bollocks. The better standard of recruits would look at it and think that they would be better off being an area manager for a supermarket where they were paid better, had health care and a company car without having to pay in so much or be abused half as much.

Simon was still very content with his life as a divorcee. The freedom from Amanda was something that he was enjoying. It is true that money was a little tighter now. He had never, to be honest, had all that much access to Amanda's family money. Her mother kept a tight hold on it and had ingrained in her daughter the need to keep tight claws on the money as well. For half the time the rich were only rich because of the fact that they kept a tight hold on their money. No, Simon was not dependant on Amanda for money, but it had helped to have had an extra amount hanging around.

Now that she was gone and now that the Government were freezing pay and destroying pensions it began to look very bleak for people like Simon who were not on high incomes. Despite the fact that he had a good deal out of the divorce he had ultimately been forced to give up the house that they had lived in and move to a more modest flat which was not particularly special. It was amazing how it became difficult to make ends meet without actually knowing how it was happening. The bills became higher and the balance between incoming and outgoing monies didn't seem to match up.

The Government only seemed to be intent on helping themselves rather than helping anyone else. They certainly were not going to help the police. The Government seemed to have decided to stick its head in a bucket whilst they then proceeded to kick it about. They were destroying the police. Some might go as far as to say that they were destroying the country.

'Don't they realise what they are doing?' Simon had asked one night when he was crewed up with George Lawrence.

'I expect so. It's probably something that they've planned because they want to destroy us and put something in our place that's run by someone that they were at Cambridge with.'

'I can't see me staying in this job. It is all I wanted to do and now it has been destroyed around my ears and there is nothing that I can do about it. It is so frustrating.'

'I would like to tell you that things would get better, but I can't see it happening. The police go through circles of repeating itself, but I have never seen the amount of damage to the police that there is now.' Lawrence seemed to be able to perfectly control the police car whilst still being able to stuff Scotch Eggs into his mouth with an amount of style which was impressive to the untrained observer.

'I have seen so much go downhill since I joined,' he continued. 'And I'm sure you have as well in the short amount of time you have been in. Morale is at the lowest that I've ever seen it. The problem is, that you can't expect the public to be given a great service when the officers are all demoralised and tired all the time. We're only human after all.'

'What's the answer?'

George seemed to think about this as he steered the car around looping country roads and balanced his food along the dashboard.

'I don't think there is an answer if I'm entirely honest.'

'There must be something that we can do. Things can't go on like this.'

'They probably can, and they can probably get a lot worse if the truth be known. The problem with the police, is that no matter what they throw at us, we make it work. We are our own worst enemies.'

'Don't the Government care about what they are doing?'

'Of course they don't care, Simon. Really? You think they give a toss about us, any of us? All they care about is making money and screwing the system. I don't mean to say that there aren't probably some people that go into politics because they want to make a difference and because they have the noblest of reasons for wanting to do so. It is just like the police; people join up here with the same intent; but the political system corrupts the politicians. They can't do any good because they are so constrained and controlled. People join us wanting to make a difference and after a while they come to the realisation that you can't make a difference.'

'I suppose.'

'They can't make a difference because the machine is too big. You're constrained by so many things. We aren't pro-active any longer. We don't have the time to be pro-active. We can only re-act. We don't have the time to prevent crime. If we're lucky, we might be able to detect it, but that isn't much consolation to most victims. They would rather it was prevented in the first place.'

'They don't want us to focus on prevention because you can't manage a deterrent; only detection.'

'Exactly. Nobody can measure how much we have put people off of committing a crime tonight just by being there. Billy Burglar might have been about to break into someone's house and we drive around the corner on routine patrol and he sees us and thinks twice and sods off back home giving it up for the night. We can't measure that because we don't know if it is happening or not.'

'If you asked most of the public, they would probably rather see a police car or an officer on patrol with nothing to go to rather than only seeing them turn up after a crime has been committed to try and sort out the pieces.'

'There's a fundamental difference between what I imagine the public want and what the management in this job want. The management love figures and as you can measure detections, they want us to focus on that; but the public don't want us to detect crime, they want us to prevent it. Given the choice would you rather be burgled and have it detected or not be burgled.'

'It's a simple choice really.'

'But not for the management because they can't prove how good they are on things that can't be measured. A member of the public stopped me the other day,' George said as he tried to open a packet of crisps at the same time as negotiating a bend in the road. 'They wanted to know why they never saw police officers walking the beat any longer.'

'What did you tell them?'

'I told them that there were less of us these days and I needed a car because I was expected to cover two towns and thirty-eight villages and that would be a little bit difficult to do on foot.'

'Goodness me, you told a member of the public the truth. They could have your balls for that.'

'Let 'em try.'

They lapsed into silence for a while whilst they continued the drive with each to their own thoughts.

'I feel so frustrated,' Simon finally said.

'I know.'

'This job isn't anything like I imagined it would be. Don't get me wrong, in some cases this is the best job in the world; but — I don't know.'

'But politicians and senior officers make it fucking difficult to do the job properly?'

'Yes, I suppose that's it.'

'We are caught in a trap where we are expected to be everything, a paramilitary army, social workers, everyone's mum and dad because their own are useless, councillors, doctors, psychiatrists — everything really. We have lost our identity.'

'Which is?'

'We are here to prevent bad things from happening to good people. It's that simple. We have lost that direction.'

Simon nodded his head and thought that this was actually rather logical. The police had become too complicated and expected to deal with too much. It should be stripped down to the basics. Every other service was allowed to do this. The fire service didn't go to domestics and the ambulance service didn't get cats out of a tree; but the police did *everything*. If you had tried everyone else then the option was to ring the police. The police spent a lot of time dealing with things that were not really police matters. The public would get a short sharp shock if the police actually went back to policing for a change rather than trying to sort out everyone's problems.

'Maybe we should just murder the Home Secretary,' Simon chortled. 'We know enough about the way things work to be able to make it look like suicide.'

'Doesn't matter we would have to take out the entire Government and even with everyone in the police on our side it would still be difficult to make it look like a mass suicide by the entire Government.'

'And then, of course, it would only mean that the Opposition got in and they would hardly make things better.'

'I suppose people might start getting a little suspicious,' Lawrence said, 'if we ended up killing off both the Government and the Opposition.'

'Could be seen as doing a great public service, though.'

'Probably get a knighthood.' They lapsed into silence for a minute.

Lawrence continued with his perpetual eating and then said 'You could probably get away with it though.'

'What murdering all the politicians?'

'No, not that. But if you were to commit a crime then we have a pretty good chance of getting away with it.'

'How so?'

'Well think about it. Firstly, we know what we look for at the scene of a crime so we would know the best way of not leaving any evidence lying around that would incriminate us.'

'I suppose so.'

'Secondly, we know so much and because of the uniform people tell us so much because they instantly trust us. Think about it, we know which places have alarms. We know where the CCTV is and which are dummy cameras. We know who has the most valuables in their houses or businesses. We poke about in the night doing things that would cause a member of the public to freak out if anyone else was doing it.'

'How do you mean?'

'Well think about it. You look out of the window one stormy, dark night and you see dark figures moving about with torches looking into places and trying door handles; or you see a car driving suspiciously slowly looking into properties. You are a law-abiding member of the public; so, what do you do?'

'Call the police.'

'Of course, you do. And if you happen to look out of your window and see the same people looking around with torches or driving passed slowly only this time the two people poking about are police officers and the car driving slowly is a police car, you just turn back from your window and snuggle down in your warm home safe in the knowledge that you are being well looked after.'

'And not remotely suspicious of the fact that the police car and officers might actually be up to no good.'

'Exactly.'

'Ah it's brilliant,' laughed Simon. 'You could get away with almost anything and nobody would suspect a thing. You can't count the number of times that people have told me that their property is empty as they will be away for a few weeks and can we keep an eye on it.'

'People would not think it all that suspicious, they would be reassured.' They both laughed at the thought of such a thing happening.

'It's a bloody good job that we are all so honest so that we would never be tempted for such a life of crime,' said George Lawrence as he tried to negotiate the opening of a packet of peanuts.

'Yes, it is, isn't it,' Simon commented as he looked through the windscreen into the darkness and the headlamps that tried to peer into the gloom of the night. Trying to find a path of light in the darkness.

Twenty

With everything that was going on and with much being said about police officers that hated their job, but for one reason or another felt that they were trapped in a vicious circle that they could not break or escape from, it was possible to overlook the fact that within the police there was a much more dangerous breed of officer than those that quintessentially hated their job but nevertheless got on with it; and this was the breed of officer that loved their job.

This may sound strange, but this breed that loved their job were far more dangerous; because what they had was ambition and ambition was a very dangerous thing to have in the police; it was a pretty dangerous thing to have in any walk of life, you only had to look towards *Macbeth* to see that. It was often remarked that you should be very careful who you decided to shit on because one day they may get promoted over you and then they would shit on you. Alternatively, you may find that those you shat on whilst you were on the way up would be there for you when you were on the way back down again.

Such a person was Chief Inspector Ian Harbour. Harbour was a very dangerous man not only because he had ambition, but because he loved the job. He lived, breathed, ate, slept, drank and would ultimately probably die in the job. He was obsessed with the job to the expense of everything else. He was not a particularly nice person either for a variety of reasons. Firstly, he never listened to music. Now you may think so what, but students of Shakespeare will know that Shakespeare taught us to be very suspicious of people that did not like music and Harbour was someone that did not ply his music at all. Shakespeare would have found him to have been a very disturbing man and would have steered well clear of him which was something that everyone did their best to do anyway.

Secondly, he didn't read books. Now again this may not strike anyone as being particularly strange; but it was a fact that if you went into a house as a police officer and there were no books to be seen anywhere then you could almost be certain that you were meeting a specific kind of person. That is not to say that murders didn't happen in libraries, Agatha Christie would submit that they did; but the general population that were book lovers were a different class of people on the whole to those that weren't. It may seem harsh, but then if you are reading this then you are probably okay.

Now the police were taught not to stereotype, but this was of course rubbish. To an extent you had to stereotype because it was very often the stereotypes that were the ones committing the crimes, i.e. the criminals. Your average police officer would tell you that on a day to day basis they entered a number of homes and probably most officers had entered homes as wide ranging as hovels and mansions. It is ludicrous to suggest that there was not a degree of stereotyping that existed when you walked into someone's home. You can tell a lot about a person by the books that they have on the shelves, the compact discs they have in their racks and the DVDs that they have. You can tell even more about them if none of these items were present.

Harbour did not have the time for books. Harbour had probably never voluntarily read a book in his life unless it was for promotion study. He would tell you that he did not have time for such things and that was because he spent so much time on thinking about *The Job*. He may have read a lot of law books in order to get where he was, but it was also a fact that he only had a very flimsy grasp on what the law actually was. He had reached a position where his grasp on the fundamentals of the legal system had escaped him and was not something that he would allow to stand in the way of getting what he wanted.

Officers that worked in the area that he was commanding would tell you if you asked them that he had single handed been responsible for destroying the morale and also for uniting everyone together against him. He had no friends in the police (nor out of it if the truth were to be told), and it would not take much prompting for officers of all ranks both higher and lower than him to tell you that they all thought that he was a bit of a wanker. He was a prime example of how it was possible to be promoted with no discernible character traits that were in anyway favourable. Almost everything human about him had been removed.

It was true that he had a wife and she was something of a mystery to a lot of people. A mystery in the sense that first of all she actually existed and secondly that she had chosen to marry such a man as Harbour. She must either be a meek and mild little thing that spent much of her time either in awe of him or doing her best to avoid him. Alternatively, as he spent so much time at work and thinking about work, she could have been living the high life shagging everyone that came along and really enjoying the freedom that his obsession gave her whilst at the same time enjoying living off of a chief inspector's salary.

The man knew no bounds at all. He had already suffered from a nervous breakdown once in his career and had obviously been too thick to learn from this and had carried on in the same manner that he had before he went wibble and was once again either heading for another breakdown or perhaps a heart attack due to the unbelievable tension and stress that he somehow managed to keep himself under. To say that he was like a coiled spring was an understatement. He was so wound up that it was a wonder that he managed to last as long as he had. It was actually as if he was the Eighth Wonder of the World as it really was a scientific and medical wonder that he was not already dead. A lot of people looked forward to the day when he eventually would shuffle off the mortal coil. It was a certainty that there would be a great number of people at his funeral who were all there just to make sure that the bastard really was dead.

Simon had been open minded when he had first met the Chief Inspector. After all, at this point in his career he hadn't been tainted. Harbour had a habit of having a meet and greet with all his officers, new and old whenever you came to *his* police station, he had a one-to-one with you in his office. Simon had just started his probationary period and was only a couple of days into his tutorship when he first met Harbour. He sat in a chair opposite Harbour who sat behind his desk.

'I don't want you calling the sergeants by their first name,' said Harbour, 'some of them will give you permission to do this, but you are to ignore this permission. That is a direct order from me. I will have formality between the ranks. This is a uniformed service and rank will be obeyed and respected.'

'Yes, sir,' replied Simon thinking that this was on the one hand a fair assessment to take, but this wasn't the army after all.

'My door is always open…' that sounded nice and helpful '… so I will know if you are fucking about out there.' Not so helpful.

Harbour continued to ramble on for a few more minutes more about some bollocks or other, but frankly Simon had stopped listening to him after the door comment.

Harbour would routinely put in fifteen hours a day every day, which really was not all that necessary for him to have to do. His biggest problem was perhaps that he just could not let go. He was permanently glued to his BlackBerry and if someone had been able to steal it from him, he probably would have died then and there more readily than being detached from life support. His BlackBerry *was* his life support. He went on leave and he took it with him and he would access his emails from the beach. He gave strict orders that on the few occasions when he had to take leave that officers were to email him tasking updates so that even if he was thousands of miles away he could still check-up to see what they were doing and that they were still disrupting criminals and stopping lots of vehicles — most of whom were innocent members of the public who were going about their ordinary day to day lives but whom the police stopped because Harbour demanded that they stop every van and 4x4 that was moving day or night in the off chance that the one in a hundred vehicle that you stopped had someone in it that was up to no good.

The powers of Stop and Search were there for legitimate reasons, but people like Harbour saw it as an opportunity to take the legislation away from what it was designed to do and to pressurise lower ranking officers into abusing the powers so that it could make him look good to the powers that be and enable him to make the promotional step to superintendent. Attitudes like this were destined to make the Stop and Search powers head for a big crash.

When he arrived at 0600 hours at the police station, he would scan the tasking updates for the previous night with a level of eagerness that was akin to what most other people would only scan the lottery results with. He was looking for two things; evidence that the night turn had not done enough; or evidence that they had been successful. If they had been successful and had caught some criminals in the act then it was very likely that he would have tossed one off there and then. A lot of people thought he was actually a sad, pathetic little figure that should probably have been pitied more than anything else were it not for the fact that he was also at the same time an obnoxious little twat. He was actually so out of touch with reality that he was known to try and give officers 'high fives' when they had done something really good and constantly signed off everything with the phrase 'happy hunting.' He was obviously too blind to realise that nobody was happy about anything under his command; or perhaps it was not that he was too blind, but actually similarly if he knew he had no friends in the police it was just that he did not care. Certainly, this pathetic attempt to be hip though was not winning him anything but derision of the highest calibre.

If you had not given the tasking updates that he was looking for then he would be on the warpath. He never actually criticised the constables to their face, of course, and this was probably because he did not have the balls to do it. Instead he would verbally abuse the inspector who in turn would jump up and down on the sergeants who would throw the shit at the constables. This was called the Chain of Command. It was worse for the inspector, of course, because she was stuck in the middle. The shit was rolling down to her from Harbour every time he decided to get a bee in his bonnet about the most trivial of things; and then she was getting the grief coming the other way from the sergeants who were telling her why it was that they thought that Harbour was a dick. In many regards this was why promotion was something that was just not worth having. Stay at the bottom and just try and get on with it the best you could. The higher you went, the less a police officer you were and the more of a politician you became; and by association the more of a prick you seemed to become if he was anything to go by.

What was also startling about Harbour was his complete and utter disregard for the law. Now the police are governed by lots of pieces of legislation but the most important is the Police and Criminal Evidence Act 1984 or PACE as it is more commonly known. PACE pretty much says what the police can and can't do in most circumstances. For instance, it covers the aforementioned stop and search powers, it covers powers of entry, it covers how you are meant to treat people that are under arrest and how they must be interviewed and so on and so on. It is there to try and prevent corruption and to stop the police from really doing whatever the hell they like whenever they like. Harbour had openly said to a number of officers 'I see PACE as more of a guideline rather than rules.'

This was, of course, completely untrue, as well as being rather corrupt. You could not just ignore pieces of legislation because it prevented you from doing what you wanted; but this was exactly what Harbour did. It put everyone else in a very difficult situation though. The PCs and the sergeants in particular knew far more about the law than he did because they were using it every day. They knew when you didn't have the grounds to stop and search or when an arrest would be illegal because the necessity was not there. This put them between a rock and a hard place though. Do you disobey Harbour and be subject to not only the wrath of the man, but also his childlike desire for revenge where he would spend the rest of your career doing everything he could to cripple you and prevent you from doing anything you wanted because you had once dared to disagree with him; or did you do something which was ultimately illegal in the hope that you might actually get away with it?

If he had known that he was not liked, and he wouldn't have cared less if he had, then he would only have taken it as a sign that he was doing his job properly. Ultimately everyone hoped that one day he would be promoted to the point where he was not operational any longer and he would quietly be shoved into an office at headquarters somewhere, or the Puzzle Palace as it was affectionately known, where he would be given the task of counting paperclips and would be unable to cause any further damage to anyone else. In the meantime, until that glorious day everyone was stuck with him much the same as you might get stuck with leprosy. Only leprosy was more attractive and there was always the chance that you might be cured of it.

One day, if he did not die before hand, he would retire. When that day came he might as well be dead for his life would be over. Nobody would care any longer about him and he would no longer have any power. He wouldn't have The Job that had been his life since he was a police cadet. He would not really have anything left to live for. A number of things could happen to him at this point. He would either eventually just drop dead because of the fact that he had nothing that was worth living for any longer. He might decide that because he had nothing left to live for any longer that he might decide to commit suicide. If that was the case then it was very likely that officers would be queuing up for miles to attend his sudden death and meticulously fill out the paperwork for it, although Harbour would probably fill out his own sudden death forms before topping himself. Or, and this was more likely, he would probably spend the rest of his days calling the police to report absolutely everything. By calling the police out to everything and anything that ever happened he would somehow in his sad little mind no doubt feel that he was still a part of it all.

Oh, beware of someone with ambition. If only he had the intelligence to have learnt from Shakespeare he might, just might, have been a better person.

There is a caveat to be added to this though. Although it was dangerous to have people with ambition in any walk of life, there were those that genuinely loved the job who didn't have ambition to climb the ranks and stab everyone else in the back. These people enjoyed being constables and doing their duty every day. They may not like the politics, but they did their best to ignore it and get on with the things that mattered: namely, the public. These people were few and far between, but they were out there, and they were to be applauded.

Twenty-One

It was fair to say that Simon had over the course of nine years now of being a police officer, become very dissatisfied with his job. He came to the conclusion that if you were in the position that he was in then you had three options.

Option one was that you just shut up and you got on with it. He had often lived by the personal philosophy of 'if you can't change it, then put up with it.' The problem was that it was becoming harder. It seemed to be one thing after another. You felt that you had surmounted one difficulty, only to have another big problem thrown in your way either by the Government or by management.

Option two was to start looking for something else to do within the police. Now this was a very positive thing about the police, you could move department and your whole job description could change. You had so many options available to you that you could move into one of these specialist departments and you might be better off for a time or you might find your niche and happily see out the rest of your career. The Government and the management were blinded to the fact that they were being stupid to try and make a round peg fit into a square hole. They did this by insisting that front line response officers should be experts in everything. They failed to acknowledge that there were those who would always be better at stop searches than others on the shift. They did not admit that there were those that would always be better at interviewing and putting files together than others. Some would be really good at traffic law and giving out tickets. You could be really good at one thing or mediocre at a lot of them. Rather than utilise the skills that different officers had on a shift they tried to force you to be something that you were not. In this case you were better off trying to get out and specialise in something that you were actually good at.

The last option was to throw your hands up in the air and leave the police entirely and go off and do something else. Something that may or may not be better paid, but something that would almost certainly mean that you were better treated. This was starting to happen throughout the country. The changes that the Government were making had started to turn a lot of police officers away from The Job and they were walking away. Police officers that would never have before dreamt of leaving the job were starting to get restless and look for other things.

It was nearly all because of the destruction that the Government had brought about. The Government's short-sightedness was really something of a marvel; they really could not see that there was likely to come a time when there wasn't going to be all that many police officers about; then who would they get to stand outside 10 Downing Street and to give the protection to the politicians that most members of the public don't even realise that they get? The truth of the matter would be, of course, that no matter how many police officers left and how the numbers depleted there would always be someone protecting Downing Street, Westminster and the politicians at the cost of not protecting the average member of the public who deserved the protection more than any politician ever would.

Simon felt that he was probably in the second camp with option two, but he was on the border and was moving to option three with a steady amount of progress. The problem that he had with moving into a specialist role was the fact that you only seemed to be moved into such roles if you were useless. This is perhaps unfair; there were a lot of decent, hardworking officers in specialist roles that deserved to be there. However, for every officer like that you could probably name another two that were a mystery as to how they had got there. Front line officers would remember these people when they were in uniform and remember them as useless officers that couldn't tell you one end of a baton from the other. How the hell did they get away with it? They seemed to be untouchable. Every organisation and every walk of life has people that are lazy, incompetent and in some cases criminal; the police are no exception. It may come as a shock to some people, but police officers were just as human as everyone else and carried the same people from all walks of life as anywhere else. They were also just as fallible as everyone else; they just didn't seem to be allowed to be; which is why such a fuss was made about it in the press when they did screw up. It was becoming possible to develop paranoia and believe that there was a campaign within the press to discredit the police. The press was quick to jump on any bad reports of the police, but were slow to report anything positive that they had done. The Government were down on the police so the press jumped on the band wagon and attacked them at the same time in order to try and win favour.

The answer as to why the lazy and the incompetent were in these roles and why people like this were promoted was really very simple. All you had to do was be good at interviews. Whenever you went for an interview within the police, they did not mark you on your ability to do the job, or what you were capable of or even what your personality was like and whether they would even be able to work with you. No; they graded you on your ability to be able to hit certain key phrases and tick boxes. If you were able to do this then you were in. Thus, it was more than possible that you had officers in certain positions that were there because of the fact that they knew how to pass interviews whilst at the same time they knew nothing about the job. Chief Inspector Harbour was really a case in point.

Simon had reached the conclusion that he was not really cut out to be front line. He enjoyed analysing things and methodically working out a problem rather than the cut and thrust of what was required for front line response. This had probably come from watching too many episodes of programmes like *Inspector Morse*, but it was nevertheless something that had slowly started to seep into his being. With this in mind he had decided to apply for CID; or as it was often called by uniform, CIDON'T, as they seemed to spend a lot of time telling uniform what they didn't do. This happened a lot. Uniform would pick up a job that was very clearly a CID matter, but when you approached CID about it, they would spend ages convincing you that it really wasn't something that would fit into their remit. If you then progressed with it yourself and managed to get close to a result then they would suddenly decide that it was something that was within their remit after all and they would sweep in and try to steal it from you.

The reason for this was because of the fact that CID were detectives. The clue was in their name. They detected things. They didn't like to take on jobs where it looked like it was not going to be possible to detect it because it would bring their statistics down. If, however, the hard graft of uniform officers had made it move towards a detection then they would be all over you to take the glory for something that they hadn't done. Such things like this annoyed a lot of officers as you might imagine. PC Lawrence had ended with a blazing argument with the Detective Sergeant over a particularly smelly burglary that CID should have taken on, but had decided not to because they didn't think there was much hope of it being detected.

'When I first came to this station twenty years ago,' Lawrence had growled at the DS. 'CID was the best department throughout the entire Force. CID here was shit hot. Now under you and your policies this department has gone from shit hot to just shit.'

The DS had fumed and looked like a blood vessel was about to burst. 'How dare you? I will have you know that my officers have got the highest detection rate in this station.'

'Of course they fucking have. They're detectives. They don't deal with all the crap we do. They don't go to accidents and domestics and God knows how many other things. Half the time they don't even go to burglaries. You would be pretty crap if your officers had the lowest detection rates in the station.'

'I find your attitude disgraceful. I am going to tell the DCI about you.'

'Oh God, run to mummy why don't you.'

'You won't be so smug when the DCI hears of this conversation.'

'Twenty years ago, the DCI was the DS here. If you want to go and tell him that when he was running this department it was shit hot and now that you are running it you have turned into a pile of shit then you go ahead. All I am saying at the end of the day is that he was a far better DS than you will ever be.'

Either the DS had never had the balls to tell the DCI or the DCI had agreed with Lawrence for he never heard anything about the argument ever again.

***

Simon had put the application for CID through the ranks. It had been approved by his Sergeant and it had then gone up to Chief Inspector Harbour. Now, this was another example of Harbour being a control freak. The method was very simple. A constable would see a job that they fancied and would put an application form together. They would then pass it to their sergeant who would either support the application or not; either way they would put their comments and justification on the form. It was then supposed to go to the inspector who would do the same. Once this was all done it would go to Human Resources.

Harbour, because of his obsessive controlling nature insisted that all applications by-pass the inspector and get sent to him. There really was no reason for this other than the fact that he simply had to know what was going on all the time and it was important to him that he interfered in things that were really not within his remit any longer. The previous Chief Inspector who had been a far nicer bloke — chiefly because you never saw him — was of the opinion that he didn't need to know about applications from constables as they were beneath him. This may sound harsh but it is true. The everyday ambitions of constables are not in the remit of a chief inspector to care about, which is why there are two ranks separating the chief inspector from the constable. If you want to get involved at that level in what constables are doing then there is no point having sergeants and inspectors. It also sends a message — one that Harbour would have been completely unaware about — that you have no faith in your middle management and their ability to manage.

The higher up the ranks you went then the more your remit changed. You were expected to do different things as you progressed and to let other things slip by the wayside. It could be seen in circumstances when sergeants made arrests. Of course, there was nothing to stop a sergeant making an arrest, there was nothing to stop any officer of any rank making an arrest; but if there was a constable there then the constable should be making it rather than the sergeant. It was not what the sergeant was expected to do any longer. Harbour was trying to retain everything from each rank and do everything. He had even recently made an arrest — presumably to prove that he could still do it. The problem was the superintendent had been furious when he had found out as he was not paying his chief inspectors to do the work that constables should have been doing.

At any rate; Simon's application for CID had been completed, passed on to his sergeant who had dutifully filled it in and then passed it to Harbour so that he could progress it. It was then that Simon had been called into the office of his sergeant.

It was coming towards the end of a particularly difficult shift where Simon had ended up fighting with a suspect at the scene of a domestic and it had taken a lot out of him. After the fight he had then spent several hours taking statements and then putting together a handover so that the idiot could be interviewed later on. It was a lot of work to do, particularly when as it was a domestic there was every chance that the wife would refuse to progress a complaint the next day. As this was all coming to an end, he then was called in to see Sergeant Baker.

Sergeant Baker was about the same age as Simon, but he had joined the police a few years before Simon and had progressed to the rank of sergeant before finally coming to the conclusion that to go any further was just not worth the effort for the small reward that came back from it. If anything, Sgt Baker appeared to be more stressed than Simon was. Sgt Baker's desk was covered in paperwork that appeared to have no order, but Baker could have told you exactly where everything was and what everything was as well. Scattered amongst the paperwork was the odd coffee mug that was either empty or had remnants of coffee still congealing inside.

'Take a seat Simon.' This was never a good sign; it is never a good thing to be offered a seat in a supervisor's office. It tends to suggest that what is to come is going to be bad news and will probably take some time to wade through. 'There is no easy way to tell you this, but Mr Harbour has decided not to support your CID application.'

This was something of a setback, Simon had to admit that. 'Any reason why?'

'He doesn't think you're experienced enough,' said Baker feeling very weary and about ten years older than he was.

'After nine years?'

'Apparently so. I don't fully understand it; the man is a law onto himself. I think it would be a good and sensible move for both yourself and the organisation, but nobody really understands what is going on in the Chief Inspector's mind.' Probably least of all the Chief Inspector, if the truth were told.

'Oh.' Simon did not really trust himself to say anything that might not include several short expletives. 'This job is really shit, isn't it?'

'Yes, it is. Every day now there is something,' Baker was a plain speaker which was another reason why it was that he would never get promoted above where he was now, it was probably a reason why he was also liked amongst those that were under him. He was well used to presenting the silk stocking full of shit for exactly what it was. 'The Inspector was in here moments ago complaining that the troops were not motivated enough.' Baker shook his head. 'How can I motivate you guys when I can't even motivate myself?'

'This job is being destroyed.'

'Yes, it is,' said Baker as he flicked a paperclip into one of the coffee mugs. There didn't seem to be much else to say at the time so Simon eventually left the office and went back to the report room where he eventually let vent to a few of the expletives that he had so far been able to keep in check. There had been no point voicing them in front of the sergeant, it was hardly his fault after all.

Baker turned back to his computer and looked at it without really seeing it. He tried to remember how he had got to where he was in life. He had never wanted to be a police officer. When he was a teenager, he had wanted to be a writer, but then life had somehow got in the way and he had never had the courage to really make a stab at being a writer. He supposed that the reason for this was that he didn't really fancy the idea of failure that much. You have to be a special kind of person to pour your heart out onto paper so that someone else could read it and then either reject it outright or then criticise your words and your life and thus slowly destroy you as well.

He couldn't really remember why it was that he had become a police officer. He supposed that it was something that he had done to please his parents because it had certainly been something that they had always wanted for him. All that reading and all that writing to end up in this shit office. What was the point? He didn't write any longer, but he did still read and that was probably the only way that he had in which he could escape. Those that were not really into reading would never understand or appreciate the escapism that you could get from reading. Losing yourself in a book and allowing your imagination to feed off of the words and the worlds of other people. As was often the case Baker found himself wondering if it really was too late for him to be able to make a go of it at being a writer. He had a great fear that he would be trapped in this role that he had found himself in, playing the part of a police officer and that towards the end of his days he would look back on his life and would be haunted by the biggest question that can haunt any person.

What if?

Twenty-Two

'Despondency.'

'I'm sorry?' This last was from PC Lawrence in response to Simon's cryptic opening.

'Everyone is so despondent at the moment. There must be something that we can do,' Simon continued as he stared vacantly into the depths of his computer terminal as if hoping that he would somehow find the answers in there.

'Oh, I see,' said Lawrence as he split open a pre-pack packet of sandwiches and delicately prised apart the bread to see if the filling was anything like what it said it was meant to be on the packet. 'What do you suggest we do? Organise a cricket match or something?'

'I don't know what we should do, but I feel that we should do something. I feel so frustrated.'

'We all do really. It's natural for this job. I would say that you will get used to it, but you won't.'

'You know what really pisses me off?'

'I would imagine that it's a lot of things, Simon.'

'Well, okay I will grant you that there are a lot of things. What really pisses me off at the moment is that drugs warrant we have just done.'

'Oh yes.'

The team had just come back from executing a drugs' warrant which had not been all that successful.

'Here are we, law abiding citizens that always pay their car tax on time and buy insurance. We never steal; we never take advantage of the system, unlike so many other people.'

'Politicians, for instance?'

'Well I wasn't going to mention them. We get up early in the morning and we work throughout the night. We work on Christmas Day and we take everything that is thrown at us. We have failed marriages and wayward children and what is it all for?'

No answer appeared to be all that forthcoming to this.

'And then we do something like that drugs warrant,' Simon continued. 'And there you have some criminal low life scum who has never worked in their life and they have a bigger house than you and I could afford even if we combined our wages. They have cars that cost more each than I earn in a couple of years. Living the life of luxury dishing out drugs to people whilst they become rich.'

'It does seem a little unfair.'

'It's more than a little unfair it's damn...' Simon appeared lost for words as he struggled to find something that fitted.

'Criminal?' suggested Lawrence.

'Yes, absolutely. In every sense of the word. It makes me sick.'

'What do you suggest that you do about it then?'

Simon thought about this one for a moment or two. 'Well I don't suppose that there is anything that we can do about it is there?'

'I wouldn't say that.'

'What do you mean?'

But PC Lawrence was not prepared to say what he meant. Not at that time.

***

Times had changed. In the shortest time the world had changed and Simon was not entirely sure as to why. Was it the case that matters were changing because of the decisions made by governments and the hierarchy? Or was it that this was what the world was always like as you got older? Simon was not really certain. It was possible that it was the latter.

In many ways for the majority of people there was always the chance that the world got worse as you grew from a carefree childhood into complicated adolescence, struggling with hormones and then moved into your twenties where you settled down and made your relationships and then your career. From there you would move into your thirties where a lot of disappointments might surface when you realised that your hopes and dreams that you had settled down on in your twenties turned out not to have happened or not to have been what you thought they were in the first place. Your forties were your time for reflection and trying to reorganise things that you had decided to change in your life as you reached the mid-way point. Your fifties were the time when you realised that age was catching up on you and you could very easily find yourself looking around you and being mentally a teenager in the body of someone in their fifties. How did I get here? How did this happen? Time has a habit of moving very quickly and you can wake up one day and find that you have missed the majority of life without realising it.

So, maybe this progression of life just made you feel that things were getting worse as you became heavily drenched in responsibility and commitment. Or it could just be that the world was in itself getting more complicated and difficult. Simon had felt that it was the world getting worse. Most of this was because of the fact that people were making life more difficult for the majority of others. The older he got the more he would look back on the past and wonder where it was that the enthusiasm had gone that he had once had. He had taken a couple of knockbacks although he felt that he could not really classify the divorce from Amanda as being a knockback; although it was possible that he could classify the marriage as something of a knockback.

It was also true that he had worked hard and jumped many hurdles in order to get into what he considered to be his dream job only to find out that it was not remotely as dreamy as he thought it would be. This was perhaps the biggest problem for him. As his faith in the police had started to deteriorate, he found that his life was entering into something of a depression. It is only to be expected. It is hard to fight off depression when everything you have pinned your hopes onto turns out to be something that you didn't expect it to be. One of the issues that would rise from this is the fact that the more depressed and desperate the situation felt then the more desperate the action would be that you might take. That was something that nobody would have been able to predict and was going to change some lives.

***

'There are times when I really, truly hate this fucking job,' said George Lawrence as he riffled through the desk drawer.

'That would be most days I would imagine,' replied Simon from the other end of the room where he was looking behind a bookcase to see if there was anything hidden.

To the casual observer their actions may have seemed strange, but they were involved in the time-honoured tradition in the police of searching someone else's house. The law permits this to happen under certain circumstances. In this particular circumstance they were conducting a search under section 18 of the Police and Criminal Evidence Act which was a very posh way of saying that the police had the opportunity to search the dwellings of some of those that they arrested when they were looking for evidence linked to the crime for which they had been arrested. In this particular instance they were searching the home of a man who had been arrested on suspicion of having stolen money from a charity. He had infiltrated the charity in question, gained the trust of those that ran the charity and then had been accused of making off with five thousand pounds of their money.

'All we seem to deal with these days is the scum of the earth,' said Lawrence as he rummaged around looking for bank statements on anything else that he might be able to find in the desk that would give them some solid evidence to put to the man.

'Nothing new there,' replied Simon.

'No; but I'm finding it gets harder the more I go through it. Every day there is some new pleb that comes up and makes you question what the point is. You take one scumbag down and then two more jump up in their place. One drug dealer is replaced by others that are worse. We're never going to win the war on drugs.'

'You don't think we should give up on that war then?'

'Of course not; we can't afford, morally, to give up on the war on drugs although God knows that we can't afford, financially, to continue it.'

'Keeps us in a job I suppose.'

'Yes, but there are times when I feel that it is a job that is not as noble as it used to be and probably not worth as much as it used to be worth either.'

'I think there are a lot of people who would feel the same.'

'Take this bloke. Stealing money from a charity. Just when you think you have reached the bottom of the barrel you discover that there is always something lower than you expected.'

Simon thought about this for a moment. 'We see more of our share of depressing things about the world. More than most other people realise exists.'

Lawrence threw some paperwork back into the drawer. 'And what do we get in the media? Attacked all the time. If it isn't the bloody politicians undermining us it's the media blaming us for everything that goes wrong in the world. Half of the tragedies that we get blamed for are actually the fault of some other agency, like social services or the like. It just seems to be that the police are the last line of resort for everyone; no matter what it is that they want.'

'Occupational hazard, I suppose.'

'Well I have had enough of it!' This last was loud and furious. Simon put down the things that he was looking through and turned to Lawrence in a rather shocked manner as he was not normally that energetic in anything that he said or did.

'Are you alright, George?'

'I'm sorry. It's just so frustrating and I'm so tired.' He sat down on one of the chairs in the room. 'So many years of this kind of thing. Over and over again, with no sign of letting up and no end in sight. I have dedicated my entire life to this job and I'm nearing thirty years of service and the world is worse now than it was when I first joined. What improvement have I made? What improvement have we made? Thirty years of knocking away at criminal activity and they have only got better at what they do. They are more perverse now than they used to be and more violent now than they used to be. Even the respect from the public is not what it used to be. So, what have we achieved in all that time?'

Simon was rather taken back at this which was so un-Lawrence like that it might have come from the mouth of a total stranger. It just goes to show you that you can work with someone for a long time and you think that you know them, but when it comes to it you don't really know all that much about people that are around you; no matter how close you are to them; or think you are to them.

'Anyway,' said Lawrence who appeared to regain something of his composure after his brief interlude of making himself clear on what it was that he really felt. 'There's nothing here.'

'No; I think you're right. Do you think he did it?'

'I don't know. I would hope not, but it's a cruel and evil world so anything is possible. Come on let's get back to custody.'

They completed their paperwork and returned to custody. They handed the paperwork over to the officer in the case, PC Helen Simpson and left her to interview the suspect and carry on with things. They then went off and had a bite to eat.

An hour later they were standing outside with civvie jackets on having a smoke when Simpson came passed with the suspect for the charity theft. She stopped next to the two other officers as the suspect walked down the steps of the police station to a taxi that was waiting for him.

'What happened, Helen?' asked Lawrence.

'No further action. I couldn't find a single thing to put to him that was concrete and there was no way that CPS would run it.'

CPS was the Crown Prosecution Service that was made up of a team of solicitors that reviewed each case that the police had and made a decision as to whether there was sufficient evidence to charge or not. They would from time to time make some decisions that the police could not understand in the least. The general guide that they went by was that they would not charge any suspect that they did not have a high chance of being able to get a successful prosecution at court. This was something of a noble sentiment as it was the public money that they were spending after all. It nevertheless did not prevent them from earning the nickname of Couldn't Prosecute Satan to fit their initials rather than their actual title.

Helen turned away and walked back into the police station. In the meantime, Simon and Lawrence watched the ex-suspect getting into the taxi. As he did, he turned and saw the two officers watching him and smiled at them although it was truer to say that the smile was more of a smirk than a smile.

'Yeah,' said Lawrence as he flicked his cigarette end down into the gutter. 'He did it alright.' This was all to do with the instinct that some police officers developed over time. It was really just to do with experience really. After so many years of doing the job it was highly possible to develop an instinct into when someone was lying or telling the truth or for when someone was innocent or guilty.

'Nothing that we can do about that now.'

'Isn't there?' Lawrence looked at Simon sideways.

'What do you mean?'

'There're always solutions that can be raised to every problem that presents itself. It's just a question of whether or not you are prepared to make the effort or to take the step that is required to get the solution.'

'I'm not following you, George.'

'No? Perhaps it's just me being a foolish old man then and not really thinking about what it is that I am talking about.'

With that he turned away and walked back into the police station leaving Simon, lost in thought, finishing his cigarette whilst he watched the taxi move away until he was on his own.

Twenty-Three

A common complaint that ran among the majority of police officers that still cared about their jobs and the level of service that they gave to victims of crime was when they were not able to bring someone that they knew was guilty to justice. There is a big difference between *knowing* that someone is guilty of a crime and being able to *prove* that they are guilty of a crime. It is a distinction that most members of the public are unable to make and in the emotive state of being a victim can take it to mean that the police officer who is dealing with them doesn't care about their case when in reality they probably do care, but they are frustrated and know that there is nothing that they can do to get the evidence that would be required to bring an offender before a court. In some cases, there may not be sufficient evidence to identify an offender and in other cases even if you have a suspect in mind you may still not have enough evidence to be able to bring them before a custody officer who would review the reason for their arrest and decide whether or not to authorise their detention. Obviously if you didn't have enough solid ground to bring them before a custody officer then you certainly didn't have enough to bring them before a court.

The second problem that frequently occurred was when you did have enough evidence to bring them before a custody officer. Once this was done and your investigation was complete you would then have to present the evidence to the Crown Prosecution Service and jump over the hurdles of convincing them that there was sufficient evidence to charge the suspect to court. Assuming that your case was tight enough to be able to do that you then had to face the gauntlet of the court to get a conviction. This might mean convincing Magistrates or worse, a jury, of their guilt.

It was worse to convince a jury of guilt because a jury was made up from members of the public who more often than not had no knowledge of the law and the legal system other than what they had seen on television or read about in detective novels. Jurors were a mixed bag of individuals. Some were diligent and paid close attention to the case making copious notes as the trial went along. Others sat there day dreaming or thinking about what they were going to have for dinner or what they would be doing at the weekend. Some were even known to make such comments like 'Well I knew he was guilty the moment he walked into the room. He has one of those guilty faces.' Now, I ask you; would you like to be tried by people like that?

A suggestion had been made that juries should really be made up of professionals who at least had some inkling of what was going on as well as some knowledge of the law and the criminal justice system. The problem with this, of course, was that this was creating an elitist jury. A jury that would only be made up of professionals who had some capacity rather than oafs who had pretty much walked off of the street and were only interested in having a little excitement in their lives or worse in some vindictive cases those that wanted to send someone to prison in retribution for something that had once happened to them in their lives. Perhaps they had once been a victim of a crime and the perpetrator had got away with it so they now wanted to balance the scales by sending someone else down. It didn't matter that this case was not linked to their circumstances. It didn't really matter whether the person who was standing in the dock was innocent or guilty. All that mattered to them was balancing the scales. That was their idea of justice.

It was a matter of long debate on whether if you were unfortunate enough to find yourself standing in the dock in a Crown Court whether you would want to be tried by experts who knew exactly what they were doing or random members of the public who did not have a clue what they were doing. Perhaps a fairer system would have allowed the suspect to be able to choose the method of how the jury was made up in their trial.

It did lead to the problem though of the lack of balance between the rights of the suspect and the rights of the victim. This was a very tricky and emotive area. Now, it is true that not all suspects are guilty and not all victims are innocent. There are malicious complaints made on a daily basis and in some cases the 'evidence' of these malicious complaints is so perfectly woven that the innocent suspect will find themselves in court having to defend themselves against something that they have not done.

Just because the police arrested someone it did not mean that the person was guilty. All the police needed to arrest someone was suspicion that they had committed an offence; or in some cases suspicion that they are about to commit an offence. In certain elements of society being arrested or even having the police turn up at your home was still seen as a stigma. There is probably some hope for society that this is still the case. For the majority of people, the arrival of a police officer on your door means either that they have come to arrest you or that they have come to tell you that someone close to you has died. Despite everything that the politicians might like to say about England being a classless society in the twenty-first century there would be a division between those who believed the arrival of the police meant arrest and those who believed that the arrival of the police meant death. It was always this way and it probably would always remain that way.

All of that to one side, however, there still remained the fact that from the moment you were arrested you had more rights than a victim did. Now if you were innocent then this was a very good thing. However, although innocent people are arrested each day, the majority that are arrested have done something to bring themselves to the police station in handcuffs — even if they are unlikely to admit it; even to themselves. When you were arrested you had to be treated in a certain way that was in accordance to the rights that you had which were laid down in legislation. The most common right that most people knew was the right to free and independent legal advice. You didn't have to pay for your solicitor. If you were going to be placed in a cell then you had a whole raft of rights from drinks and meals, to adequate heating, blankets, access to washing facilities, exercise in the open (although covered in bars) air and so on. You had the right to have your identity kept secret until such time as you were charged when it then became in the public domain.

It went further than this as well. If you were found guilty at court and you went to prison then the only thing that you really had to suffer was your loss of freedom. Now for some people that would be punishment enough on its own. For others it really wasn't such a big thing. For the vast majority life was better inside prison than it was for them on the outside. They had shelter, they had warmth, and they didn't have to buy their food or pay their bills. Most of them would have more access to education, should they want it and exercise should they need it. In many cases they could learn a trade which was a useful thing that they could then take with them to the outside world and turn towards making a life of crime that little bit more easily. Cells were furnished with televisions and computer game consoles. Prisoners had more rights than the prison guards had.

The Victorians would be turning in their grave. Of course, nobody wanted to go back to prison squalor as had been the tradition for so many hundreds of years; or at least nobody that had any power to make decisions about prisons wanted to turn back the clock to those days when going to prison was a hardship. Plenty of other people were all for stripping prisoners of every single right that they had and locking them up for twenty-three hours a day and feeding them bread and water; or alternatively bringing back the concept of hard labour and making the little darlings do something that was pointless but bloody difficult at the same time as being bone and soul breaking.

There probably could be a middle ground that could be reached. The key element that had vanished from most prison concepts was that of punishment. You were being sent to prison as a punishment, not because it was felt that you needed an easy ride. Many people would believe that the punishment had gone out of the sentence. Of course, there were those of a meek and mild demeanour that being sent to prison would be a soul-destroying experience that they would rather die than go through. These were truly the people that would be reformed by prison and would never do anything to go back into one; but they were a very small percentage of those that were 'banged up.'

There is no doubt that you had lots of rights as a suspect; but you didn't really have all that many rights as a victim and this was something that got a lot of people up in arms. A lot of people would get very annoyed about this but ultimately very little was actually done about it other than some token gestures which on their own were not really any worth. The simple fact that was overlooked for the majority of cases, was that an offender could commit a crime, get caught, get arrested, get charged, get found guilty at court and get sent to prison; but they would get over it. A victim would very often not get over the crime and it would live with them for a lot longer than it would live with the offender. Things might be getting better with victim care, but it was too slow and not enough.

There was also another option. If you were found guilty at court of the crime for which you were accused, the judge might decide, with one eye on the over population of the prison system, to give you what was called a suspended sentence. This basically meant that you were found guilty of the offence and were given a prison sentence, however, it was suspended and you were free to go. However, if you were found guilty of another crime at any point in the time that the suspended sentence was in force then you would be sent to prison for the original crime. This could happen a fair amount as career criminals that were stupid enough to continuously get caught were very difficult to keep out of prison.

You might be given a conditional discharge, where you were told to do something to prevent you from going to prison. Community service orders for instance. Or perhaps if you had been found guilty of criminal damage you might have to pay for the damage before being entirely freed from the court. There was also the possibility that you might be given a fine. You might have to also pay the prosecution's expenses. This was perhaps the most ludicrous as you could pay it off at something like a pound a week. It might never be paid off.

The Government could do something about it if they really wanted to; but they didn't want to do anything about it. That was the simple truth of the matter. Why did they not want to do anything about it? Because they were hardly ever the victims of crime was the simple answer. How many politicians were likely to be burgled? How many might be the victim of an assault on a night out when they were minding their own business? How many would be robbed of their belongings? They lived in a completely different world to everybody else. They lived in gated communities where they were protected by money. They didn't understand what it was like to live in fear of crime or to not feel safe in their own homes.

Unfortunately, this was not something that was going to change. It was once again linked to the class system that the politicians took so much time and effort in telling us didn't exist any longer. Of course it existed. There simply was no way to so quickly get rid of something that had existed for hundreds of years. It would be around a lot longer than most other things would be.

Rank and status meant that you were treated differently. Wrong by any stretch of the imagination, but it was true. It was seen in the police. There were numerous high-ranking officers of chief constable rank or above who were as corrupt as the day was long. They might get caught out taking bribes or claiming expenses that they were not entitled to do. They would do this until they were found out; and then what would happen? They would be allowed to resign and they would walk off into the sunset with a pension that was somewhere around the seventy thousand pounds a year plus range and nothing more would be said. If a police officer on the other end of the scale came even slightly close to doing anything like that then they would be dismissed instantly, lose their pension and probably end up in prison which was no place for an ex-police officer to find themselves. It was unfair; but that had a lot to do with the fact that life was unfair.

Another thing that was unfair was the fact that when someone who blatantly was guilty was found to be not guilty at court it was the police that were blamed. Now in some cases this might be valid. It might be that the case evidence that had been assembled by the police was not good enough to secure a conviction at court. However, having seen all of the hoops that police had to jump through in order to get a suspect to court it could be assumed that the evidence was probably of a reasonable quality. Add to this the fact that the Crown Prosecution Service were unlikely to send anyone to court unless they could get that conviction then you might almost assume that if a suspect had made it as far as standing in court then there was a fair chance that they had done whatever it was that they were being accused of.

So why did people 'get off' at court? It might be that despite all of the evidence to the contrary they might actually be innocent after all. It might be that the evidence was lacking. It might be that the prosecution counsel was no good or that the defence counsel was too good. It might be that the jury didn't have a bloody clue what they were doing. It could, in fact, be any number of different reasons as to why someone would be found not guilty. Almost in all cases though it was the police that were blamed by the victim, by the media and by everyone else who cared for the not guilty verdict.

The police were used to getting the blame for everything that went wrong or for all the ills of society, so in most cases it was just water off of a duck's back. There were times though when it would really grate on some officers who would become intensely frustrated that more was not done to present the case for the police. A lot of hard work and devotion was done by the majority of police officers and it was largely unnoticed and uncommented about. More could have been done to promote a better image; but instead of time spent on this the majority just preferred to get on with doing the job in the first place. No use spending time talking about how wonderful you are if you are not prepared to spend time showing everyone how wonderful you are. It hardly mattered if nobody else noticed the wonderful and helpful things that you were doing. *You* would know. It had to be reward enough on its own as there sure as hell was little other reward and thanks to the Government there wasn't really even that much of a pension at the end of your years of dedicated service now.

It was another one of those unfair things about life. Police officers would dedicate thirty years or more to intense, difficult public service where they risked their lives almost every day and they received little to no reward for it at the end. Politicians would devote themselves to doing what they wanted in the name of public service for as long a time as the public felt that they could stomach them before voting them out and in return they would receive more of a pension then the majority of them deserved. In the early years of the twenty-first century it was difficult to know if the public hated bankers or politicians the most. There were good cases against them both if the truth were told. They were very much in the same boat.

Victims would be distressed by going through the stress of court — for remember that giving evidence in court was very much like having to live through the crime once again - only to have the court decide that the person you knew was guilty was actually not guilty. It might come as a surprise to them to know that the police were pissed off as well. It would surprise a lot of people to see the police officers back in their own police room in the court pacing up and down. They knew that they had a water tight case, but it still came down to the luck of what the jury would decide to do; and to the majority of police officers, the courts and the decisions they made were a total mystery that belied understanding.

The longer you were a police officer then the longer you would see suspects (for that is what you must call them before they can become offenders or the defendant), walking away because the evidence was not there or because something had happened at court. A lot of officers didn't have much time for a lot of the defence solicitors either. Now it was true that they were only doing their job and everyone has the right to a defence. However, there were corrupt police officers and there were corrupt solicitors. The moral code stated that a solicitor could not advise a client to go no comment or offer a defence if there was an admission of guilt. The best that an honest solicitor could hope for was mitigating circumstances to explain why their client had done what they had done. The police really hated those ones that wanted to get the client that they knew was guilty off on a technicality.

Technicalities were tricky things. If they could find it, they would look for the smallest of errors that officers might have made in the gathering of evidence and they would exploit it for everything that it was worth. That is one of the chief reasons why the police had so much paperwork to complete as there were so many loopholes that needed to be closed and so much attention that needed to be presented to the detail to ensure that the entire case would not collapse later on down the line.

As stated there were corrupt officers and whenever they were found out then it would be paraded all over the news as if it was only the tip of the iceberg and the newspapers and other media outlets were nudging you and winking and saying 'Look, I told you, they are all in on it you know. It's only a matter of time.' These police officers that were found out would ultimately be sacked, but it never stopped the press from enjoying the scandal. Even police officers that had left with unblemished records who might find themselves in a spot of bother would be referred to as 'former police officer' even if the fact that they were had nothing to do with whatever it was that they were meant to have done. The press hated the police.

There was something very simple that was forgotten about the police, whether they were corrupt or as honest as the day was long and that simple fact was that police officers were human. It was a shock to a lot of people who were amazed to see that police officers ate and drank; that they also smoked and would get drunk and have sex. Vices — if you like — which were accepted in so many others without a raised eyebrow were somehow seen as scandalous in the police.

The point to all of this was the fact that the longer you were a police officer the longer you were exposed to all of these things and then ultimately it would build up and up until you either became immune to it or you felt something start to break. When something started to break you either got out and went to do something else; or you suddenly felt that it was time that you took matters into your own hands.

For PC George Lawrence something inside of him had stretched so far that it was starting to break.

Twenty-Four

We now come onto an area of the police that a lot of officers are uncomfortable with. Corruption. Now the simple fact of the matter is that there is not all that much corruption in the police. It is not the way that the papers would have you believe it is. There is no more a bent copper on every street corner than there is a paedophile priest in every church in the land. A few bad apples give a whole lot of bad press to a lot of others that are just trying to do their job and to make the world a better place for everyone to live in.

It is the same in any walk of life; you always have a minority that spoil it for the majority — no matter what it might be. A small minority of football hooligans who thought it would be fun to add violence and alcohol to football had tarnished the game for the millions of others who just liked to enjoy the sport. The same thing had happened to the vocal, violent minority of alcohol induced empty headed vandals that went on holiday in other countries and gave the English a reputation throughout the world that went against all the well-behaved people that just wanted to relax in the sun and enjoy themselves. The spoilsports didn't have to go abroad to be twats though, they were quite capable of doing it in this country. It may come as a surprise to the majority of the law abiding citizens but there was a particular breed of young male (almost always) who considered a good night out to be getting completely pissed out of their heads in a very short space of time and then picking a fight with either an innocent bystander or another drunken twat and finishing the evening off in a cell. Indeed, there were some who considered that they had not had a good night out if they didn't end it by being arrested. Each to their own. It would surprise these idiots when they did go abroad for their holidays. They suddenly discovered that no matter what they really thought about the English police, they were a lot more tolerant than a lot of other countries police. In foreign climes when they acted as they would in an English city on a Friday or Saturday night, they suddenly found that the police in this country could legally beat the crap out of them and they had a lot less rights than they did back home. Many would, of course, look at this and either hold the English police up as a paragon of virtue or look at it and say; 'You know we've got it all wrong.'

In England if you were beaten up by the police then the police officer in question could find themselves losing their jobs and being arrested and more than likely end up in prison themselves. Most police officers knew this so it was amusing to them when the public decided to make complaints about them. The most common phrase being 'I'll have your job for this.' The only real answer to this one was 'Well I suppose you must have someone's job as you don't appear to have one of your own.' The simple fact of it was that the police were not prepared to risk losing their job, their pension (such as it now was) and risk going to prison over the brief satisfaction that might be brought by kicking the shit out of some twat that really did have it coming to them.

But some people did do it. Because police officers are human. You don't become Superman just because you put on a uniform and carry a badge. If you were a twat or criminally minded before you became a police officer then becoming a police officer only meant that you were a twat who now carried a badge. Sometimes these people deliberately made the choices that led to corruption and for many others they just made mistakes as we all do and suddenly found that the mistakes that they had made had landed them in a big pile of poo.

The people within the police that investigated the complaints and the activities of the police were known as the Professional Standards Department or PSD. They had been called many things over the years and not all of them complimentary. The rank and file would often refer to them as the Rubber Heel Squad (because you couldn't hear them coming) or more often or not the SS or Gestapo. It would amuse those members of the public who thought that the police in themselves were fascist to learn that within the police there was a department that the police themselves considered to be fascist.

But why the hatred? Surely if there were corruption within the police then it would be considered a good thing to be able to investigate it, find those bad apples and get rid of them before they tainted the barrel? This was true and very few officers would argue against that. However, because even Professional Standards Officers were also human, they made the same mistakes as everyone else. One of the things that it seemed most frequently that the PSD were doing was taking it out on the easy targets and letting the more difficult ones go free.

If you made a mistake and you admitted it and threw your hands up rather than the organisation applauding you for the very honesty and integrity that they demanded of their staff, PSD would swoop in and find a way to nail you to something. This was an easy case for them because you had admitted to doing something so they didn't really have to work all that hard to hold you up and make an example of you. This is what happened when you used honesty and integrity. So, what kind of example did that lead? If on the other hand you denied whatever it was that you had allegedly done and then made a fuss and a complaint and said you were going to fight it all the way and that courts and expensive solicitors would be involved then they probably wouldn't bother with you — unless of course they had a water tight case.

Because of these double standards and a desire to nail the honest officer who was trying their best despite the fuck up that they had made then PSD had a reputation that left a lot to be desired. It was another nail in the coffin of the honest officer that was going about their business and was becoming increasingly fed up with the entire thing.

The police had once been a family and no, that didn't mean that you covered up for each other, but it did mean that you looked after each other as best you could. There was nothing like that atmosphere in the police today. Instead it had been replaced by a lot of back stabbers who were keen to climb the promotion ladder and they really didn't care if they trampled all over you on their way up. There were officers and departments that were keen to 'stick you on' so that they could demonstrate to the higher ranks that they could be heartless and were prepared to make examples of other officers even if there was no need for an example to be made. They felt that this in some way proved that you were suitable to climb the ranks when all it really proved was that you were a twat.

It was all becoming a depressing place to work. However, there really was corruption in the 1970s when it had been everywhere. The 1970s was a very strange time for the police and the reason for a lot of the corruption was over the pay or rather the fact that police officers were not paid all that much and did not have all that many advantages. Some were torn between trying to cope on the bread line or taking a few back handers from people that would supplement their income and mean that you could do things like eat and warm your house and clothe your children. The 1970s was a bad time really no matter how much nostalgia you liked to throw at the decade. The three-day week, power cuts and rubbish lying in the streets. Strikes, civil unrest and bad fashion sense. It was no wonder that the decade was rife with corruption.

The Government realised that the way to change all of this was to make pay conditions better so that it actually attracted people to become police officers and meant that those who were already police officers had no need to take bribes or backhanders any longer. This was a solution that worked and the widespread corruption that had existed as part of the norm became the extreme. The police were happier and so was everyone else. Everything would be fine so long as the Government gave no reason for corruption to come back by screwing about once again with pay, pension and conditions. Oh yeah.

The interesting thing was that the public seemed to like the idea of a return to 1970s policing if not actually a return to the 1970s as a whole. Programmes such as *Life on Mars* had shown the public that there was what appeared to be a simpler time. There was a time when the police always caught the villain — one way or another. A time when the police only fitted up people that deserved it and that if you were innocent you had nothing to worry about. They favoured the 1970s detective despite the fact that he was a chain smoking, alcoholic, sexist, womaniser, who beat confessions out of suspects.

They seemed to want this as they felt that it was the police being the police and not being social workers. These were the people that didn't want the police to hold your hand when you had done something wrong and tell you that everything was going to be okay. They wanted a police force that would slap you back into place when you had done something wrong and make you feel that you would never do anything like it again.

It must have raised a confused atmosphere for a generation of children that were told on the one hand that 'if you are naughty, I will call the policeman to come and take you away.' Thus, painting the policeman (for it always was a man then) as some kind of bogeyman that would lie in wait for wayward children. On the other hand — in some cases in the same breath, mothers would tell their children that if ever they were lost or in need of help then they should 'find a policeman' who would look after them and bring them home. It is just possible that this contradiction on what children were led to believe a police officer was led to a great deal of confusion later in life.

Times had changed from the almost mythical village bobby that knew everyone and what everyone was doing and would clip children who had been naughty around the ear and drag them home to their parents, where the arrival on the doorstep with your ear being held by a policeman would almost certainly lead to a beating. Perhaps it had changed for the better; perhaps it hadn't.

What the people who advocated a return to 1970s policing forgot was things like the Guildford Four or the Birmingham Six. Miscarriages of justice where evidence was fabricated in order to secure convictions. Had this changed? Yes, it probably had. In the world of twenty-first century policing there was simply too much paperwork that existed already without the need to have to fabricate more of it.

The true answer is that a middle ground probably needed to be found where the police were able to police again without the need to be hitting people all the time or stitching them up for things that they had not done. It was not going to be an easy thing to arrange if indeed it was going to be possible at all.

The public did still think that the police beat people up though. This was largely because they didn't understand what the police were doing. If you were on the ground being restrained by the police in the street then you probably had done something to get there. If you resisted the police then force would be used. As long as it was reasonable and justifiable and oh yes it had to be justified, then it was going to be used. Liberals and people that really didn't know better would try and interfere.

'He ain't done nothin' wrong,' one passer-by had expressed to Lawrence when he was lying on top of someone in the street trying to get them handcuffed whilst they continued to struggle after they had just beaten seven colours of crap out of someone else. There was something about some people who just felt that in that situation the offender had done nothing wrong and it was clearly police brutality that was to blame.

The system was flawed. It was possible to get very depressed when looking at it and trying to find a solution. Sometimes the solution might turn out to be something rather drastic.

Twenty-Five

'Well, all the best,' George Lawrence raised his pint of Old Speckled Hen and toasted Simon who nursed his own pint of Carlsberg and raised it in his turn in the direction of George.

'I don't know how you can drink that stuff,' Lawrence continued as he looked suspiciously at the pint that Simon was holding.

'Carlsberg?'

'Lager in general, I mean.'

'What's wrong with it?' Simon was beginning to examine his glass with a degree of unease as if he expected something horrible to be floating in it that should not have been in it; or worse still to have half of something floating in it signifying that he had probably already swallowed the other half. This is one of the worst things that can happen. Finding a slug in your Caesar salad is bad enough; but to find half a slug in your Caesar salad is a disaster.

'I find lager too acidic.'

'What have orthodox Jews got to do with it?'

'Acidic not Hassidic, you moron.'

'I'm shocked that you know the difference,' Simon was genuinely impressed by this. There were clearly depths to Lawrence's character that he strove hard to keep hidden from most people.

'I may not have gone to university and be all posh with it, but I'm not an idiot.'

'Never thought you were,' said Simon taking a large sip from his pint as this was not an entirely true statement.

'Far too acidic. I struggle to get through a pint of it and it just makes me belch and feel full of bubbles and shit.'

'Well, that's not good.'

'It's a cultural thing isn't it really?'

'What do you mean?' Simon was getting a little lost with this conversation.

'Well,' said Lawrence trying to open a packet of Scampi flavoured fries. 'When you grow up you are expected to drink lager and get out of your face on it. Ask for ale they will think that you are an old fart. Ask for a gin and tonic and they will all think you are gay.' There was a degree of logic to this when Simon thought about it. 'Could never stand the taste of lager either really. I resented every sip until I was old enough to have the balls to drink whatever I liked regardless of what anyone else might have to think about it. Isn't lager nicknamed "wife-beater?"'

'Well, what about some of the names that they have for ale? I mean they're ludicrous. What are you drinking there "nun's chuff?"'

They lapsed into silence for a moment each studying their drink of choice and slowly sipping on it. Simon was not a great one for socialising outside of work. He took the attitude that these people were his colleagues and in very few circumstances were they actually what he would class as his friends as well. He was aware that a lot of people within the police classed their colleagues as their friends; probably because they didn't actually have any friends that existed outside of the police. It was a trap that Simon did not like to fall into. Make your life centre around the police and it will be all the more difficult when you eventually have to hand that warrant card in and find out that in reality you have no life at all. It was a depressing thought.

There were also people that he worked with that he considered to be complete wankers and that he would not have wished to have spent more than five minutes with outside of work, if he could have helped it. That is why he hated shift night outs. You worked with these people all the time, more often spending more time with them than you did your own family and then you would choose to go and spend time with them when you didn't need to. There didn't seem to be all that much logic in it as far as he was concerned.

This, of course, gave him the reputation as being a 'miserable git' which was frankly something that he could live with if it meant he didn't have to put up with the shit that some people dished out when he was not getting paid to take it.

Simon's preference was to go out and spend time on an individual basis or with people that he actually liked. It caused some political incidents. Suppose you wanted to have a barbeque or you were planning some social function like a party. Did you invite only the people you liked from work and alienate those members of the shift that you frankly could not stand? Or did you invite the whole shift in order to be diplomatic and put up with people that you hated so much that you couldn't really have cared whether they lived or died? It was always a tricky one.

This is why he now found himself in a pub with George. George Lawrence seemed to have made a career of keeping people at a distance from him and keeping his private life just that — private. He didn't discuss his private life at work and it was equally possible to imagine that he did not like to talk about work when he was not actually at work. A lot of people at work did not give him any credit. They saw him as a slob who had never achieved anything within the Job. If he had once had potential, they reasoned, that he had clearly failed to reach it.

Simon had been crewed with George a lot chiefly because a lot of other people didn't think that he was worth crewing with. This turned out to be their loss. Simon had got to see through the defences that George placed in front of him that had kept a lot of his colleagues away. Too much work. He had seen that he was far more intelligent than most people would have given him credit for. He also knew a hell of a lot more about the Job than most people realised. He knew his way around legislation backwards.

George rarely put his view across, but if anyone had taken the time to ask him then they would have found out that what he said was right. He knew his stuff, but the police didn't really interest him any longer; if indeed it ever had. At some point and for reasons that were not known to all that many people and possibly only to George Lawrence himself, he had simply lost faith in the police service and from that moment on had given up on it for a lost cause.

It was a job and that was all it was; and it was not a job with a capital J as so many people seemed to refer to it as if it was some mysterious, cult religion that could only be spoken about in whispers. He went to work, he did what he had to do and then he went home and forgot all about being a police officer and did whatever it was that he did at home.

This was also something of a mystery. What did George do when he was not at work? Now the simple answer is that it was no one's business but his own. However, there are always those who feel that they need to know all that there is about everyone else. We all probably know people like that who make it their business to know what your business is. It seems to cause them no end of frustration when they come across someone like George who will listen to their probing enquiries and then politely tell them to 'Go fuck yourself.' Some people are not satisfied unless they know everything. Some people must, therefore, remain unsatisfied. The outside of work life seemed to occupy them although the general consensus of opinion was that Chief Inspector Harbour either spent his off duty time hanging upside down in his locker or asleep in a coffin somewhere in the depths of the building until it was time for him to awaken and suck the blood from someone else in order to continue to preserve his living death. This was only a theory though with no real supporting evidence.

Simon had begun to get to know George and had gradually found that he liked the majority of what he learnt about the seasoned old copper. This was why he had agreed to come and have a pint with him although he did not do this all that often. They had just finished a day shift and there was a pub just down from the police station that used to be frequented by coppers all of the time back in the days when they used to drink on and off duty as well.

Those days of CID drinking whilst they solved crime were pretty much a thing of the past now. Nevertheless, the pub was still known as a copper's pub; so, it was possible to go here for a pint every now and then without them bumping into someone that they had once banged up or have some tiresome little low-life scumbag try and sell them drugs.

'So, how are things with you, Simon?' asked George as he collected his peanuts that had skidded all over the table when the packet had burst open.

'Not too bad. Can't complain.'

'Oh, but we do complain. If there is one thing that coppers are really good at it then it is complaining.'

'Well, that's true.'

'We have good reason to complain really. We are treated like shit and get little thanks for it. See much of the ex-wife?'

Simon's divorce was not a secret. His private life had been carefully examined before he had learnt that it was best to just ignore such enquiries. Perhaps it was because when you were a police officer you were considered to always be a police officer on and off duty that made some people feel that they had the right to know everything that they wanted to about your private life. Alternatively, it was possible that there were some people who felt that they needed to know everything about your life to make up for the fact that their own life was in some way lacking in something. It was difficult to say.

'No. I'm fortunate in that regard. I believe she has gone back to Oz with her mother.'

'Australia? I didn't know they came from there.' George was possibly considering the fact that an opportunity at cheap holidays had gone flying out of the window with Simon's divorce.

'No, not Australia. Oz. As in the Land of Oz and the Wizard of Oz. She and her mother can probably contend to be the wicked witches of the east and west or whatever they were.'

George chuckled at this. 'Yeah, well we have all known people like that from time to time in our lives.'

'It's the job that pisses me off the most now.'

'I think it's pissing a lot of people off, to be honest.'

'It's a big disappointment. I came into the job with such high hopes and then they all burst into fragments within a very short space of time.'

'I've news for you,' said George as he worked his way down his ale glass. 'We all started like that and we all become disillusioned over time.'

'Really?'

'You don't think that anyone would willingly join this job when they knew how shit it was going to turn out, do you?' He shook his head. 'I've seen officers become disillusioned with the job before, but what's happening now is something different.'

'How so?'

'People are losing faith in the job. Losing faith in the government even; although that has never really been all that hard. They see everything that they have worked for going up in smoke. All that hard-earned time spent building a future and then the Government come along and with a few strokes of the pen destroy it. I suppose you have twenty years or so left before you can retire now?'

'Yeah. Twenty years. It was sixteen and I would have left at fifty-six years old, but thanks to Mr Cameron and his cronies I now have to work until I'm sixty.'

'And how ridiculous is that? This job is a hard-hitting pace and to be doing this when we are sixty is ludicrous. Cameron, or whoever made that decision has got their head stuck up their arse.'

'It's only another four years that I have to work.'

'Only another four years. Simon, what would you have to do in this world to serve four years in prison? You could rape someone. You could burgle houses until your heart's content. Hell, under the right circumstances you could probably even murder someone and they wouldn't bang you up for four years.'

'Well, that's true.' Simon looked deep into the bottom of his beer glass.

'Does it seem fair to you?'

'What?'

'The fact that we're on the side of the righteous and yet we are treated like shit all of the time, whilst those on the other side get whatever they want and do nothing for it. You don't even have to have a job and pay taxes, but they will fall over backwards to give you benefits. How many houses have you been in where they have a bigger flat screen television then you have in your house and yet they don't work a single hour for it? We slog our guts out all the time and we're lucky if we can make ends meet by the end of the month.'

'True.'

'Does it seem fair to you that we work all the hours that we do trying to protect the public and make life just a little bit better perhaps for some people than it would be if we were not around and in return we have a government — any government — because this one is no better than the last one; who rewards us by freezing our pay and getting us to pay more into our pensions to get less out of it at the end of more than three decades of service?'

'Well, if you put it like that George —'

'I do. I fucking well do. And I'll tell you something else. I'll not put up with it any longer. I say, this far and no further.' He slammed his glass down on the table as if to establish the point which only earned him a wary look from the landlord. It was possible that he knew George of old.

'Well, that's all very well, but it isn't as if you can do anything about it.'

'Isn't there?' George sat back in his chair and looked meaningfully at Simon.

'Well, there isn't is there? We're just stuck with being shafted and we have to get on with it. I suppose we could resign and go off and do something else. What else is there that you could do about it?'

'Well, I've got an idea.'

'What?'

'Play them at their own game.' George had a look on his face as if to suggest that this statement said all that he needed to say and clarified everything.

'I'm not sure I follow you.'

'I'm not sure that I trust you.'

'That seems a bit harsh,' actually Simon felt like he had just been slapped in the face. He was not sure where that comment had come from.

'You're a nice enough bloke, Simon and we get on well. In many regards we have the same opinion on a number of issues; particularly with reference to how shit the job has become.'

'Okay.'

'But there is a fine line that can be crossed. Crossing it if you're not going to cross it with me is going to land me in potentially a shit load of trouble.'

'Still not following you, George.'

'Sometimes just talking about things can be classed as conspiracy or sowing discord within the police. I could easily be sacked for that sort of thing if not actually arrested and banged up myself.'

'Well, they can't bang up everyone who sows discord about the police. There wouldn't be any officers left.'

'That's true. But as I say there's a line that can be crossed. The question is if I tell you and you're not willing to cross it with me, can I trust you to keep your mouth shut?'

'It would probably help if I knew a little more about what it was that

176

you were trying to say. I know I have only had one pint, but I feel like you are talking in riddles at the moment.'

George sipped on his pint and looked for a moment as if he had the weight of the world upon his shoulders and was trying to make difficult decisions.

'If you could break the rules and fight back and achieve something for once would you do it?'

'Hypothetically?' asked Simon as he felt the ground shifting a little beneath his feet.

'If you like.'

'I suppose it would depend on what it was.'

'A chance to give some justice back and to fight back against the way that we have been treated.'

'Sounds like a dream.'

'Possibly, but every dream has the potential to become reality. You just have to want it enough and to work hard at it. Take that wanker who we know stole from the charity. Wouldn't it be good to be able to make him give that money back and punish him?'

'Yeah, but we don't have the evidence.'

'Poh,' George waved his hands in the air. 'What would it matter if we did? If we had the evidence the court would not make him pay it back or if they did, he could get away with paying it back at about a pound a week; tying it up in legal problems so that they never saw their money again. And as to him? What would he get that was more than a slap on the wrist? Even prison is hardly a deterrent these days. The simple fact as far as I can see is that it looks like courts have stopped giving out justice.'

'So, you would make him pay some other way?'

'If I could.'

'Like being vigilantes? Everything against what we are?'

'Tricky isn't it? What if the only way to fight back is to become that which we spend all day fighting against?' George twirled his beer glass round and round on the table like some toy car as it went through ale puddles.

'Dark thoughts, George.'

'Perhaps another pint then?'

'Sure, why not?'

Twenty-Six

'Aren't you the guy that we arrested on suspicion of stealing that money from the charity?' Simon asked as he stood in the over-turned living room. It perhaps was not the most diplomatic of questions to ask at this point.

'Bloody police persecution that's what it is. You arrest me on some trumped-up charge and then I find that I have been burgled and I suppose you're not going to do anything about it?' The man was very irate to the point where he literally did appear to be going purple which Simon found fascinating to watch as he had only previously read about such things happening in novels.

'I can assure you…' Simon looked down at his notes, 'Mr Mitchell, that we will do all that we can to find out who has burgled your house. Now if I can take some details before CID get here.' That was assuming that CID would be bothered to turn up in this instance as they didn't always, but he thought it might be the best thing to say given the irate nature of Mr Mitchell.

'I don't know why I bothered to call you. The police have done nothing for me but make my life a misery.'

'What appears to be missing, sir?' Simon was doing his best to ignore the comments that were being thrown in his direction. This was an art that a lot of police officers developed with time. You had to tune out of some of the abuse or irrelevant things that people were talking about half of the time or you would never be able to function. He also found it a mystery why it was that someone would call the police and then spend all their time going off about how it was that the police were useless and didn't do anything. If that were the case then why bother to call in the first place?

'Everything,' Mr Mitchell waved his arms about in an expressive manner. This wasn't the most helpful of comments that he could have made.

'If you could be more specific, sir.'

Clearly everything was not missing as there were a lot of things still there. Granted what remained was in a pretty poor state. This was one of those burglaries where the burglar had clearly taken everything that they considered to be of any value and had trashed everything else that remained that they either could not take away with them or that they had considered was not worth stealing. The damage had been the worst that Simon had ever seen in his career so far. Someone had really done their best to ensure that whatever was left behind would be of no value to Mr Mitchell. It would take him weeks to get his house back into any form of order that he could live in and it would cost a fortune to go out and buy all of the things that he would need to replace. There was no way that the insurance company was going to cover the costs of all of this. It was a particularly vindictive crime and Simon briefly found himself wondering if this was something personal rather than a random burglary. Stealing things was one side of the story, causing the level of damage that had been caused in the process suggested either a very sadistic criminal or someone with a grudge.

'Why haven't you caught the person who did this?' This was a particularly stupid question, but one that was frequently asked. It was stupid because Mr Mitchell had only called the police thirty minutes ago and Simon had only been on scene for ten minutes so it was not entirely reasonable to ask why there had been no progress in the case.

Simon had had only one case that had been solved in three easy detections. It was a robbery. He had turned into the street and seen a man leaning against the road sign bleeding from the head.

'That's the victim,' he had deduced.

'I was walking along when I was hit over the head and my mobile was stolen,' the man had told him when they had chatted.

'That's the definition of robbery,' Simon had concluded.

'That's the man!' the victim had said pointing at a man who was about to cycle passed.

'That's the offender,' he had concluded. Three easy detections and the quickest he had solved a crime in his entire career.

'One step at a time, sir.' Simon said bringing himself back to the present. He felt that he was being particularly patient. He had no idea if George was right and that this man had stolen money from a charity, but whatever he had done or not done he was clearly an obnoxious individual and Simon didn't want to spend any longer with him then he had to. Mr Mitchell took a deep breath as if he was summoning all the powers of control that he had and was talking to a naughty child that had not understood when he had explained something several times already.

'I have three flat screen televisions missing,'

'Three, sir?' Simon felt that this was mildly excessively.

'Yes, three. One in the living room which cost me a thousand pounds alone. One in the den and one in the bedroom.'

'The den, sir?' Simon was deliberately toying with him now and having his little bit of fun. One of the ways that he often did have fun was to play the part of the thick copper. It somehow seemed to be expected of him by a certain group of people in society.

'Yes, the den, the fucking den. What's the matter don't you have a den in your house?'

'Can't say that I do sir. Least not last time I looked. What else is missing?'

'The Blu Ray machines.'

'Three of them, sir?'

'Yes dammit. Also, I am missing my entire DVD and Blu Ray collection.'

'The *entire* collection? And how many discs would that be, sir?'

It was amazing how much sarcasm could be put into the word 'sir'.

'How the hell should I know? About seven hundred probably.'

'Well that is a lot of films, sir.'

'Also, I am missing a lot of jewellery.'

'Jewellery? I thought you lived alone, sir.'

'If you must know, constable, it all belonged to my mother.'

'To your mother? Valuable, sir?'

'Priceless. From a monetary point of view, I suppose you are looking at several thousand pounds.'

Simon whistled. 'Well that is a lot of money, sir.'

'They have also stolen my laptop, my tablet, my kindle, my iPhone, my digital camera. Anything that is worth anything has been taken and you can see for yourself what they have done to the rest of the things.'

'They certainly seem to have done a lot of damage, sir. It's amazing the amount of damage that someone can cause to someone else's life.' Simon looked pointedly at Mr Mitchell and turned over a new page in his pocket notebook.

***

'Have you seen this?' demanded Simon as he waved the newspaper in the air.

'Seen what?' replied George who for once actually seemed to be not only doing something on a computer but was also concentrating on it as well. Mind you with George's lack of technological know-how and the fact that he was a confirmed 'techno-peasant' meant that his concentration could be as limited to seeing how he could turn the machine on in the first place.

'This!' Simon thrust the newspaper under George's nose. George took a few seconds from whatever it was that he was concentrating on and glanced at the newspaper briefly.

'It's a newspaper.'

'I know it's a newspaper, you idiot,' Simon pulled a chair up next to him and lowered his voice slightly even though there was nobody else in the report room. 'Have you seen what's in it?'

'Unlikely, you've only just walked in with it.'

Simon ruffled through the pages and finding the article that he was looking for laid it out across the keyboard, causing George to sigh and give up on whatever it was that he had been trying to do in the first place. He looked at the article that had been placed in front of him, but as if Simon was too impatient to let him read it out for himself, he spoke the headline aloud.

'"Anonymous donor returns money stolen". What do you make of that?'

'Not a great deal.'

'The charity that we think that guy, Mitchell stole all the money from

181

just happens to have the same amount of money returned to them.'

'Well we don't know it's the same money, do we? Perhaps it was an anonymous millionaire who read the theft story and felt that he should do something to help out those less fortunate than himself.'

Simon deflated a little. 'You think?'

'Well what do you think? You think our thief had a change of heart and decided to give the money back? Not very likely is it?'

'I don't know, but something doesn't add up to me. First of all, we're pretty convinced that he steals the money from the charity and then he's burgled and loads of high value items are stolen from him and then the money turns up at the charity.'

'So, you think someone stole the items from him, flogged them and then gave the money to charity?'

Simon sat back in his chair slightly and regarded George with curiosity.

'Don't you think it strange?'

'What? That the spirit of Robin Hood is alive and well? I think that's strange. I don't think we have a Robin Hood figure running around in the twenty-first century robbing from the rich to give to the poor. No matter how attractive the idea might seem.' George tried to return his attention to the computer. He carefully picked out what he was typing one key at a time with infinite slowness.

'Don't you think it strange that just the other night you were talking about how justice should be done and things should be put right and how it was that you didn't feel you could trust me and that there were lines to cross and then all of a sudden this news comes in today.'

'Perhaps it's proof that there is a good after all. I'm not sure that I follow what it is that you're suggesting.'

'Perhaps I'm not suggesting anything,' Simon had not entirely formulated his thoughts on this point yet. 'It just seems to me that it's a remarkable coincidence, that's all.'

'Well, I wouldn't worry about it. There are plenty of other things that you do need to worry about and this isn't one of them. Seems to me that this is one of those very rare cases where justice seems to have been done. We have not been able to punish this bloke, but someone has and the criminal has become the victim of a crime. I don't see a problem with that. *That* is justice. The donation of money to the charity may have nothing to do with this Mitchell case at all. If right has been corrected then that is all that matters.'

He returned to tapping away on the keyboard with the same level of concentration that a bomb disposal expert might have on his face whilst defusing a bomb. Simon grunted and got up and left the room.

***

It was one of those rare moments in the criminal justice system where justice did appear to have been done. It didn't happen often and it was made even more strange and unusual by the fact that the justice given out seemed to have completely bypassed the criminal justice system itself. This would make a lot of people that worked in the system very worried. The last thing that they wanted was the idea put into the minds of the public that they could go about and get their own form of justice rather than placing it in their own hands.

It is a well-known fact that the powers that be did not want the public taking matters into their own hands. They would say that this was because a society could not exist in such a state of anarchy that would rule with vigilante groups taking the law into their own hands. They painted a picture of disaster that would unfurl if this would happen. Some bleak futuristic portrait that seemed to show the streets always at night with a fire burning in an old metallic dustbin whilst tramps warmed their hands by it covered in numerous layers of clothing whilst rabid dogs roamed the streets in packs picking off small children. Quite where this alarmist image came from other than from the pages of some bleak science fiction drama was anyone's guess; but it was something that the Establishment clung to as a warning of what would happen with mob rule.

Alternatively, they would wheel out the argument that mob rule was dangerous because there was always the possibility that the mob acting on pack instinct would get it wrong and would be targeting their vigilante behaviour on the innocent. This had been seen in the past. Let local people who have a tendency to these kinds of thing believe that the person who has moved in at number six is a paedophile and then all hell will break loose. It would hardly then matter if the resident at number six is a paedophile or not. The blood was up and justice must be seen to be done. The Establishment would point out that this kind of persecution on someone who is innocent was dangerous. They would state that there are people in society who like to stir up the mob and create riots and dissent. If that meant that the odd innocent person was targeted then it hardly mattered as this was a crusade.

This was one of the arguments that the Establishment put forward for why you should put your faith in the system; for the system had never persecuted the innocent or made mistakes or stirred things up. Point this fact out and you would probably be branded an anarchist and hounded out of the hall as comments like this were obvious evidence that you were determined to bring down society and you would be after murdering the monarchy next.

The simple fact of the matter was much simpler. If the public took law into their own hands then there would be absolutely no need for all those highly paid judges and solicitors as well as a lot of other people. Now whereas the people on the top of the tree didn't care whether the people on the bottom of the tree lost their jobs they were very protective of their own jobs and their own interests. This has always been the same since the time of kings and barons.

Simple conclusion: if you as a lowly member of the mob took control of law and order then there would be no need for them to do it and they would lose their job and their authority and that would never do. You had to trust in the system therefore; even if at times the system was more corrupt than the people that it was prosecuting.

It was such a shame that those on the top of the tree didn't care about those at the bottom. It was rank stupidity really. Anyone with half a brain could have told them that if you hack at the roots and the lower part of a tree then the entire thing would eventually fall over and collapse. Those sitting on the top branches would do well to remember that they were only able to sit there because of the roots and trunk that supported them and without that they were nothing.

Twenty-Seven

Perhaps Simon's mind was a little hyper at the moment. He had not had all that much sleep lately. It seemed that the more you did shift work the more difficult it became. You would expect that it would become easier as time went by and you got used to it, but if anything, the older you got the more difficult it became to get through them. It certainly seemed to be from the scientific evidence that it shortened your life. It was going against nature, but the Government cared nothing for things like that when they were busy shafting you over pay and conditions.

Shift work was an example of where politicians were short-sighted. There had been a council meeting that Simon had attended once in his civilian capacity, he was not entirely sure why he had bothered to go. The local MP was called Sarah Newton and it didn't really matter which political party she came from as she was the kind of person that was just as likely to jump ship if she thought that she would be able to gain more from the other side of the fence. She was the kind of politician who was very much in it for herself and didn't give a toss for the people that she was meant to be representing. In this regard she was the same as most other politicians. She didn't care about anyone else as she had a private income and was from a very well educated and privileged background.

These meetings, strangely called surgeries, where she was forced to meet the public were one of the crosses that she felt that politicians had to bear; make no mistake about it she was forced to meet the public; it was *not* something that she enjoyed doing. The rest of the time she would keep as distanced from the public as it was reasonably possible to do whilst still being on the same planet. At some point during the meeting the issue had been raised over noise. Someone had made the point that there were times when the council were doing various works and this disrupted people who were on shift work. Mrs Newton had looked the person directly in the eye and stated:

'Well, it's your choice to work nights. If you don't want that disruption then you should pick a job that doesn't require you to work shifts.'

This narrow minded, blinkered view on the world was absolutely typical of a politician who obviously seemed to feel that people could pick and choose whatever jobs they wanted. Mrs Newton clearly had no concept of the jobs that were required people to work nights and on Bank Holidays and all the other times when politicians were not working. Some of them could not even understand the concept of not having a second home. Politics really did not have all that to say in its favour really. If a child told a career's advisor that they wanted to grow up to be a politician then you might consider the only thing that you could humanely do was drown it immediately. Was it really any wonder why the public had such little respect for politicians any longer?

Perhaps the lack of sleep had made him jump to conclusions, but it just seemed strange to him that so recently George had been talking about how justice needed to be done and if no one else was prepared to do it then maybe matters should be taken into their hands and then all of a sudden some form of justice did seem to have taken place. There were stranger things that happened in the world, but this was a particularly strange one. Then on the other hand maybe he was just reading too much into it. Coincidences did happen after all. It was the kind of thing that would make the unbeliever start believing in the existence of a God of some sort. It would be nice to believe that there was some kind of being or force that went around the world correcting all the wrongs that had been made. It just wasn't something that was very plausible. These things just didn't happen in real life.

All of these thoughts, and a great number more went around Simon's head as he sat in a café after he had finished work and drank slowly his flat white coffee and tried not to draw any analogies from it. He could afford the luxury of stopping in a café on his way home from work these days now that he did not have to hurry home to be with someone. Not that he ever really had to hurry home for Amanda as she would either be out socialising somewhere or would not even recognise his presence if she had of been home.

'Since when did you visit coffee shops?'

The question broke into his thoughts and for a moment he was a little disorientated as he looked up, unsure if the question was being addressed to him or whether he had picked up a fragment of someone else's conversation. He was even more disorientated when he looked up into the face of his ex-wife who was smirking down at him. She may not have been deliberately smirking, it was just the natural look that she had on her face most of the time. They do say that if you speak of the Devil then he shall appear; or in this case, she.

'I don't believe it's against the law,' he stated as he raised the coffee cup to his lips once again and noticed that the coffee was getting cold. He must have been thinking longer than he had thought that he had.

'Well you would know all about the law, wouldn't you?' sniffed Amanda as she looked around her with a disapproving air. This was something that she was particularly good at doing. Her and her mother both could look disdainfully around them whilst at a Buckingham Palace garden party. 'If you wanted to be involved in the law, then I really don't see why you couldn't have become a judge, or a barrister.'

'Jesus, we're divorced and now you still want to have arguments?' Ironically Simon got the feeling that they might be talking more now than they were when they were actually married.

'You're the one who always wanted to argue.'

'No. I wanted to discuss things, but you were the one who never wanted to talk about anything. You always preferred to keep your head buried in the sand and pretend that things were not happening. And look where that got us.' Simon didn't really see the point in having an argument about whether they used to argue or not.

'So, you still want to slag me off?' This appeared to be a word that she had learnt recently and did not fit easily into her vocabulary. This seemed to be a very surreal conversation and Simon was not entirely sure why it was happening. He had never understood Amanda all that much when he had been married to her and it seemed that now they were divorced he would continue to understand her even less than he had done before.

'You never tried to understand me,' she stated as if she had been reading his thoughts; which he would not have put it passed her to be able to do. 'You always went and did your own thing and never paid any attention to me at all. Do you have any idea of the stigma that has been raised because I had to divorce you? That kind of thing has just never happened in my family.'

'All you ever went on about was your family. You think your family is so damn important. If you have come here because you want to sling shots at each other then I can surely throw a few things at you as well.'

'I didn't come here to see you at all. If I had known you were here then I would not have come here.'

'And yet you still approached me. I had no idea you were here. You could easily have gone away without me noticing you.'

'So, you think I should run away from you, is that it?'

'I didn't say that. Jesus, I have not missed the way you manage to twist everything that anyone ever says to you.'

He remembered clearly her ability to take anything that you said and put a different twist to it and make herself out to be the victim regardless of the situation. This appeared to be a particular trait of the upper classes to be able to paint themselves into a situation where they appeared to be hard done by. You could see this by the ancestral home. 'Yes, it has thirty-six bedrooms and you really can only roller-skate from one end to the other if you want to make any progress; but dear me the cost of the upkeep you would not believe. The heating bills, the electricity bills and then of course the entire fabric of the place needs renovation which will cost a fortune. I'm afraid that we may be forced to open to the public.'

This is obviously one of the worst things that could ever happen to the upper classes. They obviously didn't consider the fact that those under them also had heating bills which were even more of a struggle to meet, even if you lived in a one bedroom flat rather than a mansion. They clung to their ancestral home, though, no matter what else was happening because they didn't want to be the generation that let it all go to hell in a handcart and were forced to sell it or, perhaps worse still, hand it over to the National Trust who might allow them to continue to live in the servants quarters whilst plebs tramped through their one time home. Oh, how the other half live.

'I suppose you hate me Simon, is that what you are saying? I certainly feel that you never loved me.' Amanda managed to drag Simon's thoughts back to the present. It always had seemed to be the case that when Amanda was talking to him he was dragged from the present into the past. He gave some serious thought to the question although he suspected that it was more rhetorical on her behalf and not something that she seriously expected an answer to though. He did, nevertheless, give it some thought as it was an interesting question.

Love was a very strange thing. How many times in a person's life were you truly in love with someone and then perhaps the relationship would break up and then years later you were left with no feelings for that person at all and could not understand what it was that you had seen in them in the first place. There was also the problem of confusing love with lust and vice versa. You could easily be in lust with someone and think it was love. This sort of thing appeared to happen very early on in life when you were getting into relationships. It was all very confusing.

Simon had been pretty convinced that he had been in love with his first girlfriend, but when he thought about her now, he could hardly summon up what her face looked like. From being the centre of his universe, she had gone to an insignificant footnote. Time played tricks on you like that. Priorities changed over the years and things which were so important once would eventually fade into a haze of nothingness. He certainly believed that he had loved Amanda once, if he hadn't then why the hell had he married her; it was a good question that he had asked himself several times during the divorce.

'I loved you. Once. You may not believe it, but I put everything that I could into our marriage, but all you were interested in was yourself and your family. You never showed me any love or affection. You were simply not interested in me.'

He believed that this was the case. He did believe that he had given everything that he could to the marriage and he would not have given up on it if he had not tried everything within his power. He only walked away in the end because the fight had been too much and it had left him physically exhausted. You can only fight for so long and then there is just nothing left in you to fight any longer. He knew that she would never believe that he had not wanted a divorce any more than she had. There comes a time though when you realise you are just bandaging a corpse and it is time to get out and do something better with your life than be manacled to a mistake.

'And so, you went off to do this police thing.'

'This police thing? At least I'm prepared to work for a living and give something back rather than you and your family who expect everything to be given to them.'

'You have no idea how it is that you have embarrassed yourself by doing this silly little job dressing up in costume.'

'Uniform.' He hated her for that. If it had been a military uniform then it probably would have been acceptable in the eyes of her family, but the police were just too low in the class system for their liking.

'You think you are making a difference. You are not making any difference other than making yourself look silly all the time.'

Simon put his coffee down and did his best to control his anger which was rising. Amanda had always made him feel like this. He became frustrated with her and he became annoyed at her attitude. It was an interesting debate as to whether or not he had actually loved her. He was not sure any longer. At the time of the marriage he would have confirmed that he loved her with his lasting dying breath. When he eventually decided that he had gone as far as he could with his marriage and realised that he was actually living a life of total crap he finally understood that he had been fooling himself as well as all the others that he had mislead into believing that he had a happy marriage.

It is easy with hindsight to see all the mistakes that you have made. It is not so easy to see things the way they really are when you are so close to them. Simon had been too close to events in his marriage to really see that it was not the happy affair that he had thought that it was. Amanda went on about the fact that divorce had bought some sort of disgrace on her family, but it had hardly been something that he had wanted either. In order to keep things going he had always made excuses for things that had happened in his marriage. The mystery to him now, amongst a whole raft of mysteries was how it was that they had ever got together in the first place. How the hell had all of this seemed like a good idea at the time.

He pushed his coffee to one side and stood up. He disliked her for a number of things since they had been married but making him spoil his coffee was the last straw really.

'I don't hate you Amanda. If anything, I don't feel anything for you at all. You're simply not worthy of the emotion and the effort that would be required to feel anything at all. Have a good life. With any luck we won't be seeing each other again.'

He then left the café before he had to put up with anything else that she might suddenly come up with that he really didn't want to hear. He couldn't see the point of her approaching to him in the first place. He couldn't see the point in her at all.

He buttoned his overcoat as he walked down the street. It was a miserable day with the sky battleship grey and the smell of smoke in the air that seemed to suggest that winter was on its way.

He had not made any difference with his life and his job. Is that what she thought? Well, perhaps it was about time that he started to make a difference.

Twenty-Eight

It will not have escaped the notice of anyone that Simon was disillusioned with his job. This was not something that was particularly unique to police officers. Many people would find disillusionment in life which often began with discovering such things as Father Christmas did not exist; nor did the Tooth Fairy and there were no such things as fairies at the bottom of the garden either, sorry kids. There was always going to be something about life that would disappoint and bring disillusionment. It simply was not what we had been led to believe it was going to be like in our childhood.

Simon was aware of the fact that there were also police officers out there that really enjoyed their job, probably. It just didn't seem to be anyone that he knew. He was also aware that depending on where you came from in the country would depend on your view. Metropolitan Forces tended to be busier, but they had more officers to spread about whereas in the rural forces you were perhaps not as busy, but there were less of you and you were expected to do everything. Some officers had transferred from the Met to Simon's rural Force and been amazed that there were not departments to take over all the work. They had been used to running about arresting people handing them over and then running about again. In the more rural Forces, they were expected to do their crime enquiries as well as run about. Arresting people often meant dealing with them as well, putting the interview into them and then putting the file together. There were also some jobs that the metropolitan Forces had ditched ages ago — usually anything that was beneath them such as a mention of Facebook, Twitter or anything regarding 'me ex-boyfriend's been texting me.' Rural Forces just didn't seem to be able to say no and almost every job that was called into the police made it through the call centre and out to dispatch. It meant a lot of police time was wasted on crap. Bottom line: if you can't sort your own life out, why do you expect someone else to be able to do it for you?

Simon didn't know what it was like in other areas, but he knew the reason why his particular Force was rushed off its feet was down to the previous Chief Constable. There wasn't much to go in favour of this man, but he had come up with a scheme which he no doubt thought was a noble idea and the idea was that officers would visit *every* victim of crime, no matter what the crime was. On the surface of it there doesn't seem to be anything wrong with this and it might be considered to be the least that the public expected, but the simple fact of the matter was that there were a lot of crimes out there and not all of them were necessary for a physical presence of a police officer. Plus, there simply were not enough officers to go around doing all this. The Chief then sat in his office feeling smug and sitting back waiting for a knighthood whilst all of his officers were run ragged.

Another thing that annoyed Simon was that everything was statistic driven now. One of the big contentions was that they were monitored on how many stop and search forms they completed. Now, the Home Office and the Chief Constable had both stated that they were not statistic led and there should not be a drive to monitor front line officers on how many people they search. The officers immediately below the rank of Chief Constable had all nodded their agreement and then ordered everyone else to keep on monitoring regardless.

This was silly as it could ultimately lead to corruption. Pretty much you had to have a good reason for wanting to stop someone going about their everyday business and search them. If you didn't have a good reason and you knew you were being monitored on this then you were likely to make up a reason which would keep the bosses happy but ultimately constitute an illegal search. The management were very slow to catch on to this and still insisted that officers get out there and 'turn people over' or 'put your hands in their pockets.' This was something that alienated the public a great deal; or to be more precise the general public didn't mind the police doing it so long as they were doing it to criminals and not to them.

One officer had been sacked for making up the names on his stop and search forms. The pressure to stop and search people had been so complete that he had gone into the local graveyard and copied the names and dates of birth off of a lot of the tombstones.

The hierarchy could not see the alienation though and felt that they had to have something that they could use to monitor their constables and their performance. What they really failed to realise by this statement was that they were basically saying how useless they were as managers. It is a well-known fact that a good sergeant will know exactly what their constables are doing and what their performance is like without the need of having to count pieces of paper. This would work up the ranks as well with a good inspector knowing what their sergeant was doing and so on and so on.

The simple fact of the matter was that there were numerous sergeants and inspectors that had absolutely no idea what those under them were doing. This was most obviously evident to the constables on the front line. They were sometimes supervised by sergeants who had no idea what they were doing or where they were. They were only interested that you returned at the end of the shift with a handful of paperwork as this showed them that you had been doing something during the day. It did not matter that you may have been thrown from job to job all day long without a chance for a cup of coffee or a bite to eat. You could be really busy like that to the point where you physically ached at the end of the shift but if you didn't have search forms at the end of the shift then you might as well not have done anything.

'There are a lot of incompetent supervisors out there,' George had said when they had discussed all of this. 'There are those that cannot make a decision and there are those that make disastrous decisions. I'm not sure which of them is worse really.'

George had munched on his sandwich and thought about it.

'Mind you. I'm not one to knock them completely. I've never climbed the ranks so perhaps it's not up to me to really criticise how good they are at their job. After all, if I am not prepared to do it myself am I in a position to criticise someone else who has tried?' This magnanimous comment had raised Simon's interest a great deal.

'Why did you never go for promotion?' he asked. George sighed and thought about that one deeply before answering.

'The simple fact of the matter is that I have been a PC for a great number of years and during that time I have seen sergeants come and go and I have seen the shit that they go through. They get it in the neck from above and they get the grief from us lot below. I guess in our position we at least only get it from one direction. The extra money and pension just aren't worth the level of crap that you are given.'

'The money and the pension probably aren't worth the crap that we're given at this level.'

'That's pretty true.'

It has been said before and it is very true that there were a number of officers in the job who had been promoted above their ability; who had been promoted above their interest and certainly a lot that had been promoted above their intelligence. The simple rule to all of this really was that you should only really seek promotion when you looked at those who were on the rung above you and thought, 'I can do better than that.' Once you had made that decision then it was time to start thinking about promotion. The problem was that not many thought like this. They were ruled by their own ambitions or their greed and they climbed the ladder of promotion and they were not suited to it in the least. They would be too blinded to see this if you pointed it out to them, of course. In fact, they would probably be very shocked about it. Most people cannot see their own weaknesses up close.

The other thing with regards to being promoted in the police is the fact that in order to be promoted you had to be prepared to swallow the corporate pill; or to at least pretend that you had. They were not going to promote you if you had even the slightest hint of individuality or creativity. You had to be devoid of any form of rebelliousness before they would even consider allowing you to be promoted. It didn't really matter if you were an incompetent twat so long as you were *their* incompetent twat.

It is also a fact of life that half the time it didn't matter what you knew so much as who you knew. You could be the best copper going and passed all of the exams with flying colours but if your face didn't fit then you were not going to get it. It really was as simply and as draconian as all of that really. In one respect the politicians were right the police did need an overhaul and to be dragged into the twenty-first century. They were just wrong in thinking that this meant length of service, pensions and wages. There were other things that should have been concentrated on that had gone to rack and ruin.

All of it would probably seem to be pretty depressing when viewed from the outside. After all the notion of the police going around being depressed, hating their job and incompetently led is not an image that is likely to fill you with all that much confidence. It really shouldn't be something to worry you though when you apply it across the board. This is not something that is unique to the police, in every job there are people who hate it and who are depressed and who are incompetently led. It is just the way of things. In all walks of life people are like this. No matter how excited you are and happy you are with your job there will always be someone who is prepared to piss on your parade.

Just remember we are all in the shit; only some of us are deeper in than others. In some cases, some of us have other twats that are standing on top of us to try and get out of it. You know who you are.

***

So, yes it was true that Simon was a bit pissed off with the job at the moment, but there were probably others who loved it with a passion. They are usually the ones that you should most watch out for though.

There is something else within the police called the 'blue lamp instinct,' which was a pretentious title given to an intuition that police officers developed. Some people were just born with this which is probably why they became police officers in the first place whereas others developed it over time being a police officer. In a nutshell it allowed you to sense various things. It allowed you sometimes to sense when you might be in danger. Something would not sit right with a situation that you were in so you would sense that there was danger about to happen and then would take appropriate action that might help you out — or might make you look like a complete idiot if you were wrong. There was also the sense of knowing when someone is lying to you. This is not something that is unique to police officers and can often be sported by teachers as well as lots of parents as well.

Some will say that it is not instinct at all, nor is it anything special to police officers, but rather it is something that just comes from experience. The more experience you have of seeing how a situation develops the more likely you are to notice how the situation in front of you will develop. The more used you are to finding out lies the easier it will become to notice when someone is lying to you. All perfectly logical really.

The point to all of this was that Simon was aware that something was not right; he believed that George was not telling him the truth and he was up to something. It was just a question of what and he had a terrible feeling that he knew exactly what it was. What he needed though was proof. This was probably something that was easier said than done. Simon was also not entirely sure what he would actually do if his suspicions were proven to be true. This was something that, if he were right, would prove to be very big. Bigger than he could probably actually handle.

***

'Are you all right, sir?'

It was a question that George was asking of Chief Inspector Harbour who appeared to be walking down the corridor of the police station with his head tilted at an angle that made him look at the ceiling. This was something of a surprise, but then there was little that would surprise George about the antics of Harbour.

'Fucking public,' the Chief Inspector replied which was not really an answer.

'Not sure I follow, sir.'

'Fucking public,' repeated Harbour as he opened the door of his office that George had been standing near. It was as he did this that George realised that he was holding a handkerchief to his face and that it was covered in blood as he appeared to be trying to stem a very large nosebleed.

'Fucking public, sir?' George followed him into the office.

'Yes, fucking public. Wanker punched me.'

'Wanker punched you, sir?' George found that when dealing with most senior officers it paid to repeat as much of what they said back to them as possible. He found this really infuriated them nicely. Harbour had dropped the bloody handkerchief on the floor and had reached for some tissues that were on his desk and was stuffing them up his nose. George had a particular hatred for this man so was finding the encounter to be one of the better ones that they had experienced together.

'Punched me, came into make a complaint didn't like the answer so fucking punched me.'

'Oh dear, sir,' replied George trying to keep the laugher out of his voice at the prospect of the first real confrontation that Harbour had probably had in his entire career. He stooped and picked up the blood-stained evidence of this.

'I would have said that he was a Yid, were it not for the fact that he was a nig-nog.'

'A nig-nog, sir?'

'Yes, a nig-nog. A bloody nigger.'

'I don't believe you can say that, sir.'

'I'll say what I damn please. Came in to complain about that fucking MP, Sarah Newton. I ask you, females becoming politicians. They should stick to the kitchen and giving birth. It's the only thing that they should be allowed to do. It's the only thing that they are good at.'

'I don't believe you can make racist and sexist comments, sir. Not in the modern police service.'

'Did you want something, Lawrence?' the Chief Inspector asked having finally realised that he was there and probably wasn't going to be of use.

'Not really, sir.'

'Then get out. I'm in a bad enough mood as it is without having to engage with a useless individual such as you. It amazes me that you are still in this job, and let me tell you if I have my way you won't be in it for much longer. Do you understand me?'

'Impeccably so, sir.'

'Get out then!'

Harbour came around the desk trying to look angry which is never easy when you have tissue stuffed up each nostril. George backed away and then found himself standing in the corridor again as the door slammed shut in his face. He realised he was still holding the handkerchief in his hands and held it up, but it was too late as he was nose to the door and he suspected that Harbour would not appreciate a knock to be given it back. George looked at it for a moment and then looked up and down the corridor trying to decide what to do with it and then in the absence of any suggestions shrugged and walked off carrying it by the very tip between finger and thumb.

Twenty-Nine

One of the things that Simon could have done in order to follow up his suspicions on George would have been to follow him. However, this is not detective fiction and the chances of being able to successfully follow George around all of the time were really something that belonged in the Philip Marlowe category of fiction. It just wasn't going to happen. Realistically it would mean having to abandon his own life so that he could dedicate all of his time to following and observing George. He would, of course, have to sleep at times as well, which would make it difficult. Added to the fact that George was not stupid and would be just as likely to realise that Simon was following him around all of the time which could certainly raise a few awkward questions.

The only way that Simon might uncover something was if he were to put George under surveillance for twenty-four hours a day. Considering that he was the only resource that he had this essentially meant he would have to do it all himself without backup and then going without sleeping, eating, going to the toilet or in any way actually having a life of his own. It wasn't a very practical suggestion.

This was part of the problem when it came to being a police officer. Very often the fictional side of policing and detective drama went out of the window for you. Oh, there were those that revelled in watching police reality and fiction shows but partly these were the ones that jerked off about the job anyway; or they were the kind of people who sat there watching it because to see all the mistakes that were being made and how unrealistic it all was.

A lot of officers didn't watch it because the fun had been taken out of it for them. It was like people that decided that they would book a murder mystery weekend because it would be a lot of fun to work like

Agatha Christie and solve the crime. A lot of police officers, if they ever went, could end up taking a look at it and then pointing at one of the assembled people and saying 'It was him.' This tended to spoil the fun for all the normal people that were present.

In reality though why would you really want to go to work all day and then come home and watch a programme about the very work that you did. If you were a baker would you really want to come home and see a reality programme about the hidden mysteries of baking and then go on a weekend baking mystery where you had to guess who had made the bagels? Well, maybe you would.

No; following George around wherever he went on the off chance that he might do something or give himself away was a ludicrous idea. It also meant that he could be following him around for ages and his suspicions may be unfounded and all that he would be doing was wasting his time. He would then get into a situation where he had reached that conclusion only to then find that he couldn't stop because if he did stop then maybe he would do something. It was like being stuck with your weekly lottery numbers and then never daring to change them because the next week your numbers could come up.

The problem then was how he could get George to reveal what it was that he was up to — assuming that George was up to something in the first place, that is? It was a tricky one and he was not entirely sure that he had the answer to it off the top of his head. He was not entirely sure that he had the answer to it after some intense thinking. Keeping a watch on George did make a degree of sense even though it did appear to be ludicrous at the same time, but how else was he really going to find out what he was up to?

Simon shook his head. He was sitting in what had been his favourite coffee house until he had discovered that his ex-wife visited as well. Strange really. He never had her pegged for visiting coffee shops like this. Perhaps she was slumming it as it was more difficult to visit the posher establishments; or perhaps she was after hooking herself up with a bit of 'rough' which would probably be enough to push her mother over the edge and allow her to inherit the entire fortune.

This belief that George was up to something had become an obsession and it was stupid. This was George that he was thinking about.

The perpetual eater and complainer who was struggling his slobbish way towards retirement. He was not Bruce Wayne and he certainly was not roaming the streets at night as Batman. Simon had let his imagination get the better of him and he blamed this on the fact that since he had become a police officer he had not had the creative side of his character utilised enough. It was not encouraged in the police and he hardly had the time to sit and write like he used to when he was studying for his literature degree. He smiled at the thought of all those useless pretentious poems that he had written as a student. For some reason if you read a great deal you felt that this somehow gave you the right to write as well. Perhaps if he had concentrated on writing then he would not have the over active imagination that he had now with regards to George.

When you actually thought about it then you could see what a completely daft idea it was. Someone had burgled Mitchell's house and that was a crying shame. Okay so maybe Mitchell had not been found guilty of the charity theft and maybe there was a chance that he was innocent and had become the innocent victim of a crime, but his instinct told him that Mitchell was rotten to the core and he had deserved everything that he had got.

Someone seemed to have taken it personally though. It had taken time to empty Mitchell's place of everything and then trash what was left. This was a job that would take several hours and most of your average criminals were in and out within a few minutes. The longer you stayed on scene the more chance there was of being caught; obviously; or the more chance there was of someone seeing something that they would later tell the police about.

Someone had taken a big risk and a lot of time and effort over the Mitchell job; and then the charity had got its money back again. Now, granted it was a big leap of faith to suggest that the two of them were connected, but it seemed highly suspicious. Okay so maybe coincidences did happen in the world; but this was one hell of a big coincidence to be expected to believe in. This level of justice was just something that Simon had never heard of before. The alleged suspect punished and punished more than any court would have done and the victim recompensed. It was simply too good to be true.

Something was going on, but then the more he thought about it the more unlikely it seemed that George was likely to have anything to do with it. This was just not the kind of thing that it seemed plausible for George to get up to. It was hard enough to get him to do work when he was paid to do it, but to expect him to do something like this outside of work was staggering.

'You know there are very few times when I'm pleased that a law is broken,' Simon said when he and George were next crewed together, 'but I have to hand it to whoever burgled Mitchell.'

'Who?'

'The bloke that we think nicked the charity money.'

'Oh, him.'

'Yeah, I'm glad that he was burgled.'

'Why?'

'I think the little bugger deserved it. He's an oily little prick that makes me shiver. I've no doubt in my mind at all that he stole from the charity and he got what he deserved because of it.'

'Nobody deserves to be a victim of crime,' said George in a flat tone as he steered the vehicle around. George nearly always drove when it came to being crewed up. He probably didn't trust anyone else's driving or maybe he just liked to be in control all of the time. He obviously felt that his seniority of years meant that he should be in control.

'Do you really think that?'

'Why else would we be in this job, but to prevent crime? You can't quantify crime. Either something is illegal or it isn't and it doesn't matter who you are, the law should apply to all.'

'Should; but it doesn't always, does it?'

'No, it doesn't.' George gritted his teeth and seemed to take the next corner a little more sharply than the training manual would have liked him to have done.

'Do you think there is a vigilante out there putting things right?' Simon held his breath although he hardly expected George to turn around and say: 'Yes, I'm Batman.'

'No, I don't think there is a vigilante out there, Simon. It's a bloody stupid idea.'

'But you have to admit it is an amazing coincidence that —'

'Yes, that's exactly what it is. An amazing coincidence. People just don't go around being vigilantes outside of films and books and things. You should know that.'

'It's unlikely, but you have to admit that it's possible,' Simon stubbornly maintained.

'No, I don't have to admit it because it's ludicrous to think that it could happen.'

'Why couldn't it?'

'Well, for one thing people just don't have the energy for that kind of thing. They are only in this for themselves. They are not going to go out of their way to do something for charity like that or for setting a wrong right. It is too much energy required. They would have to drag themselves away from X Factor or Facebook or whatever it is that you lot do these days that I thankfully am too old to get caught up in.'

'Well you do have a point there I have to admit.'

'That's the problem with society and the human race today. We have become too involved in our own lives to care about community any longer. How many of us truly know our neighbours these days? And if we did it would not have been anything like it was decades ago. It is all changed now and it isn't necessarily something that has changed for the better either.'

The conversation lapsed into silence after that as they continued their journey patrolling the night. Simon felt that he had been put firmly in his place but there was still the romantic side of him that wanted to believe that there was someone out there who could put right some of the wrongs that had happened. When he had joined the police, he had thought that this was what the role of a police officer was. The longer he had been a police officer he realised that this was not the role at all and if anything, he spent most of his days now swamped with paperwork and red tape and running around doing meaningless tasks to keep his boss happy and to make his boss look good for his boss. It was not what he felt that policing was all about; or to be more precise it was not what he felt policing *should* be about.

For a brief moment he had been swept away in the belief that there was perhaps someone out there who was setting things right who was not tied to the law or to paperwork and red tape and who certainly did not have a boss that he had to kow-tow to. For one brief moment in time he thought how glorious it would have been if that person happened to be George, but it didn't look like it was going to be George after all. George had also spoken a lot of common sense about it all and perhaps there was nobody out there after all doing all this. Perhaps it was just a coincidence.

Perhaps there was not someone out there and if there was someone out there then it wasn't George. Simon allowed these thoughts to drift through his head in the dark, silence of the car. It was then that he had his epiphany and had to stop himself from crying out with excitement which would certainly have surprised George and probably caused him to crash. His thought process had gone something like this.

Amanda was right when she said that I have not achieved anything with my life. This is not the job that I have signed up for; or that I thought that I would be doing to help people. George is right; people don't care any longer; assuming that they ever did in the first place. George is not the vigilante. There probably is not a vigilante anyway; and if there was it probably wouldn't be George.

The problem was that you could sit back in your armchair and moan about how the world was whilst doing nothing about it at the same time; or you could be a doer who didn't like the way something was, so made the decision that they would go out and do something about it rather than just grumble and hide behind their newspaper and their comfort. It was with this thought and this realisation that Simon realised that if anyone was going to be a vigilante then it might just as well be him. It was time to stand up and be counted for what you believed in.

Thirty

Okay so it was a radical idea and not something that you should really rush into; but the fact remained that if you really wanted to have a say in what was going on then you had to be prepared to stand up and be counted.

Simon did not have a particularly healthy attitude towards politicians as might have been gathered; one thing did stick in his mind though and that was an interview with Tony Blair a short while after he had stood down as Prime Minister. At the time, and for a long time afterwards, a lot of people were deriding Blair for his involvement in the Iraq War and in particular for getting the country into what a lot of people considered a needless war; but Simon had seen an interview with him where he had said something along the lines of exactly what Simon was now thinking. If you want to be considered a power to be reckoned with and to have a say in world decisions then you couldn't just sit quietly at the back of the room and expect to be accorded the same level of respect and attention as those that stood up and said, 'this is what I think, and this is what I think we should do about it.' Simon had respected Blair for that and wondered why he hadn't said it earlier.

There was only one other politician that Simon had shown any respect for and that had been John Major. There had been nothing about Major's premiership that he had found respectful. As a matter of fact he had found the man to be rather boring, after all his main legacy was the cone hotline, which had hardly been a roaring success that had lasted; but when he had lost the 1997 election to Blair and had calmly walked out of Downing Street and spent the afternoon watching cricket as if he no longer had a care in the world then Simon had found himself having the unusual feeling of respecting the man. That was the way to go. Quiet dignity and grace.

With all of this in mind Simon felt that it was probably about time to take action. Most police officers could whinge about the police until the cows came home, but what did it really achieve? It was time to take action. The problem with taking action is that it did actually require a great deal of thought. The question was what was he to do? The logical thing of getting Mitchell back was already done so that was not something that he really wanted to target. He didn't want to hurt anyone either. It is a big step to cross the line from the legal into the illegal and he didn't want violence to be a part of it. He also only wanted to target criminals. This was about setting the balance sheet straight. It was not about targeting the innocent and becoming more like the people that he was supposed to be hunting down. This was about justice; or at least if he closed one eye and squinted a bit that was what he could convince himself it was about. At the end of the day it was still breaking the law, but he would have to gloss over that bit if he was to go through with this.

As he walked home from work that morning, he pondered over why it was that he would want to do it in the first place. It was a big risk that he was taking. If he went ahead with this and tried to set the balance right and he was caught then he would be hung out to dry. Not only would he lose his job, but as a police officer caught committing crime he would almost certainly be sent to prison and that was not the most comfortable of futures to contemplate. It was a huge risk, but it still nagged at him that he was not making all that much of a difference. He also felt light headed that he actually caught himself seriously thinking about doing this. It was one thing to support someone else doing it and to applaud politely from a distance, but he was now thinking about taking a massive step that would change his life and have major repercussions.

The problem is that things like *Batman* really did not exist. Batman might be left alone as he cleaned up the streets of Gotham from all the crime, but in reality, the law would not look at it and go 'oh someone is cleaning up all the criminals for us. That's nice; shall we let him get on with it?' It just didn't happen.

So why go through with it? Was it because Amanda had niggled him with her comments that he had achieved nothing? Was it because he had become so annoyed with the Government and the way that they had destroyed the police that the only way he felt he could retain law and order was to take matters into his own hands? He didn't really know, if he was honest.

It was true that if he was caught then his life was over, but then he remembered that throughout history there was risk if you were prepared to stand up and be counted. Numerous were the people that hid away from what the Nazis were doing during the Holocaust. Easy it was to pretend that it was not happening; but there was real risk to the few and far between people who were prepared to stand up and say 'No, this is wrong.' Simon did feel a little guilty about comparing what he was thinking about to the Holocaust, however.

There was a risk of getting caught. However, if anyone was going to know how to get away with committing crime then it was surely going to have to be police officers. After all police officers knew what you looked for at a crime scene, so Simon would have the advantage over your average member of the public that had decided to turn to crime. However, they do say that when you commit a murder you make fifty mistakes that are clues for the police later on and you are lucky if you can remember five of them. As he was not thinking of committing a murder, Simon felt that he was probably pretty safe on that front. He did know the realities of what detection of crime was like though so probably had the head start over a lot of others.

The next question was what crime to commit. This was more difficult as he had set himself a strict criterion on what he wanted to achieve if he was going to turn into a latter-day Robin Hood. Some days went by whilst he pondered on this one before finally coming to the conclusion that the best that he could attack was the drug market. Drugs were an emotive subject and there were a lot of people, some of them police officers, who felt that cannabis should be legalised; but very few people could dispute how the harder drugs could seriously fuck up your life. Not only could they destroy your own life but they could destroy the lives of all those around you. Furthermore, a dependency on hard drugs would turn you to a life of crime where you would commit more crime so that you could then raise the money to go out and buy more drugs. The circle of people that were affected by drugs was wide and vast. Many people would not even necessarily know that they were the victim of drugs. A huge proportion of crime was committed to keep feeding drug habits from shoplifting to murder.

So, his target was set, now all he had to do was get on with it. Taking as many precautions as he could he decided to target someone that he knew from experience was dealing with drugs and was into frequent habits of being away at certain times of the day. He then went and bought himself a selection of anonymous black clothing which could belong to anyone, would not be distinctive and most importantly could not be tied back to him. He took the precaution of buying these items separately in different shops and only paying in cash. It occurred to him that he might be being a little too cautious, but it didn't hurt to think that way.

His next problem was what to do with his target. As he had already made his mind up that he was not going to incorporate any violence into any of this he dismissed the idea of killing off all of the drug dealers in the area. What he wanted to do was something that would disrupt them. The problem was that whatever he did was not likely to have any long-term effects. If he destroyed some drugs then they would just get more and if need be commit crime in order to get more. It was a never-ending vicious circle if he thought about it. However, doing nothing was not really an option. Yes, it was true that we never really know the consequences of our actions and something that he was to do today may have repercussions down the line that he could never have imagined; but that was true of everything, including doing nothing.

If he were to break into a 'drug den' as he had started to imagine it and destroy the drugs then there were possible setbacks that more crime would be committed in order to replace the drugs. However, there were two big positives as far as he could tell. Firstly, that would be a bunch of drugs that would be off the streets that would not find their way into the proverbial playgrounds; secondly it was a crime that the victim was very unlikely to call the police to report. You would have to be particularly stupid to call the police and tell them that 'someone has stolen my heroin, officer. I wish to make a complaint.' There were a lot of stupid people out there, granted; so, in theory anything was possible.

Now, you might wonder, wouldn't the same result be achieved by following the process of the law, arresting the druggie and confiscating his drugs and sending him to prison? The answer to that very simply was

— yes it would. However, as has been previously demonstrated there are times when the police are pretty certain about something but they just can't prove it. The evidence isn't there or CPS won't run with it; and yet you are pretty certain that they are guilty.

If Simon were to break into a house and find a load of drugs there then there would be nothing that he could do about it as a police officer as he was illegally on the premises. He would have to quickly run off and swear out a warrant from a magistrate and rush back and execute the warrant in the hope that the drugs had not already been moved off the property. The evidence would be lost and there would be little point in returning as the occupants would know that the police were on to them. It was actually a lot simpler to abandon the rules and do it this way; after all the criminals didn't follow the rules so sometimes the police were hampered by having to. Life just wasn't fair at times.

There was no rush so Simon chose his target with care. He checked the intelligence systems and from his own local knowledge picked someone that they were pretty certain was dealing with drugs, but so far, had not been able to catch him red handed. He observed the location which was handy in the sense that it was not in a busy area so there was less chance of him being spotted by any member of the public. If he was spotted and challenged then all he had to do was announce that he was a police officer flash his warrant card and tell them to fuck off before they blew the entire operation. They were not to know that it was a one man entirely illegal operation. If the police were called and caught him before he had done anything then he could probably get away with trying the same trick on them and bluff his way into making them believe that they had blundered into an operation.

Having thought of every angle that he could he then decided on a night and having parked his car some distance from the address that he was targeting made his way on foot to the property. It was a still night with not much of a moon but sufficient to be able to see by without falling into the hedgerow. He had chosen an address that was out in the countryside in the middle of nowhere really. There were a few other scattered houses around but he didn't think that there would be all that much chance of being seen by the neighbours as they probably went to bed early in order to get up early and milk cows the next day, or something like that. This showed that he didn't entirely have a good grasp of the countryside.

Having arrived at the property he stood still for a moment and listened to the stillness of the night. From time to time there was some strange noise of an animal in the wood somewhere. A badger or a fox, maybe. Hell, for all he knew it could have been an elephant. Despite living in the country for a number of years he had never really mastered it or come to understand the way of it.

He stood still for as long as he could before cramp started to grab hold of him. The long walk to the property had allowed his eyes to adjust to the dark so he felt his night vision was about as good as it was going to be although it was not doing him all that much good as there were so many shapes and shadows in the wood that he was standing in that frankly a platoon of soldiers could have been standing behind the nearest tree and he wouldn't have known about it. He had decided that the best way to approach the house was through the wood that adjoined the property. This was the best way in and out as it afforded a lot of cover on the approach. The downside was that he had to move pretty slowly through the wood as there were a number of obstacles that could crack under his feet giving away his location as well as any number of things that could trip him up and leave him with an inverted ankle or similar which would mean that he would not be able to get back to his car and would probably end up dying of hyperthermia. There was nothing quite like looking at the positive side of things!

Simon slowly crept forward towards his target having finally decided that he was safe enough to be able to get on with his task. He moved forward slowly and inch by inch drew nearer to the property. At the end of the wood there was a small dry-stone wall that he would have to climb over and then across a patch of garden and he would be at the side of the house. He crept up to the wall and crouched beside it observing the house from his position. There didn't seem to be any sign of movement and he suspected that the occupants were out. These were the kind of people that would be awake at this time of the night as they tended to lead lives that were inverted to everyone else. Getting up in the late afternoon or early evening and then going to bed when the majority of the rest of the place were getting up. You had to work nights if you wanted to commit crime.

The small garden area was littered with the usual amount of crap that he would expect to find in a place like this. It grated on him for a moment that this was a reasonably nice house, or at least it had been once, in an area that a lot of people would have killed for and it had been handed over as a council property to some low life scum who never did a day's work in their life and spent all of their waking hours shooting up drugs and making everyone else's life a misery. Looking at the place Simon doubted that he could have afforded the private rent on a place like this. It was another example of why life was unfair and perhaps another justification for why it was that he was doing what he was doing.

He dragged his thoughts back to the garden which was scattered with litter, household waste that it looked as if they couldn't even be bothered to put in the wheelie bin, but had just thrown out of the door and left to rot. Being so close to the wood it was also evident that a number of woodland animals had attacked the bin bags and their contents were scattered all over the place. This didn't so much as seem to be a recent thing either, but something that happened on a daily basis.

Also, in the garden was the obligatory rusty car that appeared to be something that certain people just had to have in the garden making it look like a cross between modern art and the eye sore that it really was. These cars were always standard types. They had been half dismantled as if someone was in the process of renovating them although no progress would ever appear to be made. They would usually miss all the useful parts like wheels, headlamps and anything else that could be taken off and sold on eBay. The car would then have a tarpaulin or similar half draped over it as if the person who put it there could not really be bothered to entirely cover it and there it would be left until it rusted into the earth and gave archaeologists something interesting to look at in the future. It was always rather difficult to work out what the dying car was. From the angle that Simon was at he thought it might be a Ford Cortina.

So intent was Simon in looking towards the house and checking for any sign of movement that he failed to allow his concentration to focus all around him so did not notice until too late that someone had crept up behind him. In fact, he did not notice it until the last moment when he detected movement and spun round and put his face right in the path of the oncoming fist that knocked him backwards. He must have banged his head on the wall because he just had a vague recollection of a dark figure standing in front of him before everything went black.

Thirty-One

Simon was something of a lifelong dedicated insomniac. If you were not someone who suffered from insomnia — and suffer was exactly the correct word — then you really could not hope to understand what it was like.

Simon felt that he had lived twice as long as everyone else because he had slept half as long as everyone else. It had been another of the points of contention between him and Amanda. Amanda was someone that fell asleep the instant her head hit the pillow and then would sleep soundly and solidly for eight hours before waking up again as if a switch had been turned on and would be as bright as a button. For an insomniac this was something that had really begun to fuck Simon off. It had not helped in the slightest that he had usually just finally managed to drag himself into a sleep when Amanda would be up as bright as the Easter bunny and Amanda was someone who worked on the principal that if she was awake then everyone was awake. It was really a wonder his marriage had lasted for as long as it had.

With all of this in mind Simon had been fascinated when he had been assaulted on duty once and a few months down the line had to go into hospital to have his knee operated on. He had been fortunate that he had spent the majority of his life away from hospitals. As such he had never been subjected to a general anaesthetic which was something that he had looked forward to. Being an insomniac the idea that someone could stick a needle in your arm and within seconds you would be asleep was a bliss that he just could not contemplate.

He had not been particularly impressed with the hospital all that much. Just before it had been his turn to meet the anaesthetist who just happened to be German, the elderly woman who was in front of him had all been but carried from the room screaming 'I don't want to do it, haven't you people gassed enough of us already?'

Simon had not considered this the best omen in the world. He had been slightly more concerned when it had been his turn to see the anaesthetist and after a general chat, he had then taken a marker pen and written on Simon's leg 'This one,' with an arrow pointing to his knee. This was not the most encouraging thing in the world. His opinion had been further cemented when the anaesthetist had got Simon to sign the consent forms for the operation to go ahead. He had no problem with this, but the doctor had handed him his fountain pen to sign the forms and Simon was very much aware of the fact that you never allowed anyone else to write with your fountain pen as the nib was formed to the way that you write and someone else could mess it up entirely.

When he had got in the operating theatre, they had all moved so fast on him he was reminded of what he had read about the famous hangman, Albert Pierrepoint, being able to get the condemned from the cell to the end of a rope in a matter of seconds. The needle was in his arm and then as he was determined to enjoy the sensation of slipping away, he concentrated hard. He just managed to be scientific enough to say:

'I'm feeling rather sleepy, but I don't know if that's because I'm tired at the moment or because of what you are…' and then he was gone. The next thing he remembered was being shaken awake by a female nurse with an impressive moustache.

All of this was in no way similar to the experience that he felt once he had blacked out outside the drug dealer's house. He had been expecting the needle with the anaesthetic, but he had not been expecting that whilst he was looking at the drug dealer's house someone would creep up behind him, then pick the forest up and hit him around the head with it.

When he had woken in the recovery section of the hospital, he had felt like he had drifted into being awake with the assistance of a cloud of angels who sang to him and escorted him into the waking world. This time he felt as if the angels were escorting him, only this time they were hitting him over the head with frying pans at the same time before throwing him back into the conscious world. He vaguely was impressed to note that the senses appeared to come back one at a time just as he had read in novels.

To begin with he had his hearing return which didn't really help him any as he couldn't hear anything. His senses then returned which was decidedly unhelpful as they told him that he had the worst headache that he had ever had in his life. It was like a major hangover without the pleasure of going through all the alcohol to begin with. He then became aware of what was around him and that he appeared to still be lying in the forest as he could feel leaves and things beneath his hands and there was something like a twig or stick poking in his back although he supposed it could have been a hedgehog. Finally, he became aware of the fact that his sight was returning and if he wanted to then he could unpeel his eyes. He wanted to, but his eyes didn't appear to want to put in an appearance at the present so they had to be convinced to open which was not the easiest thing to do in the world. It was around about this time that he finally heard the voice.

'You're pretty crap at this aren't you?'

The voice sounded familiar, but Simon could not entirely place it and was unsure where it was coming from as his eyes did not appear to want to function to the best of their ability. His brain didn't appear to want to function either as for a moment he briefly entertained that it was the voice of God that he was hearing and that he had died and this was a rather shit version of heaven. He would be very disappointed if this were heaven as he had hardly got off to the best of starts.

He lay there for a moment entertaining the thought further. Maybe it wasn't the voice of God, but he still might have died from whatever it was that had happened to him. He wasn't entirely sure that he remembered, but he knew it must be something strange as he didn't normally take to lying in the middle of a wood in the middle of the night. Wasn't his sort of thing at all.

Being dead would probably be alright. It would probably be a lot like rest days. Not having to work. Doing what you wanted. Getting out of bed when you wanted. That was assuming that you even needed to go to bed any longer. After all, if you were dead you presumably didn't need to sleep to recharge yourself. What were you recharging yourself for? No sleep? No bed? That wouldn't please Amanda.

Amanda! He wondered if she would turn up for his funeral. He suspected that she would so that she could be seen to be there. He also knew that she thought she looked good in black; well she did, but that was beside the point. He was pretty convinced that she would love the chance to stand there as the aggrieved divorced wife and the grieving ex-wife and have people pay her attention and say how terrible it was that she had been so wronged by him. She would love all of that and could get a hell of a lot of mileage out of it if the truth were known.

He wondered if there was the possibility of being able to return to Earth as a ghost. He had never really given a lot of credence in ghosts before believing that the majority of it was made up by the deluded, insane and the criminally fraudulent. Now that he was dead though he was hoping that maybe he had been wrong. If that were the case then he would have the opportunity of returning to the world and haunting Amanda for the rest of her days. He figured that he could have a lot of fun with that one.

God help God when Amanda and her mother died. If life on Earth and the Monarchy had been too beneath them then he could just imagine them wandering around heaven demanding changes and making life hell, which was ironic when you thought about it. He also hoped that heaven was a big enough place so that he did not have to spend eternity bumping into Amanda and her mother.

Hang on what had that voice said: 'You're crap at this aren't you?' What kind of thing was that to have said to you in the afterlife? Crap at what? It didn't sound all that heavenly the more he thought about it and would he really have to suffer this headache for all eternity?

'Is your head feeling any better?'

It was that voice again. Parts of his brain were beginning to come together from the different locations that they had scurried off to. It did sound familiar. It also did not make sense with his view on what the afterlife would be like.

'Sorry about that.'

It was getting more confusing now. He thought he could also smell smoke, perhaps he was in hell after all. No, it wasn't so much as smoke as tobacco. Simon felt with a bit of effort he might be able to open his eyes a little more fully now. With supreme effort of will he opened his eyes and slowly lifted his head from the forest floor and a short distance away he could just make out in the faded moonlight a figure of a man sitting on a fallen tree smoking a cigarette. Now he was pretty sure that he had not died. He recognised the man on the tree and it all clicked into place for him

It was George.

Thirty-Two

'Did you hit me?'

'Yes, I'm rather afraid that I did,' George answered. They were still in the same positions as they were before.

'Why?'

'Well, initially it was because I thought you were someone else. After I hit you and realised that it was you then I'm glad that I did.'

'That's not a very nice thing to say,' Simon contrived to be hurt by this even though his head was still ringing and taking up the majority of his attention and pain focus.

'Well, it looked like you were about to make a bloody fool of yourself,' George flicked the cigarette that he had been smoking into the undergrowth which was thankfully damp and cold enough from the November night to not cause a massive forest fire which surely would only have added to the problems that Simon felt he was experiencing that evening.

'Do you make a habit of lurking in forests and then punching people?'

'We ought to get out of here really,' said George standing up and ignoring the question. 'Can you stand up and walk?'

'I bloody hope so,' muttered Simon as he struggled to his feet and debated with himself as to whether he really felt like going anywhere with George at the precise moment as there was a high likelihood that he would turn out to be a homicidal maniac.

George slipped his arm around Simon and steadied him as standing on his feet had made Simon's head decide that it was the perfect opportunity to do some cartwheeling.

'Did you drive here?' George asked as they slowly picked their way through the brambles.

'Yes.'

'Where's your car?'

'Over there somewhere,' replied Simon vaguely waving his arm in the direction of where he thought he had parked his car.

'Best leave it for the night. We will get you out of here and somewhere warm, dry and above all light so that I can have a look at that head of yours. You probably are not really in a fit state to drive at the moment in case you have concussion or something like that. We can come back and pick your car up later.'

'You didn't hit me that hard.'

'No; but you decided to hit the wall pretty hard yourself.' Memories were queuing up to be allowed back into Simon's brain and he was not sure that he wanted them to be admitted. It was all starting to come flooding back now.

'What are you doing here?' he asked as they continued to work their way through the wood in a different direction to the one that Simon thought that he had come in from.

'Let's cover that later shall we?'

Simon tried to nod, but received a sharp reminder from his brain that it was in charge and there would be none of that nodding business going on for the time being. Lapsing into silence they worked their way through the trees unto they came to a clearing with a small dirt track road going through it; Simon supposed that it was a fire ride or something similar that had been put in to make it easier for the fire engines to get into the forest in case the whole lot were to go up in flames one day. Parked on the side of the track was George's car.

***

'Well it doesn't look too bad if you ask me,' George commented as he finished looking at Simon's head. They were sitting in George's living room having decided that it was easier to get to George's house rather than Simon trying to give directions to his own. 'You're fortunate that you have such a thick skull.'

'Somehow I knew you were going to say that.'

'You'll be fine. The skin is not broken, which is frankly a miracle as I thought you were dead the way you went down against that wall. I will get you some ice to put on it and then maybe a cup of tea will make you feel better.' George got up and disappeared into the kitchen which led off from the small living room. He came back a few seconds later and handed Simon a packet of frozen peas.

'All I have got I'm afraid.' Simon smiled weakly and placed the packet of peas on his head vaguely realising that he must look pretty ridiculous, but then immediately not caring how he looked as the coldness began to work its magic on his throbbing head. George disappeared back into the kitchen and Simon could hear the sounds of tea being made.

Whilst he sat there in the corner of the small room feeling self-conscious, he tried to look around the room without actually making too many movements that would make him feel as if his head was about to fall off. George's house reminded him very much of his grandparents' house. It had an old-fashioned feel to the place and what was very surprising given George's reputation at work, extremely neat and tidy. At work it was a mystery what was kept in George's tray and his locker was somewhere that was just not worth venturing into at all; and yet here everything was immaculate and appeared to be in its own place. Simon was also slightly surprised to see that there was a portrait of the Queen over the fireplace which he would not have expected to have found in many homes these days. He had not assumed that George was a particular establishment figure given his derision for the Government; but then Government and Monarchy are not necessarily the same thing.

George's house appeared to have had time frozen at some stage and was not the abode that most of his colleagues would have associated with George at all, which just went to show you that there could be a massive division between your work life and your home life and it was not always correct to judge the behaviour of the one against the other.

Simon was further surprised when a few minutes later George re-entered the living room with a tray of tea. At work, tea was normally made by placing an individual tea bag into a mug and making it that way. It was also very unlikely that George would actually ever make any tea at work as he appeared to have reached a period where he considered himself to be too senior in service to do anything as menial as making tea. That was what probationers were for as far as he was concerned. George now walked in, however, with what appeared to be a high quality bone china tea set which included a tea pot which was something that Simon did not think he had seen for a number of years outside of restaurants and motorway service stations — although they were made of metal that appeared to be designed to radiate heat so that you burnt to death if you tried to pick it up.

'It's Earl Grey, I hope you don't mind? You can always be a heathen and have it with milk and sugar if it will make you feel better.'

Simon was beginning to feel like he had stepped into a parallel universe and was not sure how many more surprises he could take this evening.

'How is the head feeling?'

'A lot better now, thanks for asking.'

George strained the tea (another first for Simon who had become convinced that nobody did this any longer) and then handed him a cup whilst he worked on a more puritan version for himself.

'Now perhaps we should talk about what happened this evening?' George settled down on the sofa that faced the one that Simon was sitting on.

'I think it might be a good idea.'

'Where to start though, hey? Where to start?'

'Perhaps you can explain why you punched me?'

'It's a reasonable place I suppose. I didn't know who you were and I thought that you were someone that was up to no good and was possibly looking for me.'

'Why would I be looking for you? What were you doing out there in the middle of nowhere anyway?'

'I could ask you the same question, but I think if we are honest with each other we both know that we were both out there for the same reason; don't you agree?'

Simon was silent for a moment whilst he thought about that one. It was possible that his suspicions about George had been right all along. If that were the case then by some bizarre coincidence, they appeared to have had the same job in mind at precisely the same time. If he was wrong though then admitting that he had been contemplating committing a criminal offence was not going to do either of them any favours. If they were both up to it then neither man necessarily wanted to be the first to admit it.

'What do you think I was there for?' Simon eventually opted for as a safer bet than an all-out confession. George thought about this and then stood up and threw another log on the open fire that he had started up when they had first entered the cold house.

'I think you were angling to cause some mischief to our drug dealer friend who lives at that address. I think you knew that he was not going to be there so you went to his address to cause some kind of activity to him that would hurt him personally and set him back.'

Simon smiled weakly and tried to laugh and shrug off the fact that George had hit it on the nail so perfectly.

'What makes you think that?'

'Because that is why I was there.'

'You?'

'Yes, me. You suspected me to be up to something didn't you?'

'I had my suspicions.'

'Well, they could make a detective out of you yet if it were not for the fact that you can't get into CID because your face doesn't fit.'

'That's a hell of a thing you've just admitted to, George; and a hell of a risk that you have taken by admitting it to me.'

'Maybe. However, I suspect you were there for the same thing and if you were to try and use it against me,' he spread his arms wide, 'well it's just the two of us here chatting and I can always deny that the conversation ever happened; and then it will just be your word against mine.'

Simon thought about this for a moment whilst he sipped on his tea.

'Alright, I admit it. You're right, that's why I was there. I can always deny it later as well should I have to.'

George nodded his head.

'Perfectly sensible. Well that's what I thought. Perhaps it would be a good idea if you and I had a straight chat without denying everything and beating about the bush.'

'Sounds like a plan. Did you burgle Mitchell's house?'

'Yes, I did.'

'Why?' Simon had suspected it all along, of course, but to be so blatantly told so by George was like a slap in the face all of a sudden.

'You know why. The thieving bastard stole from that charity and was getting away with it. I broke in and stole his stuff and flogged it on and then anonymously donated the proceeds to charity.'

'That was a hell of a risk. It must have taken you all night to get all that stuff.'

'Well, I admit I'm not as young as I used to be and it did take a fair amount of effort. Criminals get away with it all the time though so why shouldn't the likes of us?'

'But selling the stuff on; you could easily have been caught at that stage.'

'Just required a bit of intelligence, Simon. Most criminals are caught because at the bottom they are thick; or they are so drugged up to the eyeballs that they don't know what they are doing so don't think straight. If you walked into one shop with a load of stuff then suspicions would be roused. If you spread it out over a number of different shops then it is easy to do. I didn't bother with eBay, far too easy to get caught on that.'

'What about CCTV?'

'Well that is the advantage of this job. How many times have you been to a job and because you are wearing a uniform the owner of whatever property you are at has openly told you that the cameras are dummy or that they are not plugged in or that there are blind spots? It is just a question of choosing the area carefully and not drawing too much suspicion to yourself.'

'It's cunning I will give you that.' It was also very true what George was saying. The uniform did immediately project trust onto certain members of the public that normally would not reveal information if you put them on the rack.

'And the drug dealer tonight?'

'Similar thing. No profit from it this time to sell on though, but if I could have got in and found his stash and destroyed it then it would have been a reassurance that those particular drugs would never have hit the street. Oh, I know what you are going to say. If not that stash then he would have replaced it and sent more out onto the streets. That's true. However, I would have got one batch destroyed. Maybe that wouldn't have made any difference and he would have been tougher on security next time so I would never have been able to hit him again; but the thing is the war on drugs is something that we can never win. You lock one dealer up or take one batch off the streets and there is always another lot that will jump up in its place. You will never be able to stop people from wanting to take drugs. Whilst the demand is there then there will always be drugs; but that doesn't mean that in the war we can't win the odd battle or skirmish every now and then.'

It was a passionate appeal and Simon finished his tea whilst listening to him. It also made a lot of sense as far as he was concerned.

'How are you feeling now?'

'Much better thanks, but I think your peas have melted.'

'Well, that doesn't matter I don't really like vegetables all that much anyway. Perhaps it would be better if you stayed here tonight. It is rather late now, so much so that it's almost early. Tomorrow we can have a chat about what is going to happen next and then we can go and pick your car up.'

'I don't want to be a nuisance. Won't I disturb your wife? I'm surprised we haven't woken her up already.'

George walked over to the mantel piece and doused the fire. He then picked up a gilt framed photograph from the mantel showing an attractive looking woman. He smiled at it for a short while and traced his fingers over the glass.

'No,' he finally said. 'It will be fine. My wife's dead, you see.'

Thirty-Three

Simon slept a surprisingly peaceful night given that he was in a strange bed in a strange house after a series of very strange things had happened to him; all in all, it was very strange. After about seven hours of sleep he came down the stairs to find George in a similar position to last night, standing in front of the mantel piece with his wife's photograph in his hand. It wouldn't have surprised him at that point if George had told him that he had been standing there all night. He looked up and smiled as Simon walked into the room.

'Her name was Julia,' he said as he looked at the photograph. 'She was so beautiful and full of life, but then she got cancer and took a long while to die. She was in hospital at the end and went so quickly. I thought that was strange. How can something like the process of dying drag out so long and then the end come so suddenly that you're not prepared for it?'

'I don't know,' it was all Simon could think of to say and he was painfully aware that it was inadequate.

'The hospital rang work when she died. I was at a burglary. Harbour made the decision that I was not to be told that she had died until I had finished dealing with the burglary. Chief Inspector Harbour; he was only an inspector then, of course. He decided that he had the right to decide when I should be told about the death of my wife. He wanted his precious job to come first before anything else in the world. I fell to pieces of course when I found out. I asked them if I could have some compassionate leave and do you know what that little jumped up prick said?'

'No.'

'He said that he felt I would be better off at work rather than getting depressed at home. He may have been right, but that wasn't for him to say. Just because the Job means everything to him it doesn't mean that the rest of us should have to put up with it in the same way. He ended up allowing me to have one day off for the funeral and he had to be beaten into that he only wanted me to have half a day. I really hate that cunt.'

'You're not the only one.'

George put the photograph back on the mantel. 'I started smoking straight after the funeral.'

'You never smoked before?'

'No. Not so much as a quick one behind the bike sheds at school.'

'Why did you start?'

'I wanted to join Julia. I couldn't see any point in carrying on without her, but I've never been one for suicide. Far too dramatic for my liking. I could drink myself to death or I could smoke myself to death. Smoking won out as I couldn't strand all the throwing up from being drunk.'

'Jesus, George.'

'I wouldn't presume to know how you feel about your ex-wife or what matters were like with you, but Julia was the centre of my world. She was the beginning and the end. She saved my life and gave me a reason to get up each day and a reason to get into bed each night. She was everything to me and I just couldn't face the prospect of life without her. Smoking yourself to death seems to take far too long a time. I should have started it years ago. Amongst many other reasons that is also the reason why I hate my job. Harbour put the job before my wife and before my life. We all start out at the bottom in this job; all of us working the beat and freezing to death on nightshifts. We all do it; no matter what rank you might end up and yet you get to a certain rank and people like him seem to have that part of their brain removed that reminds them of where they came from and what it was like being in our boots. He thought that the Job was the answer to everything and the solution to all problems; and that is why I hate the job and I hate him. What gives him the right to decide such things about me?'

'I never knew.'

'Absolutely no reason why you should know,' George physically seemed to pull himself together in front of Simon's eyes as he had become hunched and Simon could have sworn that his face had become sunken and his eyes ringed with grey. 'So, how about some breakfast then shall we? We have a lot to talk about.'

***

Bacon sandwiches and strong cups of tea and coffee appeared to be what the police ran on for the majority of the time which was handy because that appeared to be George's idea of what they were going to have for breakfast. During the course of the meal they didn't talk about the subject that was perhaps upmost in their minds. Instead they talked about trivial matters until George had cleared away the table and then they sat down to talk about the more important matters.

'It isn't just the death of Julia that turned me against the job,' George continued when they were settled across from each other once again. 'I can't stand job-pissed people like Harbour, who clearly have no life outside of the job so have decided that they are going to make everyone's life in the job a bloody misery.'

'Things have been like that for years though.'

'They have. I find the hypocrisy so annoying. If you are favoured then there is nothing you can do wrong. How many times do you see "Chief Constable Good Work Recognitions" and commendations for things that you think "Hang on we do that all the time, why is this person being singled out and praised for something that we all do?"'

'That's a fair point; some people do seem to have gold shit when it comes to this job.'

'It isn't unique to this job, I know that; but this is the job that we are in so there isn't anything else that we can compare it to. We have to work with what we have got. I have seen so many officers in this job that are lazy and incompetent, but seem to get away with anything they like because they are able to charm the pants off of the person who is on the rung above them. It really fucks me off. I don't pretend to be a high flyer or someone that is going to set the world aflame. All I ever wanted to do was to be left alone and to do my job to the best of my ability.'

'They do seem to make it difficult.'

'And now there seem to be more and more people that sit in

227

specialist departments who keep issuing orders and instructions on what we should do; and all of the time it is things that will make their job easier whilst making our job more difficult. I hate this job.'

'There must be more to it than that though?'

'I don't like what the Government have done,' George shifted uneasily on the sofa. 'It seems that we are not allowed to criticise politicians any longer. Did you see that recent attack on that news reader because he said that nobody had been worth voting for in the last election?'

'Yeah, I did.'

'So, all the politicians come out of their second homes and attack him because he dares to criticise them whilst all the time, they are working to undermine us.'

'Well it's double standards. They have always been like that.'

'Maybe so; but they should remember that they are public servants the same as us and whereas they're quick to point the finger they're always slow to own up and take responsibility. If you don't want to face the criticism then you shouldn't have gone into that career. Isn't that exactly what they would say to us?'

'They think the public have lost faith in the police.'

'They want us to think that to hide the fact that the public have definitely lost faith in politicians. It's clear cut. Look at the last election; everyone you spoke to seemed to want Labour out, but there was so much entropy and apathy in the whole lot that nobody could get a majority so we landed with this circus of a coalition.'

'You would have thought that they had learnt their lesson from that.'

'They don't learn anything other than how to protect their own self interests. Two hundred years ago we have the energy and political oppositional drive to assassinate Perceval and these days people can hardly drag themselves to the polling stations let alone plan to kill off a Prime Minister.'

George had a lot of depths to him and his knowledge that a lot of people had no understanding of. He had done a good job of painting a picture of himself at work which was so distant from what he was really like that you would scarcely have believed that they were about the same person. Simon told him as much.

'Yeah, well I couldn't give a toss about what people think about me at work. Most of them are not worth giving the time of day to at any rate.'

'So,' said Simon trying to drag it back to the point. 'We seem to have both decided that the vigilante movement is worth a stab.'

'Yes, it would seem to be that way. Question is; are we going to carry on or are we going to quit it?'

'It seems a shame to walk away when we have just decided to make a stand.'

'It does rather, doesn't it? But with my wife gone and me hating the job I have nothing to lose other than my pension and the way that the Government are going that is hardly worth a piss any longer. What about you?

Simon thought about that for a moment. He certainly did not fancy the idea of prison, but that would only be a consequence if they were caught.

'What the hell. I'm in,' he finally said.

***

The idea of attacking the drug dealer's house still seemed to be a good idea so it was the plan that they stuck with for the moment. That night they found themselves in the wood once again waiting to ensure that there was nobody in the house.

'This vigilante shit is like Batman has turned out to be real,' Simon muttered as they crouched in the dark and the cold. George looked at him for a moment.

'Well, if that's true then you are Robin 'cos I sure as hell ain't.' Simon tried not to laugh out loud as it would not have seemed to have been the most sensible thing to do under the circumstances.

Whilst waiting he tried to take his mind off of the cold by thinking about what it was that they were going to do. The plan was to ensure that the house was empty and then break in, search rapidly for any drugs that might be there and destroy them. If they could do anything that made it look like it was a rival gang that had taken action then all the better. There was no chance that the matter was ever going to be reported to the police; and if it was then the full circumstances of what had happened was hardly going to be reported. On the off, remote chance that it was reported, however, then they were covered with regards to any forensic evidence that might be left there as this was a house that they had previously both done a drugs warrant on. Any contamination could be explained away by that. They still wore gloves but they were aware that there were a lot of other forensic evidence that you could leave behind at a scene. They were also aware of the fact that a lot of the tests that CSI, or SOCO as George still insisted on calling them, could run were expensive and unlikely to be wasted on a drug dealer's crime such as this one was going to be.

The chances are that even if the police did get to hear about it then it would be brushed under the carpet as nobody wanted to waste time, resources or money on investigating what was ultimately likely to be a drug debt issue or a rival gang being annoyed at another gang nudging into their territory. There was no such thing as equality under the law regardless of what people liked you to think. It was an illusion well maintained which is why every now and then someone from the upper class or a politician was thrown to the wolves and sent to prison for something, but it masked the number of cover ups that you never got to hear about. It worked at the other end of the spectrum as well. No doubt something that your average liberal person would find shocking; but then there are a lot of things that the liberals would find shocking if they only knew what was really going on in the world.

The intention tonight was to get in and out as quickly as possible. The plan was to destroy rather than to take things away with them which might have necessitated a lot of toing and froing. The only delay might be trying to locate the drugs, but they had both been on enough searches to know where people liked to hide their drugs; besides when doing a police search it had to be done neatly, tidy and with care ensuring that nothing was damaged and everything went back the way that it was found. Tonight, they could go on a rampage in ripping things apart to try and find what they were looking for and it didn't matter; in fact it only seemed to add to the justice of the matter.

'Okay,' said George finally. 'I think we're clear. Are you ready?'

'Yeah,' said Simon his breath clouding and his heart beating a lot faster than he expected that it would do.

'Let's go then.'

And they did.

Thirty-Four

If Simon had been feeling a little nervous before they went to do the drugs job then it was nothing to how he felt afterwards whilst they both waited to see if there would be any fallout about what had happened.

The job itself had gone pretty much according to their plan. They had got into the house easily enough; it is not too difficult when you know how. Once in they had quickly checked to make sure that there was nobody in the house and then had moved around in the dark using only low beam torches for light to disguise their movements from the outside.

Without the need to take care they had been able to rip and smash things which meant that they had found the drugs they were looking for in the space of ten minutes of searching. In the living room they came across a small stash of what looked like ecstasy tablets which had been hidden in a vase. Taking these, they took them into the kitchen and having boiled a kettle dropped them into a glass of boiling water which they hoped would be sufficient to render them useless by the time the owner discovered them.

Simon found a small packet of what certainly looked like cocaine hidden in the kitchen and having handed it to George he took it to the door and opening it shook the packet out into the breezy night and watched it all fly away on the wind into the garden which would make a fine coating for the morning to either arouse suspicion or be washed away.

Lastly, they discovered the cannabis factory that they had expected that they would find in the loft. There were a good forty or fifty saplings growing under the hydroponics as well as at least thirty mature plants. They immediately set about destroying them, breaking them, unearthing them and smashing the hydroponics set up to pieces.

They had not found the huge number of drugs that they might have hoped to have found, but they had certainly found more than any sane person could argue were for personal use. It was then that they had found a wad of £20 notes in a drawer which must have contained several hundred pounds. They took this with them and after having crushed a small set of scales under foot, George removed an aerosol can and sprayed the words 'GO NOW' on the living room wall. The intention being that it might look like a rival muscling in; or, as was more likely it would make the drug dealer paranoid about someone that he had double crossed or somehow annoyed in the past. That would hopefully be the outcome. They would then spend ages racking their brain (such as it was) trying to work out who it was that they had pissed off and who it was coming after them.

There was another outcome as well. With the loss of drugs it would mean that this particular pusher would be out of pocket. He would almost certainly have got these drugs from someone higher up the chain that may still be waiting for payment from when they had been sold on. That payment would now, of course, not be forthcoming, which would mean that someone higher up and far more important was going to be very angry with this particular individual and that would be a very nasty position to be in. These were certainly people that did not live within the rules of law and would think nothing about breaking the odd bone here and there or killing you off if they felt that you had betrayed them. All in all, it was potentially a good night of work they thought as they left and disappeared as quickly as they could back into the wood.

The pressure was on Simon and George now to see if the police would get wind of what had happened and if there would be an investigation. The timing had been crucial to this operation. They had planned it the night before they were due to start on an early shift. This meant that if the job was called in to the police there was a fair chance that it might not be called in until they were on shift. This meant that there was a chance that they might get deployed to it, which also meant that they might be able to cover their tracks or change anything on the crime report that they might need to if it came to light that they had made a mistake. You couldn't cover all eventualities. You could only do your best and hope that it worked out right.

At the beginning of each shift the sergeant taking the briefing would go over the crimes that had come in over the last twenty-four hours or so and this was probably one of the most tense moments for the pair as they sat there looking at the Smart Board and wondering if the result of their work was going to appear at any moment. It appeared that this was not to be the case though as the days went by and there was no mention of it.

The next thing that they had to do was to decide what to do with the money. A quick count of it had revealed that there was £500 in £20 notes that had been stuffed in an envelope in a drawer. They split the money in half and each took their half home and placed it somewhere out of the way but explainable should it ever be discovered. £250 in one place easier to explain than £500.

'We could keep it,' George had voiced.

'I did think about it, but I'm really not sure I'd be happy with some profit from drugs.'

'Well at least you could do some good with it rather than letting it go the wrong way.'

'If we keep this up then maybe that will be something to consider in the future, but at the moment perhaps something more charitable could be done with it.'

George pondered on this one for a short while and eventually they agreed that they would take the £500 and quietly drop it in the collection box that had been set up at the local hospital that were raising money for a new MRI machine. This seemed to be a good use of the money. It would no doubt come as a surprise when they next emptied the box to find a stack of £20 notes in there amongst the mostly coinage and odd £5 or £10 note that someone might have put in there. Simon began to feel that some good was being achieved; which was probably the most rewarding thing that they could hope for.

'You know,' he said to George over a pint one night. 'We could work our way through all the pushers and do this.'

'Nah,' said George shaking his head and wiping foam from his lip. 'They all talk to each other, don't they? It will not take too long for word to get around that something is going on and then one day we will walk into something where they are all tooled up; or worse.'

'True.'

'Word has probably already got around about what has happened to Jimmy; unless he is really trying to keep it under the covers so that nobody else knows about it. They can be like animals scenting when someone is wounded and moving in for the kill. One whiff from Jimmy that he is struggling and they will be all over him in an instant. It's a dog eat dog world for them and they are welcome to it.'

'Not much of a pension plan is there?'

'Most of them won't make pension age, you know that. One day they will either overdose or outlive their usefulness and be "retired". Still that's the life they have chosen so I don't have all that much sympathy for them.'

'Neither do I. They ruin enough lives so it doesn't matter to me all that much if their own lives are ruined in the process. It is the innocent people that concern me the most. They are the victims in all of this.'

'Indeed.'

Simon drank from his pint and considered how things were for a moment and how it was that events in his life had led him to be sitting here in this pub with George at this particular moment in time. 'Of course,' he continued after a while. 'If the public ever found out they would have a field day.'

'Best they don't find out then really,' said George as he continued his own pint. 'But then the public don't exactly have a great opinion of us at the best of times.'

'Well you aren't wrong about that,' Simon moodily said as he looked deeper into his pint as if he was certain that the answers to everything lay somewhere in amongst all the froth.

'The public have no understanding whatsoever of what it is that we do,' George continued. 'They have a very limited view of the police which is probably entirely based on the fact that their understanding of the police comes from traffic — which is probably where most members of the public have had contact with us in the past. They probably think that all we do is issue parking and speeding tickets.'

'Failing that they only come into contact with us because of the fact that we end up arresting them because they think that they can do whatever they damn well like because for some reason they think the law applies to other people.'

'Precisely. Most of them have absolutely no idea about the harder side of the job that we do and the things that we get up to. Most of them have never had to deal with somebody that is spread across the road after a car crash.'

'Or had to put the pieces together of someone who has jumped in front of a train.'

'I have had a long and bloody career,' George said deeply. 'I have seen so much shit over the years that most people wouldn't acquaint it with us. When I think of the hangings that I have been to; the suicides and the murders; the accidental deaths and grievous injuries and then you get some twat complaining because someone has upset them on Facebook. It absolutely staggers belief.'

'When you think about it along those lines you can see that a lot of what we are doing has a noble purpose.'

'Do you know, I remember a job I went to which must have happened fifteen years ago, maybe longer I don't know. I got called to a job that someone had heard shots being fired at this farm. Now, I didn't think anything of it — why would I? This is the country for God's sake and it's a farm. Shots are going off all the time, but for whatever reason someone thought it sufficiently suspicious to call it in to us.' George lapsed into silence.

'What happened?'

George looked up and seemed to come back from a distant past.

'Oh, I got there and there were two boys - eight and six years old if I remember correctly and anyway, they were living on the farm with their parents. Their parents had gone somewhere — I don't remember where and left these two boys with an old housekeeper or cook or something who was as deaf as a post. Took me ages to get the old bat to hear me knocking at the door. And then when I eventually got to the bottom of it, I found out that these two boys had been playing in one of the fields and one of them, I don't remember which, had wanted to play cowboys and Indians — does anyone play that anymore?'

'I doubt it,' said Simon quietly. 'Probably not politically correct these days.'

'Well, they went to play at cowboys and Indians and one of them thought that it would be much more realistic if they used their father's guns. Being a farmer he, of course had guns around the place but he was a little lax at keeping them locked up and so one of the lads went to get the gun so that they could play better; and that's what the caller heard. I didn't know it at the time, of course, this was all pieced together later. All I knew was that as I was talking to the housekeeper this little boy, this eight-year-old comes in covered in blood and he is crying and he says "Jimmy won't play anymore". So, I eventually find out that Jimmy is lying at the bottom of the field with a hole blown right through his head.'

'Jesus.'

'Yeah. And what can you do now. One boy dead the other destined to therapy and probably the rest of his life in an institution. Below the age of criminal responsibility, of course, so no prosecution, no arrest, no reckoning; but how can you survive a thing like that at the age of eight and not spend the rest of your life locked up in some nut house?'

'I don't know.'

'There probably isn't a day that has gone by without me thinking of that boy and the look on his face as he stood there covered in blood, crying his eyes out because he had just accidentally executed his six-year-old brother. And then you do public order and get some drunk twat tell you that he can do whatever he likes because he pays your wages. Where is the justice in it? No. No, the public don't understand what it is that we do.'

Simon was at a loss for words for the time being. They all dealt with difficult things in the course of their work, but dealing with things that happened to children was always difficult.

'I eventually tracked down the parents and there wasn't anyone else to go and tell them what had happened. There had been a big car crash or something and everyone was tied up so I had to go and tell them what happened. It was a lovely sunny day, bright sunshine, birds singing and I drove down this country lane and at the bottom of it was the house where they were visiting some friends. I drove down there and I got closer and closer and with every foot I travelled I thought that at the end of this road is a couple who are enjoying some time with their friends going about their normal lives and happy. They have no idea that I am the harbinger of death and I'm coming down the lane and not only am I going to change their lives but I'm going to destroy their lives as well.

After I leave, their lives will never be the same again.'

George and Simon sat in silence for a few moments each of them lost within their own thoughts. Eventually George drained his glass.

'We can't sort out all the problems of the world, Simon; but I suppose we can certainly do our small bit, which is probably more than what we will be able to achieve by sticking to the system.

'Well somebody has certainly got to do something.'

'Indeed. Well, come on, drink up, Robin. It's time that Batman was returning to the Batcave. I'm absolutely knackered.'

Thirty-Five

Before he knew where he was the approach to Christmas was upon Simon and it would soon be another year over and getting ready for a new one to begin. He took a very small degree of comfort from the fact that the turn of the year would bring him one step closer to retirement, although to be honest retirement had been put a little further away now thanks to the work of some of the enterprisingly lazy and corrupt members of Her Majesty's Government.

Christmas was a difficult time for the police. Crime would inevitably go up on a number of fronts. Firstly, there would be an increase in burglaries as your average burglar would find it hard to resist all of the extra Christmas presents that were under the tree. Naturally because of the fact that you wanted your neighbours and everyone else to be able to see your splendid twinkly lights on your Christmas tree you would put it near a window so that Mr Burglar could also see it and make a very quick assessment looking at your presents to decide whether or not they were worth breaking in for and stealing. Bearing in mind that your average burglar would break into your house to steal a packet of cigarettes it was always worthwhile. You might as well have put labels on all the presents addressed 'To Mr Burglar, Merry Christmas.'

Simon considered burglars to be amongst the lowest form of scum that walked the face of the planet. In many cases the victims of burglary would never be able to afford to go out and buy again the presents for their children that had been stolen and it would be a poorer Christmas for a lot of people because of the selfishness of the one. The irony of the burglary that George had committed was not lost on Simon and he knew that Mr Mitchell would have a poorer Christmas this year having to spend all of his money on rebuilding everything that had been taken from him, but that is what you got for stealing from charities. It was karma as far as he was concerned. Perhaps he would have a number of relatives that would be pleased to buy him many of the things that he had lost. He hoped not.

As well as burglaries there would be a rise in shoplifting as well. People would be stealing for Christmas presents, believe it or not. Some even had the chutzpah to go into the shops with a list of items that they would steal so that your average low life thief would have something nice to give their loved ones at Christmas. If you were in the know you could even provide your local thief with a list of things that you wanted and they would steal them for you for a really very reasonable price. Some of these people were career criminals; others were people that had been pushed to the line having had their wages cut and were trying to make ends meet buying food for their families and making sure they stayed warm over the coming winter. The only way they could add to the Christmas presents was to steal. For many of them it would be difficult enough to pay the rent this winter or to keep the mortgage payments up. The pressure of not being able to buy presents for their children was too much. Long gone were the days when the children would be happy to open their Christmas stocking and discover that they had a small wooden toy and a piece of fruit in there. It was no excuse when you were caught though, as these would be the most likely ones that were caught in the end.

The crime that Simon had never understood over the festive period was the drink related public order offences. Simon had trouble understanding why it was that some people felt the need to go out every Friday and Saturday night and get so paralytic that they could hardly stand, get into fights and then get themselves arrested. It was something that was beyond his comprehension, but then this was probably because he had a modicum of intelligence. He was all for going out for a good time and having a laugh, but it had to be people with a very low number of neurons knocking about in their brain that felt that getting into a fight and getting arrested was the ideal night out. The sad thing was that the women were just as bad as the men. In fact, in some cases they were worse than the men.

Come the next morning many of them didn't give a toss and would go out and do it again the following weekend. Others would sober up and wake up in their tiny little cell and would be horrified by what they had done. It was clear that these people should never be allowed to go near alcohol ever again. Whose fault was it? Certainly, it was your own fault if you allowed yourself to get so drunk that you no longer had any rational thinking ability, but it was also the fault of the Government. You may think it is a little ludicrous to blame the Government for what idiotic individuals decide to do to themselves on a weekend, but at essence they were to blame and the reason was simple: greed.

Some time ago they had introduced the all-night drinking laws which had moved away from the archaic laws which closed pubs at eleven in the evening and clubs by two in the morning. Very few people knew that these laws had been bought in for the First World War and were there to try and prevent soldiers on leave and munitions workers in the factory from getting completely bladdered whenever they could. For some reason, someone in the Government had thought that after experiencing the likes of the Somme your average Tommy might want to get pissed. It is hard to imagine why. They also couldn't have munition workers getting drunk and failing to show up for work because of hangovers and thereby disrupting the war effort. The licencing laws had been bought in and nobody had ever seen fit to remove them after the war ended. Perhaps politicians were a more sober lot back in those days and less greedy than they are today.

Many years later the Government of the day had looked towards the continent and seen how civilised the French were at drinking all hours of the day and had decided to get rid of these archaic laws and allow places to stay open all of the time. This, of course, meant that they would receive an extremely large boost in taxation from all the extra alcohol that was now being bought and sold. It was really a very good situation for them and they would rub their hands together in an excited way whilst thinking about their next pay rise and passing it off on the guise of they were only doing it for the public that they were of course here to serve.

Alcohol related crime immediately went through the roof. Government Ministers scratched their heads and couldn't work out why it was happening in England and not happening in France. The answer to that is very simple. Culture. The French are brought up to drink moderately and socially. They have no concept of the idea of going out at a weekend and trying to force as many pints of lager down their throat as it is humanly possible to do. The French would sit at their café tables and sip their red wine whilst looking towards England and silently shaking their heads.

The Government tried to rationalise what they had done by saying that people would binge drink up until eleven and the quick consumption of alcohol in a short space of time meant that they would get very drunk and very violent. By staying open longer people could moderate their drinking over a longer period and it would see an end to binge drinking. This was a noble sentiment, and was exactly what was happening on the continent. So why didn't it work? It was that little word again: culture. It did not take into account your average piss head that saw it as an opportunity to simply drink more over a longer period, but at the same rate that they had done so before. Others, and for some reason this seemed to focus largely on groups of women, realised that to go out from eight in the evening until five in the morning and drink the required amount needed to make sure you didn't know what planet you were on would cost a lot of money. The solution was to all meet up before going out and between you down a bottle or two of vodka that you have thoughtfully been able to get from the promotional display of your local supermarket that were encouraging you to go and get out of your head.

There were people who were out there who lived only for this weekend escape. All of their money and all of their time was devoted to this weekly hedonistic debacle. These were the people who had nothing else in their lives and somehow convinced themselves that they were having a good time. This is what they did and this is what your average police officer would have to face each weekend. Many resented being dragged away from the important things that the police were required to do by putting so many resources into babysitting members of the public who really should know better.

This is what every weekend was like for the police, drunken people staggering out of clubs and pubs and picking fights with other people because of some imagined slight that may or may not have actually happened; or starting a fight because they were by nature just violent individuals that really didn't deserve to be allowed to walk around draining society. What amazed most of the police officers was the fact that so many of them were unemployed and yet still managed to go out and get so drunk all of the time. Perhaps this hid a more depressing picture behind the scenes of families that were struggling to make ends meet because the male (usually) had decided to go and literally piss away the only income that they were ever going to get because he was too lazy, too drunk and too useless to ever get a real job. These are the people that without a trace of irony would then tell officers 'I pay your wages,' when the police tried to stop them from killing themselves or hurting someone else. Your average law-abiding member of the public would be horrified if they saw the scenes that went on in some of the towns and cities of this country after these drunken fools had erupted onto the streets.

Simon couldn't understand why they did this really. It certainly wasn't his idea of fun; but what he really couldn't understand was why they would do it at Christmas. Simon had worked numerous Christmas Eve's over the years and it didn't matter what day of the week it was Christmas Eve was your Friday and Saturday night combined — actually it was worse. It could be hell on earth and almost certainly was. For whatever reason the drunken fools that wasted their weekends away would do the same on Christmas Eve and yet it was *Christmas Eve.* Was there any sparkle of intelligence left in their brain that made them think that they were sailing close to spending their Christmas in a cell? Usually they would push it and push it and then once they were arrested would start wailing about spending Christmas Day in a cell when they had a little child at home that would not be able to see their mummy/daddy on Christmas now. In their own brains they seemed to think that it was the fault of the police officers that they would not be spending Christmas with their families rather than their own stupid fault. As a matter of fact, your average police officer would give the drunkard numerous opportunities to leave the area and go home before eventually having to resort to laying hands on. There are some people that you just can't help and who can't see that you are trying to help them.

It staggered belief really and was simply beyond reasonable explanations. The only explanation that Simon had come up with was either these were people that were just naturally stupid and had no concept of what they were doing or alcohol was destroying the country.

Most police officers would tell you that the majority of crime was motivated or fuelled by alcohol. Politicians liked to go on about the drug problems that the country had and the war that existed on drugs; but the biggest drug problem was alcohol.

Could you ever ban alcohol? Look to America to see how successful that had been during Prohibition. The problem was a class one once again in this classless society that had so thoughtfully been created. On the one hand you had the working class who would go out and drink pints of lager that was nicknamed 'wife-beater,' which really should be a warning to anyone. The consequences have already been described. On the other end of the scale you had the upper classes having cocktail parties, consuming bottles of wine over dinner and sipping brandy and sherry in the club every night. Strangely enough this latter group rarely seemed to erupt onto the streets in evening wear and call police officers 'cunts.' Make of it what you will.

Simon did wonder whether this was a new feature of recent generations or whether history was littered with the drunk who wanted to get out of their head every weekend and cause problems. It was possible that this was not a new thing, but he imagined that if you behaved like this back in the Middle Ages then the local Baron would just have your head cut off. He was reminded that they used to put people in the stocks for drunkenness and for a brief moment he allowed his mind to wander into fantasy at the thought of a Magistrate passing out for a sentence that someone guilty of drunk and disorderly had to spend four hours in the stocks in the middle of the city. No doubt the Human Rights people would jump up and down about this moaning about civil liberties, but it probably would clear up a lot of alcohol related crime. Interesting how these civil rights groups never seemed to jump up and down about the rights of the victim.

If you were working a night on Christmas Eve into Christmas Day itself then you would just about get a grip on the public order situation by four o'clock in the morning if you were lucky which was when a lot of families would be waking up, particularly if they had children, to open their Christmas presents. All over the country people would be getting out of bed and fighting against the cold they would hurry down to get the fire going, put the turkey in the oven, put the Christmas lights on and play Bing Crosby. It was a lovely scene. For the police around about this time the domestics would start to come in as people started to argue about the presents that they had got from each other. Started to argue over who was cooking the dinner. Started to argue about whose relatives were more important and so on. It wouldn't be unusual for someone to have been arrested by half five Christmas morning for a domestic argument that had got out of hand.

Merry Christmas everybody.

***

Another problem that came with Christmas was the shift Christmas outing which was one of the few outings that Simon never seemed to be able to excuse himself from. As a rule, he tried to steer clear of all of the things that the shift liked to do 'as a shift' outside of work. He still couldn't entirely get around the fact that you spent so much time with them and then would choose to spend more time with them outside of the work environment. It was alright if you got on with them, but you could find a very mixed bunch in the police and you didn't always get on well with them.

He was also slightly irritated by one member of the shift who for whatever reason had elected himself to be entertainments manager and would organise all of the events. He pressured people into collections for when people were celebrating births, marriages and the like and made everyone take part in Secret Santa each year. He organised all of this because he liked to be in control and he liked to be the centre of attention. It covered up for the fact that he was the least liked member of the shift. Disliked for his laziness and the fact that he would always try and find a way of getting out of doing jobs, with the inevitable result that someone else would be shafted with it. He also seemed to be able to do whatever he liked. He could come in late, go home early and get away with things that half of the other members of the team would never be allowed to do. He seemed to have the sergeants wrapped round his little finger and that tends to lead to suspicion as to what it is that the person has in hold over the sergeants. George was just prepared to sit and watch and wait for his inevitable fall which would eventually come the day he tried his tricks on with someone that was immune to his ways; when that day came there would be a spectacular crucifixion.

'What goes around comes around,' he muttered to Simon once when this officer was being particularly annoying. 'You just wait and see.'

In the meantime, the Christmas meal was organised and it was time for Simon to drag himself out and join the rest of the team and pretend that he was as merry as they seemed to be over the looming prospect of Christmas which for him just seemed to bring misery. For Simon, without a family, it was really just another working day. It seemed strange to him that there were people out there, normal people, with regular jobs and regular lives who never gave any thought at all to the idea that there were people that had to work Christmas.

Thirty-Six

All of this paints a very bleak view of what is actually going on across the country and within the ranks of the police. Most members of the public are blissfully unaware of the truth of the situation and are happy to remain in ignorance of the truth; and it is right that they should. Nobody would eat sausages if you got to see how they were made. It was the same with the way that the country was run.

Politicians would stand up in the Commons and attack people that had dared to tell the truth. If every now and then a police officer was to write a blog exploding the truth of what it was like you could rest assured that someone in the House of Commons would stand up and say it was a minority and it wasn't like that in the police at all. The question is: how would they know? Any politician that came out on a fact ignoring expedition amongst the police would never get a true representation of what was actually going on and what it was like.

From time to time politicians would come out with the police to see for themselves what was going on. They would give plenty of notice that they were doing this to allow the police to get in extra staff so it looked like resources were flush and they would inevitably go home by about one in the morning so would leave before the action really started. They would go away thinking that all was well. Sergeants and inspectors would hand pick the officers that the politician was allowed to come into contact with whilst they were out. There was no way that they would allow a politician to come into contact with someone that would actually tell the truth.

It was all rather bizarre really as this only served to mask the truth of the situation rather than actually taking the politician showing them the truth and saying 'look you broke it, see what you have done? Now what the hell do you propose to do about it?' The police were very good at shooting themselves in the foot and not defending themselves enough. The police were also one of the few jobs that meant you were criticised by the public for doing your job and criticised by the hierarchy within the police for not doing your job. You couldn't really win if the truth were known. There was always someone who was prepared to stick it into you.

There probably were a small group of people somewhere hidden away in a cave or something who never got out all that much who thought that actually politicians were really doing a very good job and were easy targets. If such a group of people did exist then they really were a very small minority who would probably keep their mouths shut when faced with the majority of the rest of the country that would probably have gladly brought back stoning for politicians that crossed the line.

Nobody can deny that it is probably a very difficult job, assuming that you were doing it properly. It obviously was impossible to please everyone in politics so you had to accept the fact that no matter what it was that you did you were going to piss somebody off. It wasn't really policy decisions that annoyed people all that much, although brainless out of touch policies that showed that you only had the faintest of grasps as to what was going on in the country didn't help. No; what really annoyed everyone, was the corruption.

The sex scandals and the expenses fiasco had damaged politicians to a point where recovery was likely to be difficult if not impossible. To an extent though it was their own fault. One of two things were happening. Either, politics attracted a large number of people that were either sex addicts, sexual deviants and downright liars; or decent people went into politics and almost overnight were corrupted by the power and ended up being sex addicts, sexual deviants and downright liars. In reality it was probably a bit of both.

The reason for this was clear to see across the board. We don't really need to spend any time talking about Parliament; we can take that as read. If you turned your focus to the police then there were two interesting groups. Firstly, it was a given fact that if you climbed sufficiently high enough up the ranks then you ceased to be a police officer and you became a politician. The number of chief officers that had got themselves involved in scandal over expenses or being caught lying could only have secured them a place in the Cabinet immediately. It was like they couldn't help themselves. There they were at the top of their game and they were milking if for everything that it was worth.

Some argument had taken place recently because the idea was suggested that officers of a certain rank could be graduate entries from university and as they were managers, they didn't really need to be warranted police officers. Police officers across the country jumped up and down at this in anger. They might be many things but they took comfort from the fact that the person sitting in the chief constable's chair of any Force had once been at the bottom of the pile and had worked nights, walked the beat and done all the things that every other officer had done; granted they may not have done it for all that long a time, but they had nevertheless done it. You couldn't enter at certain ranks; every police officer entered at the bottom and worked their way up. If you suddenly introduced people who were not police officers at these high ranks then they simply would not understand what it meant to be police officers having never experienced it and the results would be disastrous. There was truth in this, but it was slightly flawed by the fact that those of such high rank were so distanced from being on the front line that they really didn't have a clue about the police anyway so ultimately when it came down to it, it didn't really matter.

The second group of people who were worth looking at were the police commissioners. These were people that had been bought in to be crime commissioners who were civilians and could sack chief constables if they wanted to. The public didn't want them. This was clear by the fact that so few voted for them because they really didn't care or understand what it was that they were meant to be doing. In the short time that they had been in several of them had already been involved in scandal and allegations of expenses fiddling — why? The answer was simple, because they were politicians.

***

The Right Honourable Sarah Newton, Member of Parliament, was a politician who has already briefly appeared within this narrative. It is possible to see that a lot of negative things have been said about politicians and it is probably time that the record was set straight. There are MPs out there who entered politics because they wanted to make a difference and do good. These people are dedicated individuals that work hard and truly are servants of the people. They put in long hours and are involved at numerous different levels of government. They work hard all of the time to ensure that the people they represent have a voice. They stand up for the things that you need and when you are in difficulty, they will fight your corner for you. They are noble people and they work hard. They earn every penny of their salary. They do not fiddle their expenses. They are not involved in sex scandals and they have never broken the law or asked anyone to lie for them. These politicians bemoan the fact that they are never heard of. Why? Simply because of the fact that the press and the public prefer to hate their politicians rather than admire them. These politicians are just as disgusted as you are over the scandal that goes on in politics. Like the police, these people are in a thankless job with the uphill, almost impossible task of trying to do what is right. These people are magnificent and should be applauded and it is important to know that Sarah Newton was not one of these people.

The word that you would probably use for Newton was hypocrite. She would get very annoyed and agitated when politicians were criticised and she would stand up and be very vocal about defending her colleagues whilst at the same time being guilty of all of the accusations that were being thrown about. Her belief was that you could do whatever you liked so long as you didn't get caught out. Play the indignant party until such time as you were caught out and then if you were caught out you could break down in tears and blame someone else for why it is that you did whatever it was that you were caught doing. She had once been embroiled within the expenses scandal and had gone on *Newsnight* and cried her eyes out to Jeremy Paxman claiming that it was the pressure of working so hard for your country that you couldn't always keep track of what it was that you were doing and, of course, because you were so busy with serving the needs of the many you had to rely on others to assist you with the paperwork and it was hardly your fault if some of those people were a little less scrupulous than you were yourself. Judging from the look on his face Paxman had believed her about as much as Simon had when he was watching it.

She had fiddled her expenses and she was not alone in having done this. Why had she done this? Because it was the norm, everyone was doing it so what could possibly be wrong in the fact that she was doing what everyone else was doing? If she wasn't involved then she would actually have been at a disadvantage compared to her colleagues and there was no way that she was going to allow that to happen. It was a mystery to Simon why it was that politicians so felt the need to fiddle expenses. It was almost as if they couldn't help themselves as if it was some kind of addiction. Perhaps they should be pitied rather than ridiculed.

There were so many things that the public hated about politicians that it was almost impossible to nail it down to one thing if you had to. Simon ultimately settled on the fact that what he hated most about them was their sense of self-righteousness and if there was one thing that Sarah Newton MP could do well it was self-righteousness. In her own mind her being a Member of Parliament was her God given right and she was entitled to everything that came with it, all of the perks whether they were legal or not.

She had an expensive lifestyle to keep up. She did have two homes that needed to be run, but that was because she was to all intents and purposes separated from her husband although in the public eye they were still together. He lived in one house with his young boyfriend who was only just legal and she lived in her other home where she was able to entertain a number of callers and indulge in the freedom that she wanted so much. She despised her husband for the potential scandal that he had created and the deal was that he kept his mouth shut and out of the way but would make public appearances with her on demand in return for her allowing him to live at her expense; or rather the expense of the public for that is where the money came from.

You might pity her for this situation and wonder why in the modern times that we live in she just didn't divorce her husband and fall back on public sympathy which could only really do her a lot of good. The answer was that her husband knew too much about her and if they were to divorce, he could easily make public her cocaine habit and the fact that she had a tendency to use male and female prostitutes from time to time.

In this regard she was really just your typical politician.

Newton was just as dangerous as the likes of Chief Inspector Harbour as she too was fuelled by ambition and one day saw herself as being Prime Minister and did not care who she had to sleep with or stab in the back, or possibly both, in order to get there. Really, she had no redeeming features at all; unfortunately, some people are just like that. It is the way that they are. She lacked empathy; she could just not see things from anyone's point of view other than her own and couldn't understand why other people would not be working for the benefit of her.

Presumably this is why she had gone into politics in the first place.

Thirty-Seven

The Christmas work-do was something that could be depressing at the best of times, but Simon really wasn't in the mood for it tonight. You might get the impression that he hated his colleagues and dreaded the idea of spending time with them, but this was not the case. Despite the steady destruction of morale which the Government and the police hierarchy had seen fit to implement as policy, there was still a huge amount of comradery amongst the troops that were on the front line taking the shots from all directions. It wasn't politically correct to refer to them as troops any longer, but political correctness or not, that is what they were. It had surprised Simon exactly how much humour there was and there was a special bond that existed between colleagues that were in the same boat as you were.

The simple fact of the matter though was that the team were divided into groups. There were those that you were friendly with and perhaps socialised outside of work with, and would actually class as friends more than colleagues. There were others who you were not really friends with although you were still pleasant and worked well with. These were not necessarily people that you would see outside of work, but had no issues with crewing up with and working together. The last group were the ones that you couldn't stand the sight of. You would prefer not to be seen dead in their company outside of work and you despised the idea of crewing up with them. There were, fortunately, not all that many of the last group and those that might end up in it were officers that were either lazy or incompetent. Being crewed up with them would mean that you would have to do all of the work or it could mean that if the balloon went up you would be on your own because they were about as much use in a tricky situation as a chocolate fireguard.

They had gone for a curry for their Christmas meal which was not exactly a traditional meal to have during the festive season, but curry along with kebabs seemed to feature as the staple diet of preferred food for the majority of police officers. Every now and then there would be ridicule of the police for not being fit. It was hardly surprising really as the shift pattern meant that you had to eat a lot of crap, missed meals frequently and of course there were medical reports which indicated that shift patterns and working nights in particular were exceedingly bad for your health. All in all, you had to be pretty insane to want to do this job for the so little back that you got for it and the amount of grief that was now evidenced that you had to go through.

It had surprised Simon a great deal that George had turned up for the Christmas meal. He seemed less inclined to mingle with his fellows than Simon was. Once the meal was over and they were free to wander into the bar they were able to talk to each other. Having made sure that there was nobody in the immediate area and that the nosy members of the shift in particular were preoccupied with trying to work out the latest gossip, they convened to discuss what was likely to happen next.

'You still want to continue with this?' Simon had asked.

'Do you want to pull out?' George knew how to answer a question with a question. Any police officer worth their salt was good at asking questions, but not so good at answering them.

'No. There's something to be said about quitting whilst you're ahead, but I don't think we've gone as far as we could yet.'

'There're a few things left that we could do. It would be rather difficult to know when to stop really.'

'There's a danger that we might get a taste for it and end up liking it too much,' commented Simon as he sipped at his two fingers of gin and top up of tonic.

'True.'

'I still think we should only target individuals that have no sympathy within the public gaze though.' They thought about this for a moment.

'Banker, maybe?' asked Simon.

'Well, it's true that they're top of the list of people that are in general despised by the public. I'm rather impressed myself really at how they manage to bring the country to its knees and get bailed out by *us* and still manage to retain an air of arrogance.'

'It would be enormously satisfying to have a pop at them.'

'Nah,' George shook his head. 'Too complicated. I think we would be overstretching ourselves a little too much if we tried to do a bank job.'

'Of course, if we were to do something like that it might change the motivation slightly.'

'How do you mean?' George sipped on his pint and despite having just eaten a meal opened a packet of crisps which he then liberally doused with Worcestershire sauce.

'Well so far what we have done we have done for justice and to set the record straight.'

'Yes, ripping a bank off would arguably be justice as well.'

'Yes, it would, but then the motivation might also be to keep the money for ourselves. Instead of doing all of this for the nobler of reasons we would just become robbers who wanted to vanish into the night with a sack load of money.'

George thought about this. 'Can't say that we didn't deserve it. Doesn't look like the Government are going to give us fuck all.'

'What are you two talking about?'

This last was from Katy Waterhouse who had suddenly appeared next to them at the bar and scared the shit out of Simon who almost choked on his drink as he had been in mid-sip at her appearance.

'Not a lot,' George said who appeared to be the epitome of cool.

'Honestly,' said Katy as she collected her drink order. 'You two are as thick as thieves these days. Always chatting in dark corners.' She chuckled to herself and walked off whilst the other two shared a look and a smile. Before anything else could be discussed between them they were joined by Sergeant Baker who appeared to have had a little more alcohol than he perhaps should have had.

'Lads.'

'Skipper.' They both acknowledged noticing the pecking order and the fact that Baker had referred to George as one of the lads despite being at least ten years younger than him.

'Enjoying yourself?' asked George.

'Shit job though ain't it?' was Baker's reply which was unusual as they had not even mentioned the job. It seemed to be something of an obsession with most police officers, however, that they couldn't stop talking about the job; either positively or more often than not negatively.

'Why did you become a police officer?' Simon asked this as it was a question that he had been asking himself a lot lately, chiefly in the hope that he would come up with some kind of answer that would not have meant that Amanda had been right all along. He asked it of Baker as the man always seemed to be so down with the job that it was more of a mystery as to what he was doing there in the first place.

'I fell in love.'

This was not perhaps the answer that he had been expecting, so they waited in silence to see what Baker might say next. Intrigued despite themselves.

'I was fifteen at the time, because that was my age you see?' They both nodded wondering exactly how much he really had drunk. 'Fell in love with this wonderful girl. Would have done anything for her I would. Didn't have much money at the time. Well I was fifteen, you see? She liked this video and I wanted to buy it for her as a present, but I couldn't afford it, so I nicked it, you see?'

'Shoplifting?' A rather obvious question, but they were both taken back by this startling revelation which had come from their normally strait-laced Sergeant.

'Yeah, I never got caught or anything; but I later felt so guilty about it that I felt the need to somehow reset the balance and rectify it all. Of course, I didn't tell my interview board that this was the reason why I wanted to be a copper.'

'I suppose they may have frowned upon it,' said George with a smile.

'Could have done. Can't remember what the video was now. Long time ago.' Baker seemed to stare off into the middle distance for a short while as if trying to summon up memories that had long since slipped from his grasp. 'Can't have been all that good.'

'And do you feel you have made amends now?' asked George with a twinkle in his eye. All he got in return was a snort and then a moment longer of silence.

'Do you know what they're thinking of doing now?' Baker asked all of a sudden.

'Who?'

'What?'

Both questions were equally valid.

'I read the other day,' Baker continued ignoring the question of who? 'that they're thinking of putting adverts on the side of police cars now.'

'You're kidding?' said Simon wondering exactly how much Baker really had drunk this evening.

'Straight up, I kid you not,' he continued.

'What the fuck for?'

'Well as you know the Government in their infinite wisdom have cut back on policing budgets and told us all that we have to cut hundreds of thousands of pounds and save money. Now the immediate knock on effect of this is less officers on the front line. However, in desperation to try and keep the money coming in, some chiefs are looking at sponsorship.'

'Unbelievable.' George was shaking his head in desperation.

'Totally true. We can re-coop money by having *Police — sponsored by Tesco* written down the side of the cars.'

'Well I suppose every little does help.'

'I swear to God,' Baker continued. 'I've absolutely no idea what this country is coming to any longer. Cameron has fucked us all over big time.' He shook his head and wandered off elsewhere.

'Well, that's different, I grant you,' said George as he watched him go. 'Nothing really surprises me about all of this anymore.'

'I always think that things can't become any more farcical than they already are; and just when I think we have reached the very depths of it; I find that there is still further that we can fall.' Simon shook his head and drained the remainder of what was left in his glass.

There wasn't all that much left to the evening after that. Baker had managed to puncture some of the atmosphere by reminding them of the stupidity of the situation that they were in and so they had gathered their coats and discreetly slipped away leaving Katy on the dance floor doing some things that she would ultimately live to regret when she sobered up. Simon and George stood outside and smoked a cigarette whilst contemplating the evening and what the future might bring.

'Politicians,' said George suddenly.

'What about them?'

'They're hated just as much as bankers. Who would trust a politician these days?'

'Well, probably nobody. What's your point?'

'Maybe that should be out next mark; a politician. What do you think?'

Simon thought about this for a moment whilst taking the last drag on his cigarette. 'I think that if you think a banker is too hard a target to get to, then how the hell are we going to get to a politician?'

George reflected on this for a moment whilst he finished his own cigarette and then immediately reached into his pocket and lit himself another one. When it was alight, he turned again to Simon.

'There are probably ways. All it takes is a little thought that's all.' And with that he waved and with one hand in pocket and the other hand occupied with his cigarette he walked off in a cloud of smoke into the damp Christmas night.

Thirty-Eight

'This isn't really going to be as easy as you thought it might be, is it?' said Simon as he gazed in wonder at George's log fire which he was fascinated by, as like so many things in George's house he had not seen the like since his grandparents had died in the late 1980s.

George sat on the opposite side of the fire and stared into it for some time without answering, seemingly without even having heard the question.

'I grant you, it probably is more of a challenge than I had let on it was,' he eventually commented.

'A bit more of a challenge?'

'Quite a lot more of a challenge, if I'm honest,' he consented as he continued to look into the flames.

'How do we get at a politician?' It was a question that Simon had asked several times over the last few days and there had never been an answer returned. 'Okay, so we get the guy who stole from the charity and return the money to charity — that's justice, I can see that.'

George grunted.

'We then hit the drug dealer which is again a no brainer, self-explanatory.'

Another grunt.

'All of that I can see and understand as fitting in with the justice element of what we have been trying to do.'

'Do you think hitting a politician would not be justice?' George finally commented as he leaned forward to poke at the fire as it appeared to be faltering slightly.

'No, I think it would. It certainly would be to us because of the fact that the politicians of this country have given us a right royal screwing over. A lot of the public would probably like it as well because there is no sympathy for politicians out there at the moment. I just wonder if we are setting our sights a little too high.'

'You think we should aim a little lower then?'

'Well, we agree that a banker is a bit out of our league and virtually untouchable. I think a politician might just be in the same bracket.'

'Possibly. So, what do you want to do; hit a paedophile?'

'We have to think very carefully about what it is that we want to achieve here George. We hit Mitchell—'

'I hit Mitchell, you mean?'

'Granted, you hit Mitchell because of the fact that you were convinced of his guilt and he had escaped justice. Hitting him was a means of balancing the records. I've no problem with that at all.'

'Good. Bit late if you had really.'

'So, Jimmy the old drug dealer gets hit to take the drugs off of the streets and to hit him where it will hurt him the most. With any luck we might force him to leave the area if he thinks he has muscled into someone else's territory as well.'

'Granted; although I doubt we have put him out of action.'

'That was never the intention to put him out of action. There is only one way to put someone like him out of action.'

'I don't want anything violent.'

'Exactly. I agree with you if we resort to violence then we are no better than the scum bags that we are supposed to be putting away in the first place.'

'Of course,' said George thinking it over. 'There are those that would say that having crossed the line that we have and by having done the things that we have done that we are no better than them now anyway.'

'True; but I still think we have to live by some moral code even if the criminals don't. There isn't even honour among thieves any longer these days. It's a dog eat dog world.'

'Okay; so, what about a paedo then?'

'Again, it comes back to what you want to achieve. It's a given fact that the public hate any crimes to do with children and sex crimes are right up there so it wouldn't exactly get a lot of sympathy if you were to do something against a paedo, but what? We can't resort to violence ourselves and if we "out" one of them publicly then we could run the risk of being the catalyst of causing the vigilante mob to be the ones that do the violence.'

'But it wouldn't be us doing it?'

'It wouldn't be us doing it, but it would just be semantics. We would have been the ones that started it rolling so we might as well have just done it.'

'And we don't want to do that.'

'What about if we planted incriminating material on someone and then had them prosecuted legitimately?'

'We could, but then if they are "at it" then we shouldn't really need to plant anything and if we did to an innocent person then we would be no better off than things were back in the seventies. Plus, of course, there is the problem of where we get the "stuff" from. We can hardly make it walk out of the evidence room any longer when everything is audited so much and could so easily be traced back to where it came from.'

They both lapsed into silence once again.

'It's actually quite difficult to break the law when you are still governing yourself with so many rules,' Simon eventually offered up.

'You're not wrong. I still favour the idea of hitting a politician hard though.'

'Okay, well what would be hard for a politician?'

'Losing face? Being caught out at something?'

'Could be,' Simon nodded. 'However, that sounds like due process of law. You might as well just hunt them down the traditional way.'

'What if we found something and leaked it to the press?'

'Found during a burglary, you mean?'

'Yeah.'

'Problem would be that would the press touch anything gained in a less than legitimate manner?'

'Well, look at the phone hacking thing.'

'True and I doubt they will have learnt any lessons from that.'

'The problem,' said George thinking over his own argument, 'is that it would all be dependent on actually finding something incriminating during a burglary.'

'And we can't actually be sure of that.'

'No, we can't.'

They both stared into the fire for a few moments as the wood cracked and popped. The gaze was intense as if they were both hoping that the answer to the questions that they wanted would somehow be located in the flames.

'Of course, if we did find something incriminating,' Simon said after a while. 'We don't have to hand it to the press; we could use it to our own advantage.'

'Blackmail?'

'Why not?'

'Hell of a risk of being caught by doing that though.'

'Would sort the pension out.'

'Tricky business blackmail though.'

'Well nobody ever said this would be easy.' They resumed their staring into the fire.

'There could be another way, of course,' Simon said after a while.

'What would that be?'

'Well, so far everything we have done and everything that we have talked about, is about setting some injustice right.'

'Yes?'

'Well, what if we changed our operating policy slightly?'

'How do you mean?'

'What if we decided to do something that would make us better off?'

'Explain.'

'Okay well hear me out. What if we decided to do a job that resulted in us having enough money that we could leave the police and either not have to work again; or could result in us doing what we wanted to do rather than being stuck in a thankless job that is getting worse day by day?' George thought about this for a moment.

'Don't you think they might get suspicious if we suddenly leave and have a lot of money to throw around?'

'Well yes they would which is why you have to be discreet about it and not turn up to work on your final day in a Lamborghini.'

'Lamborghini? Fuck sake, how much money are you thinking of taking?'

'Okay, well maybe not that much.'

'I can't see us being able to do any job that is enough for us to be able to retire from the Force with. You're just talking a shed load of money and that means a big job that is a little more than we can probably get away with.'

'Okay, well what if we went with not enough to retire on, but enough to supplement the income and pay off a few bills and live a little more comfortably than we can at the moment due to the Government? We could even steal it from a politician to make it more about justice.'

'It's not a bad idea, but with the amount of money that you are talking of taking it wouldn't last for all that long.'

'So?'

'So, eventually it will run out and you are going to want to do another job and then suddenly this becomes a way of habit and part of life.'

'It could do.'

George stood up and went into the kitchen from where Simon eventually heard the signs of more tea being made. After a few minutes he came back in with a tray and spent a few minutes fiddling about with the items on it without saying anything. Simon knew better than to say anything himself at that particular moment in time.

'What I'm not sure I like,' George said as he eventually settled down with a cup of tea in his hands. 'Is the fact that it's a huge shift from doing things because it's right that someone should do them, to we are doing it for our own gain and to help ourselves. That isn't really why we started this off in the first place. Well it certainly isn't why I started this off anyway.'

'I see your point.' They lapsed into silence once again. 'I'm not sure what we're going to do then.'

'Perhaps this is just the natural end of things,' George said as he drained his tea. 'Perhaps we aren't meant to go any further than this.'

'Do you believe in such things?'

'I don't know. What I do know is that we have managed to get away with what has happened — so far, at least. I don't know if there is such a thing as fate and if we will be tempting it, to be pushing it any further than we already have. You know as well as I do what will happen to us if we get caught at any of this.'

'Of course I do.'

'So, all I'm saying is maybe this is the natural end where we finish things off. I admit that I would love to have a crack at a politician as a means of getting back at them after all the years of grief that they have given me and the country.'

'I agree, it would be nice to hit one of them as a payback for all the lies and shit that they come out with whilst being so pompous and fucking self-righteous all of the time.'

'It would be good. It would be the ultimate fix, but at the moment I just can't think how we would be able to do it.'

'No, neither can I.'

And with that they returned to silence as they each tried to mull over the problem of how you can bring low someone who is pretty low to begin with. Perhaps if they had not fenced themselves in with so many scruples it might have been easier to find a way out of their current impasse, but that was the problem. They had set themselves some stern rules that they were not keen to break. Yes, they had broken the law and by the strictest definition of the term that did make them criminals; but what separated them from most criminals is the rules and the morality that they had. Criminals no doubt had a morality of their own, but when you saw the kinds of crimes that they would happily commit then it became rather difficult to work out what that morality was.

Thirty-Nine

'Sarah Newton.'

'What about her?' replied Simon as he sipped his tea in front of George's fire once again. It was fast heading towards spring now although the winter had been milder than Simon had expected it to be and it was not all that cold, yet still George insisted on his fire and Simon seemed to take a great deal of comfort from it. In fact, he realised that he was starting to spend a lot more time at George's house than he was at his own cold flat. Not surprising really and George really didn't seem to mind all that much when it came down to it.

'She's a horrible woman.'

'Well of course; she's a politician.'

'We should target her.'

'But we've been through this, how are we going to target her or any politician for that matter? They're too far out of reach.'

George mulled on this for a while whilst he sipped his own tea.

'Speculative burglary.'

'You what?'

'Let's break in and have a nose round and see what we can find. We may come across something very worthwhile.'

'And we may not.'

'True, but at least we will have had a go. Of course, there is the negative publicity if we don't find anything.'

'How do you mean?'

'Well,' continued George whilst he tried to eat a biscuit at the same time. 'If we find anything then she is likely to keep her mouth shut as she is not going to want to find herself all over the tabloids. However, if we don't find anything then she will scream bloody blue murder at how useless the police are as they have allowed someone to break into her house.'

'You can never win with someone like that. She is exactly the kind of person who sees things entirely from her own point of view. She has no consideration for other people. She's the kind of victim that expects all the stops to be pulled out when thanks to the like of her in the first place we don't have the resources to be able to pull out the stops on every single crime that gets reported to us. Nevertheless, they expect us to work miracles when we have no evidence to go on.'

'Posh people can be worse than the beanies to deal with. Beanies may not pay any tax and in general be useless to society but the upper classes treat the police like servants.'

'But if the evidence isn't there then there isn't much that we can do about it is there?'

'No, but then maybe the evidence should be there.'

'Not sure I am following you, George.'

'Just mulling over an idea in my mind that's all. Leave that one with me; you will have to trust me. I do think that Newton should be the next target and possibly the last target as well.'

'The last?'

'There is only so long that I feel that we can get away with this. We're tempting fate rather too much as it is.'

Simon thought about this as he gazed into the flames. George was right, of course, but he suddenly felt that he might miss it. For the first time in his career he was beginning to feel that he actually might be making a difference. It was just amazingly ironic that in order to feel like he could make a difference he had to cross the line to the other side of the law.

***

The decision had been made to target Sarah Newton and as it was likely to be the last job that they were going to do then the plans were drawn up carefully and they waited until they knew that they would be able to get into the house when it was unoccupied. This was not such an easy thing to do as there always seemed to be someone who was hanging around. Eventually though the waiting paid off and it was on a cold night that they stood crouched in some bushes at the bottom of Newton's garden watching the house to ensure that there were no signs of life.

It was handy that Newton was so stuck up and hated the public so much that she had decided that the best thing was to live in the country where she wouldn't be disturbed by neighbours. No chance of any witnesses or onlookers who would be able to be useful to the police later on.

When they were sure that nothing was going to happen, they slowly crept up the lawn towards the back door of the house. They didn't need torches as there was a full moon that shone down from a cloudless night and provided them with more than enough light. Rather too much light if they had been honest, but you can't have everything.

'I've got a bad feeling about this,' Simon whispered when they reached the back door.

'Ah, it'll be fine,' said George as he unravelled the small tool kit that he had brought with him.

'Maybe we should go back.'

'We're here now.'

Before any further argument could be mustered, he took a small glass hammer from his bag and lightly tapped it on the window pane in the bottom corner which immediately shattered. He knocked it out as quietly as he could and reached in to feel that as he had suspected the key was in the lock on the inside of the door.

'People never listen to crime prevention advice,' Simon muttered trying to cover up for his ill feeling.

'People like her never listen to anything but the sound of her own voice, she no doubt feels that she is above everything' George replied as he pushed the door slowly open. 'Come on, let's be quick.'

They hurried into the house and began to look around. George went straight to the living room where he rummaged in his seemingly endless pockets and pulled out a folded sack which he unravelled on the floor.

'What are you doing?' Simon whispered.

'Trust me.'

'I do trust you, but what are you doing?'

'Simon, this is not time for a debate. Do you trust me?'

'Yes.'

'Then find anything you can that looks like it's of value and put it in the sack.'

'Why?'

'Just do it,' he looked at Simon. '*Please.*'

Simon shrugged and then nodded. Not for the first time he had the distinct impression that George had his own agenda and that he was not always someone who was going to share it with someone else. He would say that he had not led him astray so far by trusting him, but then that was a difficult thing to say after you had both just broken into someone's house and were filling a sack with their most expensive items.

George looked at his watch and then picked up a couple of expensive looking ornaments and threw them into the sack that was beginning to fill up nicely. He then looked around the room.

'Right, that's enough. Let's get going?'

'Get going? We haven't done anything yet.' Simon was getting more and more confused and didn't like the fact that he felt he no longer had the slightest idea what was going on.

'We've done much more than you can imagine. However, it will now be very prudent if we were to leave as quickly as possible.'

Simon shrugged and went to pick up the sack.

'Leave it.'

'What?'

'Leave it, we're not taking it with us.'

'George, what the hell is going on?'

'We're leaving Simon, unless you want to stay and explain what you are doing here to our colleagues when they arrive any minute.'

'What?'

'Silent alarm. We triggered it when we came through the door. I estimate our colleagues will be here within the next two minutes or so. So, if it is all the same to you, I think it's time to go, so will you get a fucking move on?'

Simon all but ran to the door that they had come in by and the two of them raced down the garden to the wooded area that they had been observing the house from moments before. They pushed their way into the woods and when they were a safe distance from the house, they sat down near the trunk of a large tree in order to catch their breath.

'All this running, I thought I had put all that behind me,' George panted.

'Do you mind telling me what is going on now?'

'All will be revealed. We need to get fully away. Once they discover that the house is a confirmed break, they are going to get a dog out. Now the timing has been perfect. Due to our lovely Government wanting cut backs the last dog went off duty an hour ago. They won't pay them to be on all night long now. They are going to have to do a call out by which time we should be long gone.'

'I know all about dogs, what I don't understand—'

Simon broke off as the flashing blue lights peppered through the trees from the road that was a couple of hundred yards away. The two cars drove quickly onwards into the night heading for the house.

'I warrant that they are going to be rather busy.'

'I still don't understand.'

'Not here. Later. Now come on.'

They quickly made their way off towards where George had parked the car some distance away. Having arrived after seeing another couple of police cars silently screaming towards the house they as quietly as they could slipped off in the opposite direction where they hoped that they would not bump into any of their colleagues. Simon was none the wiser as to what was going on.

'So, are you going to tell me what is going on now?' Simon asked when they were safely in the car and on a main road some distance away from Newton's house.

'Not at the moment.'

'And why not?'

'Because I'm not sure what is about to happen. Things have been put in place and I have no idea how they are going to pan out at the moment. I think it best that for the time being at least we just keep things on the basis of the less you know the better.'

'Why?'

'Because if the shit hits the fan over this job then there is no sense in both of us going down.'

'Why would the shit hit the fan over this job?'

'Just an instinct that I have,' George continued to manoeuvre the car through the night and didn't appear to be about to be further drawn on what he was thinking. Simon found it very frustrating but knew that there was nothing that he could really do about it. If George had made up his mind that he was not going to say anything then there really was nothing that Simon would be able to do to get him to change his mind.

Simon lapsed into silence and spent the rest of the journey thinking about how livid Sarah Newton MP was going to be when she found out that her house had been broken into. It is distinctly possible that she would have been annoyed to have learnt that the police were not camped outside her property day and night protecting it from strays and vagabonds. After all there was a police officer outside 10 Downing Street all the time so why couldn't there by one outside of her house?

Simon had always thought that the police officer detailed to stand outside Downing Street was a waste of resources that could have been best used elsewhere. If the public knew how much money and how many resources were dedicated in the Westminster area alone to ensuring that politicians would feel safe there would be an outrage. So many officers wasted on these egotistical megalomaniacs when they could better be served in walking the beat and making arrests of people that had violated the law.

It is doubtful that he would have continued to feel like this if he had known that in the space of a week the investigation into the burglary at Sarah Newton's house had revealed some evidence that meant that a small gang of officers were heading towards the police station where Simon and George worked, intent on making an arrest.

Forty

Politicians would like to convince us all that they have abolished the idea of a two-tier society where there is still division by class. There is some truth that we don't have one end of society that are waited upon by butlers whilst the other end are forced to go down a coal pit and have their children die in poverty any longer, but the divisions are still there even though they are not as clearly extreme as they once were. If there is any doubt in your mind over that then just consider how many people in the higher echelons of politics had been to Harrow or Eton? How many had been educated at Oxford or Cambridge? It is true that you could make it without having been to these places, but you were in the minority and would always be looked upon as an outsider and with suspicion from your peers.

This prejudice in class was seen in the Sarah Newton investigation as well. The break in had been discovered at four-thirty in the morning. The highest-ranking officer on duty at that time had been an inspector who was the duty inspector for the county. She had attended the scene by five o'clock in the morning and had immediately got on the telephone to the on-call superintendent, who had appeared to be banging his head against the wall at the same time as listening to what the inspector had said. It was half past five when the superintendent had decided to put the call in to the Assistant Chief Constable. The ACC had been enjoying a rare piece of quality sleep where he had been dreaming that he no longer had the word 'Assistant' at the front of his title. Having listened to what the superintendent had said he had spent several moments debating with himself as to whether he should call the Chief Constable. It was now six o'clock in the morning and the ACC debated that the Chief would be in the office within the next two hours so he could leave it until then before telling him what had happened. However, he ultimately concluded that if the Chief found out that his assistant had known about this incident two hours previous to him and had not elected to tell him then he was probably going to end up in a load of shit. He decided to make the call. The Chief called everyone into the office early and spent twenty minutes balling them all out about how it was that this had been allowed to happen. Nothing reasonable at this, of course, as it was hardly the fault of any of the officers that the place had been burgled.

The difference in class here is that nobody would have woken the Superintendent, let alone anyone else, if it turned out that it was *your* house that had been burgled. It is possible that the duty inspector would have heard about it, but even that is doubtful and they certainly wouldn't have turned up at the scene. Now it is true that if your house is burgled then the chances are that the Chief Constable is not going to get in a lot of shit about it. It is almost certainly the case that the break-in to Sarah Newton's house would result in the shit flying in a lot of different directions.

It went without saying, therefore that no expense was to be spared into investigating this particular offence. The Chief Constable spent the majority of the day in his office answering telephone calls from increasingly higher ranking and increasingly more irate people from Westminster and Whitehall who all appeared to want to know what kind of shoddy organisation it was that he was running anyway. The Chief ended the last telephone call and put his head in his hands and sighed. He took an aspirin and thought about his life. It wasn't meant to be like this. It was meant to be fun at the top. He was meant to be able to sit at the top and delegate everything that he didn't fancy doing to the people underneath him and then if the flack got him and he had no way out he could resign and walk away with a very substantial pension and lump sum. He just hadn't expected that it might be time for retirement as early as this, but he could see that those bloody politicians were going to make this a resigning matter. It didn't matter that they could shag their way through the country, lie in court, take bribes and back handers for asking questions, set up companies that would favour them when they lost their seat, or any of the other things that they did; they would never resign, but rather they would hold onto power until it was finally wrestled from their torn and bloody fingernails. Well, look at Thatcher. It really wasn't all that fair as he felt that he had so much more that he could have given and now his career was almost certainly over. Someone would want heads to roll for this, and it was clear that he would be the one that would have to take the flack.

Money was no object in the investigation and the Chief had made it very clear to his officers that he would be taking a very close personal interest in the investigation. He was desperate to get a detection on this job so that he could show the powers that be in Government that although this outrage had taken place on his watch, he had been able to sweep in and get a result. With any luck then it would show that he was in control and that meant that he would still be able to progress his career to the highest possible outcome and collect a knighthood along the way.

It was his dream that he had held for some time and he was pleased to know that it was still in his grasp when the senior investigating officer had told him that there was significant evidence at the scene of the burglary which should, with luck, lead them to be able to identify a suspect, or two, and make an arrest. He was delighted about this and with satisfaction passed the information onto the Home Secretary who seemed to spend most of her day ringing him up to have a go, rather than whatever it was that she was meant to be doing.

You can imagine how the Chief's face fell as well as all his dreams when the senior investigating officer came to see him a few days later and told him that the evidence gathered did provide them with a suspect that they could arrest; when she told him who the suspect was, that was when the Chief's world started to collapse into small pieces that he doubted he would ever be able to put together again.

The Chief had not liked the news that had been passed to him, but he was a professional and even though he could see that his entire career was now over, he mustered enough strength to agree with the course of action that the Senior Investigating Officer had proposed. Whilst she went off to muster the troops together the Chief spent twenty minutes looking into the middle distance where he could see his knighthood disappearing over the horizon and wondering what it was that he had done wrong to find himself sitting behind this desk on this particular day. He sighed deeply and pressed the intercom.

'Yes, sir?' came the tinny voice of his staff officer over the intercom.

'Get me the Home Office would you, David?'

'Yes sir.'

'And then you had better get the IPCC and that fatuous Crime Commissioner lined up for a call as well.'

'Certainly sir. Would you like the Commissioner after the Home Office?'

'No. Let the little prick wait.'

He sat with his head in his hands again whilst waiting for the call to the Home Office to be put through. He didn't feel that he deserved this. It was bad enough that a politician should be a victim of crime on his patch; but that the evidence should point towards the fact that the person responsible for the crime was one of his officers was outrageous. He tried to keep as calm as possible and controlled. He knew that if he went anywhere near the officer in question then he was going to castrate the man. What chance did he have of a knighthood now?

'The Home Office for you, sir,' his staff officer told him over the intercom.

The Chief sighed and picked up the telephone.

***

The arrest of Chief Inspector Harbour for the burglary of Sarah Newton's house caused a great deal of surprise amongst the ranks. It was unexpected as well as very exciting to think of the horrible man as being responsible for such a thing.

'Well it doesn't surprise me,' one officer had said to another when they had met in the mail room soon after the arrest had been made. 'He always seemed to be very shifty to me. Wouldn't put anything passed a man like that.'

'I don't know,' the other one said. 'He never struck me as having the kind of personality to do something like that.'

'How do you mean?'

'Well, the man always seemed to me to lack imagination, creative flare. I wouldn't have given him the credit to be a master criminal.'

'Not a master criminal though is he. The silly wanker got caught.'

They completed the posting of their individual letters and went their separate ways.

Harbour's office had been sealed off and then emptied of all his files, his computer and everything else that was in his office on the off chance that there might be something in there that would be of use for the investigation. Even if there was nothing in there which proved that he was a burglar he had better hope that everything else was in order in his affairs as Professional Standards would be going through everything he had with a fine tooth comb looking for evidence that he was guilty of *anything*.

The person who was most surprised by the arrest of Chief Inspector Harbour was Chief Inspector Harbour who was pretty certain that he was innocent. The second most surprised person was Simon who had been convinced that his number was up and that they were coming for him. The person who was least surprised was George who had taken it all in his stride with a smile on his face.

'Well, he is finished now,' said George as they walked out of the station and towards the pub at the end of a shift one day.

'I don't see why,' replied Simon. 'We know that he didn't do it don't we.'

'Do we? Do you think it will matter? You know as well as I do that they will be desperate for a result on this case. Problem is the result comes with a price. One of their own Chief Inspectors committing crime. I would imagine that will be the end of the Chief Constable. Can't see him surviving this one.'

'You think he will resign?'

'I don't think they will leave him much choice. Bad enough that the crime happened in the first place, but then to find out that one of your senior managers is the suspect. Not good publicity that.'

'I don't understand why they arrested him.'

'I should imagine that they had their reasons,' George puffed on his cigarette whilst they walked. 'Of course, all that previous stuff about him having a nervous breakdown is bound to come out. Shows that he is not stable and in his right mind, of course. Probably had another breakdown and decided to go on a crime rampage. Tragic case. Perhaps he should be pitied more than punished.'

'You know something don't you?'

'I know lots of things. I know that he doesn't have an alibi for the night of the break in.'

'How do you know that?'

'Contacts, old son.' George tapped the side of his nose.

'What about his wife?'

'Turns out that she was out shagging one of the sergeants, believe it or not. That is certainly what rumour is saying. Fact is that she will not be providing him with an alibi. Maybe all the years of being with him has finally got to her. Either way I hear that he is taking the arrest and the fact that his wife appears to have left him rather badly.'

They walked in silence for a while each to their own thoughts as George completed the cigarette.

'Still, I don't know what they will do with him now that they have got him,' said George as he circumvented a puddle. 'Even if they decide that the evidence is insufficient to charge him his career is over now. Suspension whilst this is investigated and even if they decide not to charge him then he is going to be punted away somewhere where he can be allowed to rot and slowly forgotten about. Providing that this doesn't make him go completely gaga of course. Tragic really.'

'Couldn't have happened to a nicer man really.'

'Totally agree. I think it's karma. He had it coming to him the way he went around being a twat to everyone.'

'I still don't understand what led them to Harbour,' said Simon as he ground out his own cigarette.

'No? Well it turns out that they had good DNA evidence at the scene to suggest that he was responsible.'

'What DNA evidence?'

'Turns out that they found a blood-soaked handkerchief which tested for his DNA. Well as you know when we join up they take a sample of our DNA to eliminate us from crime scenes that we attend; or implicate in this instance.'

'How the hell did a blood-stained handkerchief with Harbour's DNA get at the scene?'

'It is something of a mystery isn't it? It does rather seem to suggest that he was there. As I say, it may not be enough to send him to court, but I should think it is enough to screw him over. Certainly leaves him with some questions to answer as it does rather suggest that he was there.'

Simon stopped walking and stared at George with a degree of what could only be described as admiration.

'The target was never Sarah Newton was it?'

George stopped and turned around and looked at Simon.

'The target was Harbour wasn't it? All along you had him in your sights.'

'Well,' said George as he stubbed out his cigarette. 'He shouldn't have been such a heartless twat when my wife died then should he? Come on, I will buy you a pint. I want to talk to you about this paedophile that I have been thinking about. I think I know a way that we can set the balance straight without resorting to violence.'

And with that they walked into the pub.

Also by the author

Apnoea ISBN: 978-1-78830-127-5 (2018)
The Write Stuff ISBN: 978-1-78830-445-0 (2019)